LUCIANNA

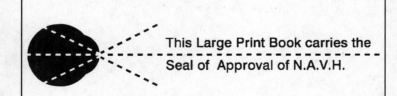

This Large Print Book carries the
Seal of Approval of N.A.V.H.

THE SILK MERCHANT'S DAUGHTERS

LUCIANNA

BERTRICE SMALL

THORNDIKE PRESS

A part of Gale, Cengage Learning

GALE
CENGAGE Learning®

Detroit • New York • San Francisco • New Haven, Conn • Waterville, Maine • London

GALE
CENGAGE Learning®

LIBRARY OF CONGRESS CATALOGING-IN-PUBLICATION DATA

Small, Bertrice.
    Lucianna : the silk merchant's daughters / by Bertrice Small. — Large print edition.
      pages ; cm. — (Thorndike Press large print romance)
    ISBN 978-1-4104-6285-5 (hardcover) — ISBN 1-4104-6285-4 (hardcover)
    1. Large type books. I. Title.
PS3569.M28L83 2013b
813'.54—dc23   2013032225

Published in 2013 by arrangement with NAL Signet, a member of Penguin Group (USA) LLC, a Penguin Random House Company

For Marilyn, Candy, and Bernadine.
Thanks for being such good friends.

PROLOGUE

Orianna Pietro d'Angelo had been amazed at how easily her third daughter, Lucianna, had accepted her parents' wishes. Orianna had not wanted any of her four daughters married to ordinary men. She wanted men of titles and wealth. The eldest, Bianca, had run off with a Turkish prince and was no longer spoken of within the family. The second, Francesca, had been left widowed with two children, and refused to accept a second husband. God only knew how she was raising her son, the young Duke of Terreno Boscoso, without the strong influence of a husband. But Francesca was so headstrong.

And now here was Lucianna. Her dower portion was down to virtually nothing with the sudden competition from Milan in the silk trade, which had affected Giovanni Pietro d'Angelo's own silk business. At sixteen, she was already in danger of becoming an old maid, and then there was the youngest sister, Giulia, already fourteen, who would also be in need of a husband very shortly. Giulia now preferred to be called Serena, which was her second name. She thought it more elegant.

Their financial situation known, there had been few offers for the beautiful Lucianna. Several, even given the family's straitened circumstances, were considered unsuitable. One, however, came from a wealthy bookseller, Alfredo Allibatore. He was quite elderly, with a grown son who helped his father manage their business, which consisted of bookbinding as well. Under normal circumstances, even Signore Allibatore's son would have been considered too old for Lucianna.

But the bookseller was the most respected in the city, and known as a good man. There was simply no other choice.

Told of her impending marriage, Lucianna accepted her parents' decision meekly and agreed. Orianna didn't know whether to be stunned or relieved, but Lucianna assured her parents she completely understood her situation, and thanked them for finding her a decent husband. A meeting was arranged between the prospective bride and her elderly groom.

Alfredo Allibatore, while pleased, was still curious why such a lovely young woman would accept his suit. Once they were alone, he asked her, and Lucianna told him quite candidly.

"I am sixteen, *signore*. I must marry or enter my mother's favored convent. I have no mind to be a nun."

"I am old. I cannot service you as a proper husband would. There will be no children of our making, Lucianna. Can you live such a life, my dear?"

"Yes, I can," she told him. "In your house I will be the mistress. I will not have my mother, good woman she is, fussing over my unmarried state." She smiled at him. "With the example of my two older sisters before me, I am not eager to allow passion to rule my life. I prefer a quieter existence, *signore*. I hope you are not offended by my candor. It is my one fault, I fear, and you should be warned of it if you are to take me as your wife."

He chuckled. "I find your candor refreshing," he told her. "I believe that we shall do very well together, Lucianna."

They were wed two weeks later. There was no need for a long engagement, and they were happy together. Lucianna kept Alfredo's home beautifully. She was good company, intelligent, and amusing. His two daughters were nuns, and they did not see them after the wedding. His son and daughter-in-law were relieved to have someone taking care of their elderly parent. They welcomed Lucianna warmly. And three years later, at the age of nineteen, Lucianna became a widow when her elderly husband died a peaceful death while holding his wife's delicate hand.

The estate had been divided fairly. The shop and some coin had been given to her stepson. He was pleased. His two sisters received a stipend for their convent, and Lucianna became a very rich woman with a house and a great deal of gold coin. And she followed the directive of her sister Francesca. She quickly disabused her mother of any ideas of remarriage until it was her choice to do so and she did the choosing.

"At this moment I choose not to remarry, Mama," she told Orianna. "I would like to enjoy the freedom that being a respected and respectable widow has brought me. I need no passion or the drama it brings into one's life. I thank you for your concern and your good thoughts, however."

"Let her be," Giovanni Pietro d'Angelo said. "She is not her sisters. When she is ready, it will be the right man, and she will quickly learn that passion has a place in her life." He put a comforting arm about his wife's shoulders. "After all, *cara mia,* you did."

"Gio!" she scolded him gently, but she knew he was right. Despite her reluctance to marry him all those years ago, he had become a very good husband to her, and she was finally ready to admit to her good fortune. He was a patient and wise man. They had done well together.

CHAPTER 1

It was odd being without Alfredo, Lucianna thought, now that his funeral was over and his will read. She was alone for the first time in her life. Of course there was Balia, her serving woman. Balia did not come from her father's house. She had been one of Alfredo's servants. Lucianna didn't want someone from her mother's staff who would feel it her duty to report to Orianna.

Lucianna had asked her son-in-law, Norberto, if she might help in the shop, and he was happy to grant her request. His children were too young to help him, and his wife, Anna Maria, did not want her girls to be seen as shopkeepers. Their son was only six. Norberto did not like dealing with their clients, and he was happy to have Lucianna do so for him. People liked his stepmother, and her family's prestige added luster to his business, he felt.

For Lucianna, it was something to do. She

was not bored when she spent time in her late husband's bookselling shop. She had always enjoyed Alfredo's company there. He was an educated and clever man who had taught her a great deal in the brief course of their marriage. She did not enjoy Norberto. She could not tell what he did or did not know, for he spoke little, preferring to use his hands in the intricate and delicate art of bookbinding, which required all his attention. He excelled at working with the elegant leather. She also suspected he did not believe in women having too much knowledge. Still, he was pleasant enough. She had believed he was just a trifle in awe of her because of her family. She had always been polite and kind to Norberto as a result, which had pleased her husband.

"You are my angel," Alfredo had frequently told her, and Lucianna would laugh.

"I am simply practical, and I do not believe in being unkind to frail creatures," she once responded to him, and he laughed again.

"He is a bit of a frail fellow, isn't he? His mother had far more to do with raising him than I did, and Maria Clara was a gentle woman. You are different, my young wife."

"How so, Fredo?" she had asked, curious.

"You are strong like your mother, but

kinder," he told her. "You are intelligent as well. If your father had not lost so much gold to the Milan trade, you could have had a prince, and I am well aware of it. Yet you faced your situation without complaint and accepted an old man for your husband with good grace. I remember the stories of Francesca, your sister, who mocked her suitors until the Medici sent her away. But still, she did wed a duke."

"The eldest of us made no complaint and did as she was bid," Lucianna had reminded him.

"Rovere blackmailed your father with some indiscretion, I am certain," Alfredo Allibatore had told his wife. "I cannot imagine for what, as your father is a discreet man. He would have never let his daughter go to that debauched monster otherwise."

"Yet he did, but I did not know for several years after what Rovere's spur had been, for I was too young for such talk," she had told him. "By then Bianca had fled Rovere, and when he was murdered, she eloped with Prince Amir, much to my mother's shame. We don't even know if she lives today. I barely knew her. We are eight years apart in age. She has never really been a part of my life. I do not believe I should know her if we came face-to-face. It was said she was the most beautiful of us all, however."

He had surprised her then by telling her, "Your elder sister lives in an Ottoman principality called El Dinut. I bind books now and again for her husband, Prince Amir. It is said she is the love of his life. I believe it to be so, judging from the book of his love poems I just bound for her. They have one child, a daughter."

"Have you ever met him?" she asked, curious.

"No," Alfredo responded. "The prince sends his books to be bound from his home across the sea. I am paid by a small bank here in Milan. The books are returned to him via one of the prince's vessels."

It was the first and only time he ever surprised her. She had told her twin brother, Luca, who said even their mother knew Bianca lived. She simply chose not to discuss it with her other children. Lucianna had thought that was rather mean-spirited of their mother, but she said nothing more to her twin. They all knew that Bianca had been her mother's favorite, and that by following her heart Bianca had disappointed her mother greatly.

So now Lucianna was alone, and she wondered if Prince Amir knew of her husband's death, and whether he would still continue to send the Allibatores his books for binding. Only time would tell her the answer to that. If he did, perhaps she would send her sister a letter when the books were returned to him.

The months slipped by, and Lucianna's life remained a quiet and uneventful one. The new year came and went. It was a chilly, rainy winter in Florence. Her little sister, Serena, came to visit one afternoon in the company of her ancient nursemaid. Serena was much too old to have a nursemaid, but, while realizing this youngest daughter of hers must marry soon, Orianna could not quite bring herself to settle upon a husband for Serena.

"I'm going to end up an old maid," Serena complained. "She was quick enough to marry you and our other sisters, but cannot seem to find the right man for me. Grandfather has given up on her."

"Is there anyone you particularly like?" Lucianna asked.

"Not really, but I simply must get out of that house. I am sixteen, and she treats me as if I were a babe of three. My opportunities to meet anyone are very limited. I go to church with Mama daily, but no one stands in the square waiting for me to pass by as they did with Bianca. Papa's great fortune is mostly gone, and it is known my dower is small."

"I would gladly supplement any dower our parents can now afford. Is it that bad, Serena?"

"I have heard Papa discussing letting Marco have the business, and retiring to the villa in Tuscany. He says he would rather grow grapes and make wine than try to make bargainers appreciate how much finer our silk is compared to Milan's."

"Oh dear!" Lucianna exclaimed. "I fear he is serious. Papa loves the silk trade and always has."

"Worse," Serena said. "He doesn't want to return from the countryside when we go this summer! I will be wed to some grape grower or farmer's son!"

"Not if our mother has anything to say about it," Lucianna said, laughing. "Go to the country with the family this summer. If Father insists upon remaining, I will ask our mother to let you come and keep me company now that I am alone and widowed. Believe me, she will bring you herself rather than have you stuck in the country. And she will come often herself to visit us both while she tries to get Father to return to the city. Florence does not compare to her beloved Venice, but she is not about to spend the

18

remainder of her life growing grapes."

"I do not know what I would do without you, Lucianna," Serena said gratefully.

"*Matrigna,* forgive the interruption, but we have a new customer arriving shortly. He is an Englishman recommended to us, and he is here in Florence to purchase silk cloth for his king. I apologize I did not tell you earlier," Norberto said, coming from his workshop. "He seeks a book of poetry. Good afternoon *Signorina* Serena."

"Good afternoon, *Signore* Allibatore," Serena responded, curtsying politely to him.

"You do not wish to speak with such an important new customer?" Lucianna inquired, already knowing what the answer would be, but asking anyway.

"Oh no, no, no, *matrigna.* You are far better with those who seek books than I am. Papa always said so."

"Then I shall give him our best service, and *grazie,* Norberto," Lucianna responded as her stepson scurried back to his workshop.

"What a funny man," Serena noted. "I have always thought so."

"He is just shy, and quite awed by the name 'Pietro d'Angelo,' " Lucianna explained. "He is actually very kind and a wonderful workman. Without him, Alfredo's

19

shop could not continue on."

"How did you bear being married to such an old man?" Serena asked boldly.

"We were friends, never lovers, little sister. And by being his wife, I married as our parents dictated and escaped their palazzo, not to mention our mother," the older girl explained.

"Do you mean you are still a virgin?" Serena dared to inquire.

"I am," Lucianna replied.

"Does our mother know?" Serena asked.

"She never asked, and it was not something I chose to discuss with her, Serena. Now stop asking questions, or I shall not take you to live with me next autumn, though perhaps you would prefer a lovely winter in the countryside. Hmm?"

"No, thank you! And now my lips are sealed."

The shop bell rang and a tall gentleman entered.

"Go back to my apartment quickly," Lucianna ordered the young girl. She wanted no one believing Serena was a shopgirl. "Good afternoon, *signore.* Is there something in particular you are seeking?"

"Si, signorina," he responded.

"It is *signora.* I am the widow of Alfredo Allibatore, *signore.*"

His Italian was rough. "Poetry," he told her.

"In Italian or English?" she inquired politely.

"You have both?" He sounded surprised.

"We are a bookshop, *signore*. We keep books in all languages," Lucianna explained to him. "Might you be more comfortable if we spoke in English?" And she smiled at the look of surprise on his face.

"God, yes!" he answered gratefully.

"Then let us do so. I am quite conversant in your language."

"How . . ." he began.

"I am considered highly educated for a woman," Lucianna told him. "I speak my own tongue, English, and French." She led him to a shelf of exquisitely bound books. "Poetry in several languages. Please feel free to browse, and if you have any questions, I shall be glad to answer them, *signore*." Lucianna turned back to her counter.

She couldn't help but notice him. He was not what she would call handsome, but he was very attractive in a serious sort of way. His face was long, with a dimpled chin. His hair was black, not simply dark, or even the deepest brown. Black. When they had spoken at the counter, she saw he had light gray eyes, and his skin was fair rather than ruddy or dark. His cheekbones were high and his nose long and very straight. He had the most fascinating thick black eyebrows, and thick black eyelashes. It was a serious face. She liked it because it was different from any other face she had ever known or seen.

"I understand you have come to Florence seeking silk. We have the finest," Lucianna said, daringly opening a conversation.

"Aye," he said. "The stuff in Milan isn't of a quality I would want for the queen and her female relations."

"You are a seller of silk, then," she said.

He laughed. "Nay, *Signora* Allibatore, I am Robert Minton, the Earl of Lisle, the king's friend. I volunteered for this particular duty because I have never been to Italy before and wished to see it. I have no interest in political office, as so many others surrounding our young King Henry do. The king's treasury is not particularly full at this moment, but he is very fond of and generous to his bride. She wished Italian silk, and so here I am."

"I hope, then, that you will visit my father's establishment," Lucianna said. "He is Giovanni Pietro d'Angelo, and the premier silk merchant in Florence, if not all of Italy."

"Ah, yes, he has been most highly recommended," Robert Minton told her.

"You need no one else if you purchase your silk from the Pietro d'Angelos," she told him.

"How did a successful silk merchant's daughter end up married to an ordinary bookseller? Did your parents permit you a love match?" he boldly asked her.

Lucianna laughed. "Nay," she said. "It is a long story, and you are not really interested in it, I am certain. Have you found your book?"

He didn't need to know that the failure of the Medici bank had caused her father to lose a great deal of his monies, and that she didn't have a respectable enough dower to attract a better name.

Interesting, the earl thought. But then they had just met, and he was not really entitled to know such personal information. "Yes, I have found a book, but I should like it rebound in a richer leather with gold," he explained to her.

"I will call my stepson, who does the binding. If you tell him exactly what you desire, he will see it done properly. Norberto, please come and speak with our new customer about rebinding his purchase."

Robert Minton was very surprised to see a middle-aged man hurry from a side room.

Obviously the fair Lucianna's husband had been a much older man. *What a waste,* he thought, and then turned to the bookbinder. "I wish it bound in the softest, finest, deep green leather. You will decorate it with gold about the edges discreetly. The cover will be inscribed as follows in gold lettering: *To Her Majesty, Queen Elizabeth of England.*" Then he realized he had been speaking in English, and he looked to Lucianna.

She quickly translated to her stepson, who nodded and said something that Lucianna translated back to Robert Minton. "Norberto said he understood exactly what you require, and he is honored to be chosen to do this work for you. The book will be ready for you in three days, my lord."

"Grazie," he said to the bookbinder, who nodded and then, taking the book, scampered back into his workshop.

"He is shy, which is why I manage the shop," Lucianna explained. "Alfredo taught me so that when he no longer could, I could."

"Would you attend Mass with me tomorrow, *signora,* and then perhaps afterwards walk with me?" he boldly asked her.

"I cannot, *signore,*" Lucianna said. "My husband is not dead a full year yet, and I yet mourn him."

"When will he be dead a full year?" he asked her.

"The fifth of next month," she replied.

"Then I must wait until then to escort you to Mass," the Earl of Lisle said, with a small smile that Lucianna couldn't help but return.

She wondered a moment if her mother would approve, but then she realized it was not necessary to ask Orianna. "I shall look forward to it, my lord," she told him. He was attractive and well-spoken. She wanted to know him better, and going to Mass with this Englishman could hardly be considered scandalous.

He bowed a small bow, and then said, "I shall return in three days for my book, *signora.*" Then he was gone through the bookshop door.

Lucianna found herself disappointed to see him go. She would have liked him to remain and speak with her longer. There were no more customers that afternoon. She found her sister upstairs waiting for her. She had been embroidering.

"He was handsome, the Englishman," Serena said.

"I thought him attractive, but hardly handsome," Lucianna replied. "Where is old Esta?"

Serena nodded her head. "Snoozing. It's all she does anymore."

"I shall suggest to our mother that you have a proper serving woman," Lucianna. "I saw the family litter waiting outside from the window when I came up. It is time for you and Esta to go before it gets dark. Awaken the old lady. I will fetch your cloaks."

When Esta was full-awake and in her cloak, Lucianna said to her, "I think it is time my sister had her own serving woman, don't you, Esta?"

"Bless you, *signora,* if you could but convince your mama," the old nursemaid said. "Your papa has promised me I may live out my life at the villa, which would please me, as that is where I was born and raised until your mother chose me to look after my young mistress. I will be happy to go home and not have to return again to this dirty city," she said frankly.

"Good, then you will support me when I approach Mama. I shall do so before you go to Tuscany in a few weeks," Lucianna promised. Then she escorted Serena and Esta to their waiting litter, and watched as the litter made its way down her street.

"Bless you!" Serena said as she climbed into the vehicle.

Lucianna smiled. Orianna was really trying to keep her youngest child — *the baby*
— as Serena had always been known. But
her three older sisters were wed, though two
were widowed. Her oldest brother, Marco,
was a husband and a father. Her second
brother, Giorgio, was a priest of some
importance, now stationed in Rome. And
Lucianna's own twin, Luca, debated between marriage and the military.

He was at their grandfather's in Venice
right now, inspecting the available young
heiresses. Luca far preferred Venice to Florence, which pleased his elderly grandparent,
who was a prince. Luca was an outrageously
handsome young man, and his charm made
him very popular with both mothers and
their daughters. From what her mother said,
Lucianna suspected her twin brother would
find a wife in Venice and settle down there
in Grandfather's palazzo.

Despite being the youngest son in his im-
mediate family, Luca was likely to be given
his grandfather's title when the old man
died, and he would inherit his palazzo. That
would not please Mama's sisters, but then,
they only seemed to spawn daughters. Her
Venetian aunts had given the Pietro
d'Angelo children fourteen female cousins.

Lucianna wondered if the English earl

would visit Venice. One could not come to Italy without seeing Venice. Of course he would go to Venice eventually before he returned to his northern clime. He simply had to go. She sighed. She had never met a man except Alfredo that she really liked. But she did like Robert Minton. She wished she hadn't had to refuse his invitation to attend Mass, but she could not be seen with him right now without causing a scandal. And when he left Florence, would other men consider her being with him an indication that the widow Allibatore was now accepting callers?

She didn't want to be importuned by men seeking a rich wife, or a mistress. Why was there no simple way for a woman to speak with gentlemen without becoming involved or suggesting a scandal? Wasn't there a way for women and men to be just friends?

Being seen with a man would encourage her mother to go looking for a suitable second husband for her, especially now that Lucianna had her own wealth. Whatever happened, she wanted to control her own life.

Her bed beckoned. It had been a long day. Lucianna called to her serving woman, and she was shortly abed. She fell asleep quickly.

CHAPTER 2

She saw him at Mass the following morning. Their eyes met, but other than that he made no approach, either inside the church or outside of it afterwards. He was there the following morning.

Should she be flattered? She wasn't certain. All his appearance said to her was that he was a devout man, but to her maidservant, Balia, it said a great deal more.

"He likes you!" she crowed as they walked home from San Piero. "If you permitted, he would walk out with you. I see the longing in his eyes to know you better, mistress."

"You have a great imagination, and a romantic nature," Lucianna replied. "We have spoken briefly once. About books. Nothing more. Besides, I could hardly walk out with a strange gentleman while I am still in mourning."

"You are a good and respectful lady," Balia said. "Master Alfredo could not have had a better wife in his old age, but the master is dead. He was an old gentleman, and you a young girl. Is it not time for you to find a bit of happiness?"

"It is expected of me that I mourn my husband a year. I am glad to do so, for he was more than deserving, Balia."

"I cannot argue that," Balia agreed.

The following afternoon, the Earl of Lisle came to pick up the book of poetry he had ordered rebound for his queen. "Good day, *signora,*" he said, greeting her with a smile. "I have come to get my purchase. May I see it first?"

Lucianna handed it to him, watching as he took the volume and examined it closely, turning it over in his hands. "I hope it pleases you, my lord."

"It is exquisite, the leather beautiful, the lettering perfect. Please thank Master Norberto for me. He is a true artist, *signora.*" He handed it back to her for wrapping and drew out his purse, never showing any distress at the price she charged him.

"I hope your queen will treasure it," Lucianna said. "When do you plan to return to England, my lord?"

"Not for another month or two," he said. "I would see Rome and Venice before I return."

"My grandfather lives in Venice," she told him. "I have never been to Rome, however."

At that moment the bell to the shop door jangled, opened, and, to Lucianna's great surprise, Orianna Pietro d'Angelo entered. Lucianna wasn't quite certain what to do, but the earl was quick. "I shall bid you good day, *Signora* Allibatore. And I shall see you on the sixth of next month." With an elegant bow, he departed with his wrapped package, nodding politely to the visitor as he went. The door to the shop closed behind him.

"Who was that attractive gentleman, and why was he not speaking Italian?" Orianna wanted to know.

"He is an English lord, Mother. The Earl of Lisle. He purchased a book of poetry and had Norberto rebind it to his fancy," Lucianna said.

"Ah, that is the gentleman. He purchased a large quantity of your father's finest silks this morning. And he paid with gold as easily as if he were counting out pennies," Orianna said. "Your father told me he was buying the silks for the English king to give his bride."

"The book was also for his queen," Lucianna told her mother. "I am so glad Father got his custom."

Orianna looked closely at her daughter. "Perhaps you recommended your father's silks to this man?"

"It might have come up in the conversation," Lucianna said.

"Thank you," Orianna responded, smiling. "It was a large order, and he was pleased. You have a head for business, Lucianna. More than Marco, certainly. I wish you would leave this dusty bookshop and help your brother. Could not Norberto run it?"

"He is too shy, Mother. He simply wishes to do his beautiful binding, nothing more," Lucianna told her mother. "Alfredo loved his business and his books."

"Alfredo was a good man, and he did very well by you, I will admit," her mother said. "But you have no children by him. Your first loyalty should be to the Pietro d'Angelos, who are your blood kin."

"I will consider it, Mother," Lucianna told her parent. When later she thought about it, she realized she should far prefer to work with her father's silks than within the old bookshop. Still, she had no intention of moving back into her mother's house. She knew Orianna's real intent was to marry her off again to another suitable man. Yet she could remain in her own house and hire someone to manage the bookshop while she helped her brother Marco.

Marco was a good man, eleven years her senior. He had a lovely wife, Maria Theresa, and three daughters, but Lucianna knew he also kept a mistress, Clarinda Pisani. Her brother was charming, but far more interested in his pleasure than in managing the business their father had built up. Giovanni Pietro d'Angelo was becoming an old man now. He wanted a little peace in his life, and not the responsibility of a business, but he knew that Marco was not entirely responsible. He would not admit it even to himself, but Orianna saw it. She saw the two men needed help.

Lucianna, to Orianna's surprise, seemed to have business sense. She had obviously learned it from her late husband. Lucianna, in her mother's opinion, owed it to her family to help them. She had, after all, been clever enough to direct this English lord to the family's silk establishment, where he spent his king's gold lavishly. Her beauty would draw other rich men to their silk shop. Perhaps there was another wealthy man among them who would offer for Lucianna.

Lucianna told her mother she would consider helping out her father and her brother, and she actually was considering it. The bookshop was quiet, for Florence was not particularly prosperous. Books were not a necessity, as was food. People had little to spare on luxuries like books. But the one thing Lucianna determined was that she was not going to give up her home, and so she agreed to help her brother.

"If someone wishes to purchase a book," she told her stepson, "it will be you who must come from your workshop to help them. I have no experience hiring people, and I see no necessity in spending the money to pay someone. It is that, or I must close the shop, and then how will you gain your trade?"

Norberto's wife was not pleased upon hearing this news. "How can you thrust that responsibility upon him?" she demanded of Lucianna when she came to visit the shop. "You know how frail he is, but then, I suppose it is better. There has been talk, you know."

"Talk?" Lucianna said. "What kind of talk?"

"Well," Norberto's wife said, "there is no denying you are a beautiful young woman alone much of the day with a man not your husband. I have had to defend my husband's good name on several occasions, Lucianna."

Lucianna laughed, and she laughed until her sides ached while her stepdaughter-in-law stood, looking outraged. Finally she managed to say, "If there has been *talk,* it cannot involve me. Certainly my loyalty to Alfredo could suggest nothing more than my faith and devotion to him. I defy anyone to suggest anything else. I would hardly take up with his son upon my husband's death. I am insulted you would even suggest such a thing, Anna Maria!"

"I am only saying what has been said," her stepdaughter-in-law replied. "I certainly know you would hardly take up with a crooked little man like my Norberto. But if you are no longer in the same shop, it cannot be said of you."

"Wash day and fountain gossips," Lucianna muttered.

"Will you continue to live in the house?" Anna Maria asked.

"Of course. Where else would I go?" Lucianna asked her.

"I thought you might return to your father's house, and then we would move into this house."

"God and Santa Anna forbid I ever live with my mother again," Lucianna said with a laugh. "And if the gossips say Norberto comes upstairs to see me smile and they compliment him for being a loving stepson to the poor and lonely widow his beloved father left, Anna Maria, say they are ridiculous."

"You want me to approve of this licentiousness?" Norberto's wife was totally infuriated by Lucianna's suggestion. "How dare you!"

"Go home, Anna Maria. I am fast wearying of this conversation."

"You are *dismissing* me?"

"I suppose I am," Lucianna said. "Please go now." Poor Norberto, she thought, as his wife stormed from the shop. He would have to listen to Anna Maria's version of this argument when he went home this evening, even though he had heard every word the two women spoke today from his workshop.

"I am sorry," she heard her stepson say as he came forth. "I told her such gossip was ridiculous. She agreed it was, but I could not dissuade her from speaking with you. Anna Maria does not know when to cease her gabble."

"I am sorry you will have to listen to all of it again when you go home," Lucianna said to him.

"I shall work late tonight," he told her with a smile.

"Then I will have a servant bring you a

36

hot meal," she said to him. "You work hard, I know, and such work cannot be easy."

"Thank you," he said, and returned to his workshop.

The next few weeks went by quickly. Though loath to spend the money, Lucianna added two litter bearers to her staff so she might use her chair whenever she chose. As they were relations of her own servants, she felt comfortable with them, and they were grateful for the employment in the tight Florentine economy.

By good fortune, one of them had an educated son who was more than happy to run the bookshop for her, which pleased both Norberto and his wife. Having another man in the shop would cause no gossip that involved her husband, Anna Maria said. Heaven only knew what would be said of her mother-in-law, she noted meanly, but of course that was not her concern. Lucianna laughed.

She rode her litter each morning to church, and most mornings the Earl of Lisle was there to offer her a nod and a smile. She then was taken to her father's retail shop, where she first put their books in order and watched over the shop during the day. Her father came less and less to his place of business, and Lucianna found herself managing it as Marco spent more time with his mistress.

"What will you do if I get sick?" she asked her brother.

"You do not get sick," he reminded her.

"There may come a time when I am no longer here," she said. "What will you do then, Marco?"

"Why would you not be here?" he said. "You do not get sick, and you have said you do not wish to remarry." His logic made perfect sense to him. "What else would keep you from your duties?"

"Perhaps I might decide to travel," she said. "I could visit Bianca in her mysterious El Dinut, or Francesca in Terreno Boscoso. I might go to Venice to see Luca and decide which of his hopefuls is the right girl for him. We are twins, after all."

"You cannot leave the shop to travel," he said again, with what he hoped passed for perfect logic.

"Why not?"

"I would not let you," he replied with a warm smile, "and as I am your big brother, you must obey me, as you have no husband to guide you, little sister."

"I think it is I who guide you, Marco," Lucianna told him, and she did not smile back at him. "I will have to speak to our mother about this if you do not listen to me. My mourning is over now. I will have suitors whether I wish to wed again or not. There will always be gentlemen who seek me for a wife, and for my gold, Marco. I have never been in love. But what or who is to say that I could not be in love one day? You must spend more time in the shop, and less with your mistress, Clarinda, Brother. If the shop fails after all these years, who is to give you an income? I do not believe your wife would be content to have no income to spend on her finery, and that of your children, or you on Clarinda. She will not remain with you if you cannot support her. She will seek another protector."

Marco looked shocked by his sister's words. Being without funds had never occurred to him. He had never been without enough coin to spend. He did not, however, intend to be lectured by his younger sister, who, he was discovering, was much wiser than he. Not that he would ever tell her so. Women were not meant to be in full charge. This was not her household. This was his business.

"I shall come in each morning," he said. "The whole morning. But I must have my afternoons with Clarinda."

"It will do for a start," Lucianna said

sweetly. "Thank you, dear brother. Father's shop should have your touch, not mine. All I do, I do in your name, Marco."

He smiled then, well pleased. "As it should be, dearest Lucianna."

Pompous fool, she thought to herself. When had Marco become so overblown? Their father was not so. It was his very good nature in dealing with servants and noblemen alike that had won him his excellent reputation as a fair man. "We are all God's children," he would say. "Equal in his eyes."

"Well, not in mine," his wife would murmur. "Really, Gio, you can hardly consider the kitchen boy or the vegetable seller in the market your equal. And certainly not mine! Do you forget that I am the daughter of a prince?"

And her father would reply drolly, "No, my dear Orianna, I never forget you are the daughter of a Venetian prince. How could I?"

Overhearing, the children would giggle to one another. Lucianna realized there was a great deal of their mother in her eldest brother. Not in Giorgio, who was more influenced by the church, but perhaps in Luca, who preferred the strict life of a soldier. Her oldest brother was simply not as good at dealing with people as he should

40

be. He had not always been that way, but as their father put more and more of the responsibility of his silk trade on Marco, her brother had changed. Well, no matter. She was here to gently guide him, and hopefully he would learn from her without ever realizing she was teaching him.

Her mourning period was officially over now. She was not surprised to see the Englishman enter the shop one morning. "I have not seen you at San Piero recently," she greeted him.

"I have been in Rome and Venice," he told her. "I will soon have to return to England, as the seas grow rougher as the autumn deepens. But not, of course, before we have attended church together, and you have walked with me in some pleasant park, *signora*. I shall be the envy of Florence with you on my arm."

He smiled, and Lucianna was glad she had the counter to clutch, else she was certain she would have fallen. Her knees grew weak at the sound of that deep, almost musical, warm voice. "You flatter me most shamelessly, my lord. I shall, however, be pleased to attend Mass with you, and perhaps even walk in some pleasant park. I know just the one, as it happens."

"Tomorrow?" he said eagerly.

"Oh no, my lord, for tomorrow I must work," she told him.

"Such odd words coming from a lady's lips," he said. "Why are you here in your father's retail establishment and not in your snug little bookshop, *signora*?"

"My father needed my help, for my brother finds it difficult to manage everything. The bookshop did not really require my services, although you may rest assured that I will watch my accounts carefully each week. And my stepdaughter-in-law was most delighted I chose to go. I am told *there was talk,*" Lucianna told him, smiling.

"Talk? What kind of talk?" he asked with all the innocence of a man.

"Talk," she emphasized, rolling her eyes.

"God's nightshirt! You and Norberto? Surely you jest, *signora*. It is ludicrous and ridiculous to consider such a thing even privily."

"I know." Lucianna giggled. "My poor stepson was mortified."

Robert Minton, Earl of Lisle, burst out laughing. "I well imagine that he was. Well, *signora,* that settles it. You and I must be seen in public on several occasions as soon as possible. Poor Norberto's reputation must be saved, and restored."

"We can attend Mass together on Sunday," Lucianna said, "and walk together in the park afterwards."

"Shall I come to your house and bring you?" he asked her.

"No, no, I shall meet you at San Piero," she told him. "It is better I arrive alone, else we should cause the kind of talk that would make my mother most unhappy. People are quick to jump to conclusions here, and more often than not, the wrong conclusion."

"Such gossip is not local to Florence. King Henry's mother is the Lady Margaret Beaufort. She bore the king when she was barely thirteen. His father, her second husband, was Edmund Tudor, who had been killed in battle a few months prior to the king's birth. Many feel she has too much influence on him."

"Does she?" Lucianna asked, fascinated by a girl who had borne her only child at thirteen to her second husband.

"If she does," the earl replied, "he considers her words, for he is a loving son. But the king's decisions are his own, I firmly believe. You will see when you come to England."

"I am not going to England," Lucianna said.

"I think that you will. One day," he told her.

"It is unlikely I shall every leave Florence and its environs," she told him. "Unlike my mother, I enjoy my city."

"You will like England. It is green and beautiful."

"I like Florence," she said.

"Have you never traveled?" he asked.

"My sister Bianca traveled, and Francesca traveled, but I was married in Florence and have never been anywhere else," Lucianna told him. "My husband was an elderly gentleman and could not travel even to my family's summer villa, or down to the seashore where there is a small seaside villa that belonged to one of my grandparents."

He was surprised to learn she had never left the Florentine environs. She seemed so educated.

"I don't suppose travels in books or searching my globe counts," she put in.

"I suppose it is better than nothing at all," he told her. "Shall I tell you about Rome and Venice?" he asked her.

"I do know something of Venice. My mother is the daughter of Prince Alessandro Venier," she told him. "But I should enjoy hearing of Rome, and your impressions of Venice. To my mother, it is the most perfect city in the world. My two older sisters' stories of it were mostly humorous.

They lived with our grandfather at one point. That was where Bianca had the opportunity to flee with her prince, and Francesca made such a mini-scandal with some boy she fancied herself in love with, but of course she really wasn't." Lucianna laughed.

"Your sisters sound like naughty wenches," he noted, smiling.

"In that, my mother would agree with you," Lucianna said.

At that moment the shop bell rang, and its door opened to admit a fat gentleman.

"Ah, *Signore* Piscelli," Lucianna greeted him, stepping from behind her counter and past the earl. "My father said you were in need of some fine silks." She ushered him to a chair. "Please sit, *signore,* and I will have what you require brought forth."

"Thank you, thank you, *Signora* Lucianna," the fat gentleman said. "I am quite comfortable now." He raised the small glass of wine a shop servant had hurried forth with. "Please continue with your other customer. I am content to wait."

"You are most gracious," Lucianna said. "The earl has completed his business. Silks for the English king." Then she turned to Robert Minton. "Thank you so much for your generous custom, my lord," and she ushered him smoothly from the shop with a smile.

"Masterfully done, *signora,*" he said as he bowed and departed.

He should return to England soon, he thought, as he walked along the busy streets back to his lodging. He had already been gone for several months, but he had sent the silk ahead with two of his servants before he departed for Rome and Venice so Henry would not have to wait. As a rule, Henry was not a generous young man, but Robert Minton knew that came from having little as he grew up.

Few seriously believed Henry Tudor, son of Margaret Beaufort, would ever be England's king. King Edward had had brothers and two living sons. But Edward died unexpectedly, and his brother Richard, Duke of York, took the throne. At that moment Richard had been the king's only living brother. As for the little princes, they disappeared, leaving only Richard. Many believed Richard had murdered his nephews, especially among the Tudor adherents. Robert Minton did not.

Richard loved all children, and he had always been the favorite uncle. Such talk was said to tar Richard's memory, to make him a villain, to make Henry Tudor England's savior. If anyone had killed those poor boys, it had been someone aligned with the Tudors' aspirations. Robert Minton did not voice his private thoughts aloud. He had grown up with Henry Tudor, and he knew him too well. Henry was ambitious, but he was not a man who would stoop to murdering children. So Richard of York became the villain to Henry Tudor's savior. After Richard's death in battle, Henry became king, and all other possible suitors for England's throne found themselves lodged in the Tower.

Robert Minton had found among the Pietro d'Angelo silks a particularly fine dark ruby brocade, which he purchased for the king's mother and sent along to the Lady Margaret Beaufort with his compliments. She was not a woman for bold colors, but the dark red brocade would both please and flatter her. She had always treated him with kindness when he was just a minor earl's heir. Far more important boys had surrounded the young king back in those halcyon days when they were growing into men in Brittany, where Henry had been sent by his mother for his own safety.

He wondered what she would think of his fascination with the beautiful Lucianna Pietro d'Angelo. She would smile and tease him, saying, "Are none of our English girls good enough for you, Robbie?"

But she would like the young woman he suspected Lucianna was, a woman who valued tradition and was sensible, much like Lady Margaret herself.

Robert Minton had never met a girl like Lucianna before. She was still young. She could not yet be twenty. God's blood! He didn't even know her age. But before he left Florence, he would know as much about her as he could.

In the morning, he reached San Piero to find her already there. Boldly, he joined her, and their eyes met briefly. They stood together, saying the words of the service almost as one. The priest placed the Host in their open mouths. And afterwards Robert Minton took her arm and escorted her from the church. He saw the attention paid to them as they walked down the stone steps of the church together — the murmurs, the fingers pointing at her gown. It was no longer a color of mourning, but a sky blue that flattered her gold hair with its red high-lights.

She greeted those who greeted her, introducing him politely and moving on as quickly as she could, which amused him. She seemed well versed in how to deal with the curious. "We are likely to meet my mother next, for someone will already be on their way to tell her they saw us. We are making it easy for her, for we shall walk in the park by my family's home, proving to my mother that there is nothing to be concerned about," she told him.

"Would she suspect otherwise?" he asked, amused.

"Of course she would. I am a beautiful and rich widow. I will be sought after by men both unscrupulous as well as deadly dull and respectable," Lucianna said in humorous tones. "Orianna Pietro d'Angelo is a woman who would see her children protected and happy, as she believes is proper. My two older sisters managed to push her from their lives, for she will meddle. It will be harder for me, for I am right here in Florence, where she may appear like some busybody faerie godmother at any time, alas. So 'tis best to let her believe she still maintains some small charge over me, my lord, even if she does not."

"Yes, on our brief acquaintance I considered your mother to be a lady of strong principles," he said. "I find myself amused to see that you understand her so well, and know how to manage her."

"It took many years, but mostly I learned

from the behavior of my two older sisters, and the mistakes they made in dealing with our mother," Lucianna admitted. "You must understand Orianna. Daughters of Venetian princes do not as a rule wed merchants, even wealthy merchants, but our grandfather had many daughters, and our mother was the youngest of them and had the smallest dower to offer. My grandfather liked our father despite what he considered his shortcomings, and he offered this Florentine merchant his daughter in marriage. Our mother was in love with a married man at the time, and there was danger of a scandal. Rumors of such a possibility had already caused several suitable families with younger sons to withdraw even the hope of a marriage between their families. So our mother was quickly wed to the Florentine merchant, and departed Venice. She has never forgotten it was her behavior that cost her a Venetian marriage. So we, her daughters, have to be better than she was."

"Yet your oldest sister fled her marriage, I am told. Your mother could not have been pleased with that," he said.

"That is a tale for another time," Lucianna told him. "We are here now," she said as she led him from the street past delicate wrought-iron gates and into an exquisite small park. "We Florentines love our small parks. My parents created this one, and it is open to the public. Our family's reputation is such that the park is kept peaceful. Any who would misbehave are ejected, and forbidden to return."

They strolled now along a graveled path on either side of which there were lime trees. There were beds of roses here and there. The roses were so naturally fragrant that they perfumed the air about them. Robert Minton didn't believe he had ever been in such a romantic place in his life. They came to a marble bench, and he drew her down onto it with him. Birds in the trees about them sang.

"This has to be a dream," he said, "and if it is, may I never awaken."

Lucianna laughed softly. "I do not believe anyone has ever said such lovely words about the Pietro d'Angelos' little park, my lord."

"It's exquisite! So much so that it could not possibly be re-created anywhere else."

"If you sat here in winter with a cold rain beating down upon your broad shoulders, my lord, you might consider otherwise," she told him. "Ah, do not look up, but here come my mother and my father, enjoying the beauty of their creation, no doubt,"

Lucianna said.

Robert Minton, Earl of Lisle, burst out laughing. "You are really a most outrageous girl," he said.

"I am a woman, my lord. A beautiful widow woman," she said.

"No, *signora,* you are a girl, not yet a woman, and your blush reveals the truth of my observations. Do not deny it."

"Ah, Lucianna, my lord of Lisle," Orianna Pietro d'Angelo purred in greeting.

"Daughter. My lord," Giovanni Pietro d'Angelo said to each.

"Mother, how lovely to see you. Roberto invited me for a walk in the park after Mass, but then he admitted to knowing no park. I told him I knew the loveliest park in all of Florence, and so here we are!"

"I was told you arrived at Mass together, Lucianna," Orianna said, disapprovingly. "And that you were dressed inappropriately."

"I was most certainly not in Roberto's company when we arrived, Mother! I came quite alone. How dreadful of someone to spread such a rumor. I am outraged. Am I to have no life of my own? My mourning is over for Alfredo. Believe me, every fortune hunter in Florence will be approaching me. Will there be unseemly gossip about them too? As for my gown, do you find it unseemly?"

Orianna looked at her daughter's modest sky blue garment and shook her head. "No, I do not," she admitted. Then she said, "Will you and the earl join us for dinner?"

"It would be a pleasure, *Signora* Pietro d'Angelo," Robert Minton quickly spoke up. "I am honored that you would invite a stranger into your home for a meal." He stood now and bowed to both of Lucianna's parents in a show of respect.

"Oh," Orianna trilled girlishly, "it is really our honor, my lord."

"We shall not argue about it, my dear *signora,*" the earl said with a smile.

Lucianna stood up. "Then come, and let us all add to the gossip by walking together to the palazzo," she said, trying not to show her irritation. What on earth did her mother expect to accomplish with this invitation? Now that Lucianna had fulfilled her obligation to her late husband, she wanted a private life, and that did not include having dinner with her parents and the earl. Well, perhaps with the earl.

CHAPTER 3

Robert Minton enjoyed his time with the Pietro d'Angelos. Once inside their beautiful palazzo gardens drinking wine, he found himself quite relaxed. He could not say the same for Lucianna, who, he realized, was waiting for her mother to begin some sort of interrogation, but oddly, Orianna asked little. He found Lucianna's younger sister, Serena, amusing and filled with gossip that she obviously quite relished. His host invited him to view a painting of his entire family.

"It was painted many years ago before they were all scattered," he said, almost wistfully. Then he lowered his voice. "Orianna will not have it displayed in a prominent place any longer because of Bianca's behavior. So I keep it in my library, where she seldom comes," Giovanni explained as he opened the door to the room, ushering the earl inside. "I enjoy gazing upon my seven children in happier times." Then he pointed to a paneled wall.

The earl walked closer to view the painting. It was a charming family portrait, and it was obvious they were all very happy. "Bianca is the dark-haired girl?"

"Yes. She was fourteen. Marco, fifteen. It was just before I was forced to give her in marriage to an unsuitable man. I will not say he was a gentleman, for he was not. Lucianna will tell you the story. The boy with the sweet smile is our Giorgio; he was eleven. Francesca, the one with the proud look, was nine; Lucianna and her twin brother, six; and our youngest, Serena, four." He chuckled. "The boys didn't care, of course, but the girls, even the smallest, were so proud of having their portrait painted."

"It is a fine family, *Signore* Pietro d'Angelo," the earl said, complimenting his host. "I am particularly charmed to see *Signora* Lucianna at such a young and vulnerable age."

"Giovanni," the silk merchant said. "I think perhaps we shall be more than just friends one day, Roberto. Besides, you are now considered a valued client of my establishment." The older man smiled. "No explanations are required at this time, Roberto. We shall let life lead us where it will."

"I would, nonetheless, like your permission to court Lucianna, Giovanni. You should know my attentions to your daughter are honorable."

"Lucianna is a widow, and she will make her own decisions, Roberto. I can no longer claim any influence over her, although Orianna would argue with me in that respect." He chuckled. "I am grateful for your confidence. It would be my suggestion, however, that nothing be said at this time to my wife. She will begin having a trousseau sewn for Lucianna before the fact. And if you take Lucianna to wife, my lord, I question if she would want to live in England. Of my four daughters, she is the one who loves the city best."

"Then I must see that she learn to love England as well," the earl said. "Your guild does not have a representative in London, do they? The Milanese are planning to send one in order to spare their cloth merchants having to wait for English custom, and to make it more convenient for our merchants. If you do not send a representative to London too, the Milanese will take all your trade, thus ruining the Florentine silk merchants."

"I was not yet aware of this," Giovanni

Pietro d'Angelo said. "I must call a meeting of my guild and present this to them. If Milan sends a representative to London, then so must Florence. No one will want to go, of course, and leave their businesses to their sons alone."

"Send Lucianna to represent Florence. She knows your business well. Certainly better than your heir does. Your fellow tradesmen know and like your daughter. I would even go so far as to say they trust her. Milan will send some stuffy fellow who will have difficulty dealing with our merchants. Florence's representative will be a beautiful woman who speaks our language with an absolutely delightful accent, and she will charm her way among our merchants."

"There will be some among my guild who will be difficult to convince that sending a woman is the right thing to do," Giovanni said.

"Convince them that it is. Remind them that the English king sent his representative to purchase silks for his queen in Florence, and it was your daughter who sold him a large order, though that is not quite true. The Pietro d'Angelos therefore have a small amount of influence with the English now, which means that silk merchants of Florence do too. They should not deny that prestige, Giovanni."

"All of this to gain my daughter's company in England?" The silk merchant laughed, unable to help himself. "You are a very clever man, Roberto, but your idea actually has merit." Then he sighed. "I shall have to go back to my shop full-time if I let Lucianna go to England. My son is well meaning, but a dunce where his mistress is concerned. A more scheming baggage I have never known, but Marco is enamored of her. It is to be hoped she will eventually find a wealthier protector, and then Marco will be sent packing, but until that time, he has not the wit or the will to concentrate on the business."

There was a knock upon the door, and a servant called, "The mistress bids you and the English lord to table, *signore*."

"We had best go, lest we incur Orianna's displeasure," the silk merchant said with a small smile.

The two men hurried to the dining room and took their places. A priest at the table offered a blessing, and everyone sat. The meal was well cooked and delicious. The wines served were quite good, and the earl complimented his hostess.

Orianna smiled, quite pleased. When the

last of the goblets had been cleared from the table, Lucianna announced that they must be going. "It is not yet dark," her mother said. "Remain a bit longer."

"No, Mother," her third daughter replied. "You have been very gracious to us, but it is time to leave." She stood up, looking to the earl.

He could see desperation in her eyes. "Indeed, we must go, *signora,*" he agreed with Lucianna. "Your hospitality has been most pleasant, but even I am wise enough not to walk your streets in the dark. I often wonder why the streets of cities become so dangerous after the sun has set." He took Orianna's elegant hand and kissed it, bowing.

"I believe Roberto is wise, my dear, and careful of our daughter, which I know you appreciate," Giovanni Pietro d'Angelo said in smooth and placating tones to his wife. He knew the game she was playing well. Having fed her guest, and filled him with wine, she was now ready to pounce. Lucianna knew this game too, which was why she was so intent on hurrying the earl from her parents' palazzo.

Orianna sighed dramatically. "Very well," she conceded, "if you think you must go, then you must. I hope you will come again, my lord." And then she smiled her most charming smile at him.

"I would be honored," Robert Minton said, bowing again. Then he turned, taking Lucianna's arm politely, and they departed the Pietro d'Angelos' palazzo, walking quickly to regain the little green park.

"Thank heavens!" Lucianna smiled. "I freed you before she was able to begin her interrogation. She will be most annoyed with me for it, I fear. She doesn't know half about you that she wants to know."

He chuckled. "I could see how stressed you were in her presence," he noted. "Your mother is a most formidable woman." He chuckled again.

"And always has been," Lucianna told him. "Francesca drove her half mad with her determination to have her own way. She is much like our mother. My sister has now become the noble widow, guarding her son like a tigress and ruling Terreno Boscoso in his name. She will not take another husband, and her council is in firm agreement with her, which has our mother stymied, for she would see Francesca re-wed but cannot stand against the royal council of Terreno Boscoso."

"So she will now concentrate upon her other widowed daughter," he said, smiling.

"Yes, Santa Anna, help me," Lucianna admitted with a small smile. "I wish there were a way I could escape her."

He said nothing about his conversation with her father. She wished to avoid Orianna's machinations, but she had said nothing of leaving her beloved Florence. If the silk merchants of Florence could be persuaded to send a representative to London, and she was their chosen one, then her mother might protest, but she could not stop her daughter, for while he knew Lucianna would protest such an assignment, he also knew she would go.

"Come," she said to him. "We will walk along the river for a brief distance. The day is fair."

"May I interrogate you as your mother would have done to me?" he asked her.

"I will not guarantee to answer all your questions, my lord," she told him with a little smile.

"You wed to please your family," he said. It was not a query.

"I did. The economy had made it impossible to have the sort of enormous dower that my two older sisters had. Both Bianca's and Francesca's behaviors had made many families wary of seeking my hand. Would I be like my sisters? Independent and deter-

61

mined to have my own way? Alfredo wanted a wife who would take care of him in his old age. He made no secret of it, and he decided a young pretty one would give him more pleasure than a cranky older woman."

She laughed. "It was so like him to be direct. He asked my parents for me. They were thoughtful enough to ask me. We met several times, and frankly, I liked him. He was quite forthright with me. He was too old to enjoy conjugal relations, and we would not have them. He wanted to know if I could accept it, and I agreed I could. So we were wed. He was kind to me and generous. I was not unhappy with him."

"You do not want passion with a man?" he asked her, curious.

"I did not want it or believe it possible with a man past eighty," she told him. "I have been sheltered by my family, as all respectable women are. I have never been in love, but if I were, I should want children with my husband," she told him.

"I am relieved to hear it," he responded. She was a virgin, even as he had already suspected. Untouched. "You want love in your marriage? Most marriages are arranged for the best interests of the families involved, Lucianna."

"I know," she admitted, "but Bianca loved

her prince enough to give up her family. As for Francesca, she insulted every suitor who sought her hand, and when the heir to Terreno Boscoso chose her for his bride, she ran away, and had to be brought back. Of course, the little fool was quite happy with him, and then he was murdered by a servant. They say her wrath was ferocious. She now rules her duchy for her little son. She might remarry, but will not, and her council backs her, much to our mother's irritation. With two such sisters, and a small dower, I was not eagerly sought after. I was happy to marry Alfredo. It took me away from my mother's house, and my husband and I were good to each other. He often called me his angel, but I called him my knight for rescuing me."

The earl smiled. "Your late husband, God assoil his good soul, sounds like a fine man," he said to her.

"He was. He left Norberto only his shop, and a small amount of gold. He left me his house, and a great deal of gold," Lucianna said.

"And now your mourning is over, and you will be besieged for your hand," he said. "Will it please you?"

"Not particularly," she replied. "I shall have to waste my time chasing off fortune hunters who will all believe I am just being coy by sending them off. One thing Alfredo told me before he died: I was not to wed again unless I was madly in love. 'Let none but a man you trust have charge over you,' he said. I agree, and I shall follow Alfredo's most excellent advice," Lucianna said.

"I asked your father this afternoon if I might court you," he told her, much to her surprise. "He said that must be your decision, although your mother would disagree if she knew. We thought it best to say nothing to her. Will you let me court you, Lucianna?"

She was actually very surprised by his candor. "I would prefer it better if we might just begin as friends," she told him. "I am not ready to think seriously of marriage yet."

"I understand. You like the freedom being a widow has given you," he observed.

Lucianna laughed. "I do not know if I quite like it yet that you understand me so well," she said, and though she made light of it with him, it did disturb her. "Besides, how can you court me? You must return to England very soon."

"I can come back," he answered. "I can write you wonderful long letters while I am gone. And while I am not here, you can entertain all those gentlemen fascinated by your beauty, and more enchanted by your fortune."

"Does my fortune not interest you, my lord?"

"I have my own fortune. Any fortune you possess would remain yours as my wife," he told her. "I am delighted by your beauty, but more so by your intellect and charm. A woman needs more than skill in bedsport to be my wife, although I realize that will not necessarily be so with other men."

"You are not at all like Florentine men," she observed. "It is both intriguing and frightening, my lord."

He stopped in their stroll, and taking her shoulders between his two hands, looked boldly down into her face. "Be intrigued, Lucianna, but never be afraid of me. I have never before been so charmed by a lady as I am by you."

"Nor has any gentleman been so direct with me but my husband," she responded. Then she said, "It is getting late, and the light will soon begin to fade, my lord. I think it best you escort me home now."

"I agree," he told her, and together they departed the path along the river Arno so he might bring her to her house. They did not speak again as they walked, but once at her door he said, "I will see you on the morrow at San Piero, Lucianna, if you will permit."

She nodded, saying only, "Yes." Then she entered her house, closing the door behind her.

Balia hurried down the stairs upon hearing her enter. "Gracious, mistress, where were you so long?"

"The Englishman and I decided to walk in a park. I chose the one my family built, for I knew someone would have already hurried to fill my mother's ear with the knowledge I was with Roberto. It was easier in his presence to answer the few questions she was able to ask. She insisted we have our meal with them. Afterwards he and I walked along the Arno."

The Englishman likes you," Balia said.

"So he has said to me. Come with me on the morrow to Mass so we may stem the worst of the gossip," Lucianna said.

"You should have taken me this morning," Balia scolded.

"I did not wish to walk in the park with you," Lucianna said with a small smile, and Balia laughed.

"No, I do not imagine you did," she replied, "but you must consider your reputation, mistress. A man who enjoys a woman's company usually has eventual seduction on his mind."

"You could very well be right," Lucianna agreed. She was not yet ready to tell her faithful servant that the English earl had even more on his mind. "I will be most circumspect in my public behavior, I can promise you. Now bring me some warm soup, for I find I am chilled."

Balia hurried off to do her mistress's bidding as Lucianna settled herself in a comfortable chair. "Well, Fredo," she said, speaking to her deceased husband, "what do you think of this Englishman? I have to admit his charm has won me over, but I need to know more of him. How many men appear charming, but are really villains? My mother, of course, would be delighted to see me take such a man as a husband. Oh, the crowing she would do if I were wed to an English earl, a personal friend of their king. She would make certain every family reluctant to offer one of their sons to me would suffer with the knowledge of their foolishness. Then she would go seeking another titled son-in-law elsewhere for Serena. I know — I must be patient, as you were ever advising me, Fredo. Well, I promise you that I will be."

Balia brought her a small cup of hot soup and then left her to her thoughts. They were many. If Roberto actually asked her to marry him, she would have to leave Florence and go to England with him. She wondered if she could do that. She could if she loved him, Lucianna thought. And she had never heard it said that England was a savage or uncivilized place. It was green and fair, if Roberto was to be believed.

Of course they had been at war with themselves over two ruling families, but that matter was now settled with the death of the Yorkist heirs, and the reign of the Lancastrian king called Henry VII. Fortunately, her earl was a member of the Lancaster faction. His person and his lands were safe from confiscation. But the question still remained: could she learn to love him enough to leave Florence? To even leave her family? Family was all-important, and unlike Bianca and Francesca, Lucianna was not certain she could be without them.

The soup finished, she called for Balia, who prepared her for bed.

Once in her bed, and Balia gone to her own little chamber, Lucianna considered further. How was the wife of an English lord meant to behave? Would she be part of the court? She doubted that the high-born ladies of the court would easily accept her, if they accepted her at all. Would that make her a detriment to Roberto? Even Orianna would seriously consider such a thing and worry.

But her eldest sister, Bianca, had loved her prince enough to step into a new world. She had obviously thrived, if one was to believe Marco, who had managed to see her once after she had gone. Even Marco would not have lied in that matter. Even if their mother pretended not to care, she knew Orianna did, but more so their father.

And Francesca had gone to Terreno Boscoso to wed the duke's son and heir. She had been one of three maidens he would choose from, and Francesca had been the most blasé about the whole matter, much to Orianna's distress. Yet the old duke's son had chosen her, fascinated by her beauty and independent attitude. Francesca had been happy before her young husband was murdered. And she had no desire to return to Florence.

But England was a long way away, Lucianna thought. Still, Bianca's home was certainly as far, but Terreno Boscoso was a part of the Italian states. Lucianna sighed. If she could love Roberto, then she could certainly be as brave as her sisters. And she did want children one day. *And passion.* She knew nothing of it, admittedly, but she knew that a woman who found passion was a happy and content woman. While her brief marriage with her husband had been pleasant, Lucianna could not recall having really been happy and content since her childhood summers in the Tuscan countryside.

She finally fell asleep without realizing it, and opened her eyes in the morning as Balia gently shook her shoulder, awakening her. "Time for church?" she murmured sleepily.

"Yes, mistress," Balia said. "I think that pretty rose gown will do nicely this morning."

"Nay, something a little bit more subdued. I don't want to appear to be celebrating the end of my mourning. I could see several women were shocked yesterday by my sudden change into color again. Perhaps the dark green with the fine lace," Lucianna suggested.

"The old crows would like you to keep to black for the rest of your life," Balia muttered.

"And keep myself hidden in the bookshop." Lucianna chuckled. "I know, Balia, I know. While I have always been most careful in my behavior, I am still one of the scandalous Pietro d'Angelo sisters, and they must keep their sons and brothers safe from me."

"You are nothing at all like your two older sisters!" Balia said indignantly.

"No, I did not run away with an infidel, nor do I rule a duchy for my little son," Lucianna agreed, "but I married a man who could have been my grandfather. Why would I have done such a thing except to inherit his wealth? And what kind of a life did the poor man live with me? Have I a secret lover? Did I hasten Alfredo's death?"

"Mistress!" Balia was shocked.

"Now, Balia, do not deny you have heard this idle chatter, for my sister Serena has and has reported it all to me," Lucianna said.

Balia flushed. "I have," she admitted, "and refuted it all to the teller's face, but they didn't want to believe you were a good wife to the master. Nor, had I explained to them, would they have understood that you and he became good friends." She rehung the rose-colored gown and drew out a dark green silk decorated at its neck and sleeves with fine lace that had been made by the nuns at a local convent.

"Let them think what they will," Lucianna said. "I know I was a good wife to my husband, and his family knew it. That is all

71

that matters. Still, for a few weeks I shall maintain more subdued colored gowns so that my neighbors may grow used to the idea that the Widow Allibatore has, after a full year, put aside her mourning." She looked at the gown Balia was holding up. "Oh yes, that will do nicely. Do we have some nice roses in the garden I might wear in my hair?"

"When does the Englishman return to his country?" Balia asked.

"Soon, I believe," Lucianna told her. "I shall miss his company, for he is charming and amusing."

"He has remained longer because of you," Balia said.

"I think he has remained because he likes our city," Lucianna answered her.

"You are naïve if you believe so, and I know you are not," Balia replied with a twinkle in her eye.

And it did become obvious that that was exactly why Robert Minton remained in Florence. But soon the weather began to grow colder and wetter.

"I cannot remain any longer," he told Lucianna as they sat one day by her fire. "I cannot leave my estates any longer. My majordomo cannot manage without me, though he is a good man."

"And I imagine the king needs you too," she answered.

"Nay, I am Henry Tudor's friend, nothing more. I do not meddle in politics. Politics is a dangerous and tricky business. I want no part of it, Lucianna. I would marry, and have children. Being the patriarch of a family, the lord of a large estate, is a far better life. The whims of royalty quickly turn friend to foe. I am at my king's beck and call, but we spoke much of this when we were young men in Brittany. I told Henry Tudor then I would always be there for him, but I would not involve myself in his governance. He said he understood, and that he wished he might live his life as simply. His mother, of course, would have never allowed it. Making him king, wedding him to Elizabeth of York, ended the hundred years of quarreling between the house of Lancaster and the house of York."

"You are a clever man to keep a king for a friend without involving yourself in his rule," Lucianna told him. "I admire you for it, Roberto. I am sorry you must leave Florence, for I much enjoy walking with you along the river, and in the parks. I will miss you, if you will permit me to say it."

"Will you give me your permission to come back?" he asked, seriously.

"Will you come back, Roberto?"

"For you, Lucianna, aye. I will come back," he said.

"Then I shall wait for you, my lord," she responded with a smile.

"You must, however, give me something by which to remember you, *cara,*" he said to her. And leaning forward in his chair, he pulled her towards him, and kissed her.

Lucianna's head spun. The kiss was not a gentle or quick kiss. It deepened with each moment he held her, and something stirred within Lucianna, and suddenly flared, causing her to feel heat suffusing her entire body. To her surprise, she shivered. His kiss softened before he took his lips from hers, but he still held her gently.

"That was your first real kiss, wasn't it?" he asked.

Briefly speechless, she nodded, finally saying, "Alfredo's lips never touched mine but once, briefly, the day we wed. He always kissed me on the cheek, or the forehead, or my hand."

"Then I certainly have something very special to remember you by until I return, Lucianna. I am honored, sweetheart."

It was the first time he had ever used such a serious endearment. Lucianna felt a thrill race through her. Then she said teasingly,

"If that is the art of kissing I shall have to attempt to experience more of it."

"No!" he said fiercely, and then, softening his tone, continued. "You must not encourage other men to kiss you, Lucianna, lest you tarnish your reputation. You do not want the gossips suggesting that you are loose in your behavior."

"No," she agreed meekly with him, "of course not, Roberto." But even as inexperienced as she was in the romantic relationships between men and women, Lucianna knew his explanation wasn't the full truth. "I shall be very mindful of my behavior while you are away," she promised him. Certainly a man did not kiss a woman like that unless he had some tender feeling for her.

He took his leave of her then, this time depositing a gentle kiss on her cheek. She watched him go, and then with a sigh she closed her front door, turning at the sound of Balia's voice.

"He is gone then for good," her serving woman said.

"No, he has promised to return," Lucianna said. "I hope he will."

"Sometimes gentlemen make promises they intend to keep at the time they make them, but then they do not," Balia told the young woman. "I hope you will not be disappointed, mistress."

"He will not disappoint me," Lucianna replied firmly.

CHAPTER 4

She missed his company, but Lucianna quickly found herself bombarded by bouquets sent by admiring gentlemen pleading for her company. They would join her at the Mass without her invitation, and she sent them away, complaining to the priest at San Piero of their intrusion into her devotions.

"But, *Signora* Allibatore," he said to her, "did you not allow the English gentleman to join you?"

"After he first requested my company weeks ago, I explained to him I was in mourning for my husband and would not entertain the idea of such a thing until my mourning was completed. He graciously accepted my words, and he asked again once my mourning for Alfredo had concluded. As he was a good customer of my father's, I considered it would be proper to permit his company at the Mass. Now that Lord Lisle is gone, these bold fellows think they may have my company easily, without my permission, Padre, and they cannot."

"I understand," the priest said immediately, but then he added, "Of course, some of them might be interested in courting you, *signora.*"

"They are far more interested in the fortune my dear husband left me," Lucianna said candidly to the cleric, "and you know it to be so. I am not yet ready to socialize, except with my family. My mother will advise me if I decide I should like to remarry."

"You are a good daughter, *signora,* to trust your parent," he approved.

"I was a good wife too," she said sharply. "There has never been any secret as to why Alfredo wed me. He wanted a pretty caretaker, and after the examples my sisters set, I was happy to be the wife of this good man, despite his great age. We were friends, though such an idea may shock many. He was kind, and he was generous. I tried to be the same in return, which is why I have honored his memory so faithfully. I am not yet ready to be assaulted by fortune hunters in church or elsewhere," Lucianna told the priest. "Speak to these men, or I shall be forced to deny myself the Mass each day."

The priest was very surprised by her frank

admission. Her husband had never had anything but the most loving and kind words for her. The *signora* had obviously felt an equal devotion to the elderly bookseller. "I will do so personally, *signora*," he promised Lucianna.

"*Grazie*," she said, and then returned home.

After some weeks had passed, Orianna came to visit her daughter one Sunday when she knew Lucianna would be home, and not in the silk shop trying to teach Marco what he must know but was no longer interested in learning. "I have begun to hear gossip that disturbs me, Daughter," Orianna began.

Lucianna knew exactly what her mother would say, but she asked sweetly, "What can that be? I am most circumspect in my life, Mother, going to Mass each day, looking after Father's shop six days a week. What can have disturbed you that you would pay me a special visit?"

"Why will you not accept the gentlemen who would call upon you, or their floral tributes, Lucianna? Your year of mourning is concluded."

"I am not interested in playing the *civetta*, Mother. Is that so very wrong of me? Would you have me fill my house with flowers and men I do not want?" Lucianna hated defending herself. When was Orianna going to leave her to live her own life as she saw fit?

"You are a well-to-do widow, Lucianna, and still young enough for a husband. You have a fine fortune to recommend you."

"I am not interested in a man who needs my *fine fortune* to recommend me. If a man can find nothing more about me than Alfredo's gold, then I certainly do not want him. At the moment, shocking as it may seem to you, Mother, I do not want to remarry."

"He is not coming back, Lucianna," her mother said.

"Who?"

"Do not play the innocent with me, Daughter. You know exactly who. Your Englishman. I know that you liked him, and why not? He was handsome in a rough way, and he had charm. If I had been you, I should have liked him too and entertained romantic thoughts. A man like that, however, isn't interested in taking a silk merchant's daughter to wife. Whatever he promised, he will not be back, Lucianna."

"I suppose if I had been you, Mother, I would have been assailed by romantic thoughts," Lucianna said. "But I am not you. I found Roberto charming and a good companion. Nothing more. And I will not even entertain marrying again until that dunce who is my brother stops daydreaming constantly about the wondrous Clarinda and learns how to manage Father's silk business. It is not that difficult if Marco would pay attention, but he does not. I pity his good wife."

"A good wife ignores creatures like Clarinda, and he is the envy of all his friends for having such a beautiful mistress."

"If I remarry, no husband will permit me to continue in Father's shop. How long will Clarinda remain by his side when he cannot buy her the latest bauble she wants? If Marco does not pay attention to our business, there will be no money. No mistress's undying devotion extends past a man's ability to gift her lavishly," Lucianna said. "When he was younger, he was enthusiastic to learn how to be a successful silk merchant, Mother, but once he met Clarinda, it all changed."

"She helps him forget," Orianna said slowly.

"Forget? What does Marco need to forget?"

"*Her.* He has always held himself responsible for her unfortunate fate, despite the fact she forgave him."

"Perhaps if you would speak her name

instead of referring to Bianca — yes, Mother, my oldest sister, Bianca — in such terms as *her,* he might feel truly forgiven. He knows how much you love her, and how her willingness to give up everything for Prince Amir hurt you. Tell him that you forgive him too. He will never be the man he was meant to be until you do."

"How clever you are to understand me so well, Lucianna. I am not sure I like it. And I believe we were speaking of the Englishman, were we not?"

"But, Mother, there is nothing to speak about with regard to him," Lucianna said. "Do not make excuses for me that do not exist just because I choose to remain a widow."

"I shall never have any grandchildren until Serena weds. It is to be hoped she will prove more amenable than the rest of you have," Orianna grumbled.

"You have three grandchildren," Lucianna said, laughing at this self-pitying outburst by her mother. "Bianca has a little girl, a princess, which should certainly please you, and Francesca has a son and a daughter. If you want more, then let Serena have a hand in choosing who she would wed," Lucianna advised her parent. "I know you wanted, hoped, that your daughters would marry well, and it did not quite happen as you would have willed it. I'm sorry."

"I can see I will make no headway with you. You will do as you please, Lucianna. I hope your choices will be wise ones."

Lucianna escorted her mother to the door and opened it. There stood a young gentleman, a bouquet in his hand. She sighed.

"Oh, *Signore* Parini," Orianna cooed, "have you come to visit my daughter?" She smiled warmly.

But before *Signore* Parini could open his mouth, Lucianna said in the most dulcet of tones, "Unfortunately I am not accepting visitors today, *Signore.* Farewell, Mother." She shut the door firmly behind them both. Orianna eventually would have her head for that little piece of business, Lucianna thought. But Guido Parini was probably the dullest man in all of Florence, and she was not of a mind to entertain him on her one day of freedom.

Balia came forward, laughing softly. "That was nicely done, mistress, but she will not be pleased by what you just did."

"No, she won't," Lucianna agreed, "but she'll get that poor man to escort her home, walking by her chair litter, and he will give her the flowers for herself, which will please her."

"I listened while you two spoke," Balia said. "You may have surprised her with your reasoning, but she will still seek to see you remarried as quickly as possible now that your formal mourning is over. Do you think she is correct? That the Englishman will not come back to Florence?"

"I don't know," Lucianna admitted. "But there is no harm in waiting for a brief time. Especially if I am going to be importuned by men like *Signore* Parini."

"I do not see how you are going to escape these eager gentlemen," Balia said. "And your mother will not be happy until she sees you wed again, I fear."

When Giovanni Pietro d'Angelo learned of his wife's visit to Lucianna, he knew it was time for him to act. Since the Englishman had told him of Milan's decision to set up a representative of their silk trade in London, Giovanni had been investigating discreetly if such a thing was actually coming to pass. He had finally learned it was indeed.

The Milanese planned next spring to send the son of one of their silk merchants to England to represent their silk guild. It was time to call a meeting of the guild and present this danger to his own guild members. He fully expected opposition, and he got it.

"Let them," one of his members said.

"If we do not have our own agent representing Florence, we will lose a great deal of business," Giovanni warned them.

"We are already losing business to Milan."

"We will lose more. If you were a busy merchant in London, would you want to leave your business and family to travel to Florence?"

"I'd travel anywhere, anytime, to avoid listening to my wife and my mistress complain," one man said, and there was much good-natured laughter at this remark.

Giovanni smiled. "I imagine we all would at one time or another, but if there is an easier way of obtaining our fine silk for English merchants, why should we not pursue it?" he asked them. "It will not require an enormous outlay on our parts. A small shop in a good location, a single representative, a fine supply of our fabrics, and smaller samples showing the various colors available. If we divide the small cost among us, we then have an excellent advantage."

"Where did you learn this information regarding Milan?" one of the silk merchants asked him.

"I heard it first from the English lord who purchased such a large order from me for his king several months back. He had visited Milan first, and was told it. After he passed his knowledge on to me, I investigated the rumor myself, and learned it was true."

"We must pay for the man representing us. London is an expensive city in which to live," another of the silk merchants said. "We need someone knowledgeable, and someone who can speak their language. Who among us has someone like that who fits that description and is willing to part with them?"

There was a deep silence. No one spoke up, and Giovanni Pietro d'Angelo knew he now had the advantage over them. He had not been certain until now, but now he knew.

"I would send my daughter Lucianna," he said quietly. "She is very knowledgeable of our trade and speaks English quite well."

"A woman?"

"The bookseller's widow?"

"Impossible! We will be a laughingstock."

"Why?" he demanded of them. "Because she is female? She knows our business. She speaks their language."

"What does Orianna think of this?" one merchant dared to ask.

"She'll have your balls for even suggesting such a thing," another said boldly.

"My wife does not manage my business, nor this guild," Giovanni Pietro d'Angelo said icily. "If you are foolish enough to allow Milan to get ahead of us, I will send her myself to represent my silks only, and I will end up being the only successful silk merchant remaining in our fair city. It is your decision to make, good sirs." He had no intention of arguing the point all evening.

"To send a woman to do our business is unusual," Carlo Alberti, a well-respected silk merchant said. "I cannot deny, however, that Lucianna, your daughter, knows silk very well. She is a credit to you and to our guild. Will you compromise with us, Giovanni, and send a man with her? My wife tells me that Orianna is unhappy that your Luca follows a military career. He is your daughter's twin. Could you not persuade him to give up his warlike pursuits to learn the business of our commerce? He might accompany his sister to London. She could teach him our trade. Considering your oldest son's disinterest in silk, and your second son's religious vocation, it could do you no disservice to have another heir, with a well-rounded knowledge of silks."

The other merchants voiced their agreement and approval of such a plan. Thinking for a moment, Giovanni Pietro d'Angelo decided that Carlo Alberti's idea was a rather excellent one. Why he hadn't thought of it himself, he didn't know. "I will agree to your proposal," he said, "and send Luca with his sister. Now let us vote on the matter."

They voted. While a few disliked the idea, the majority voted in favor of opening a small shop in London to represent their guild, with Lucianna Pietro d'Angelo and her brother Luca as their representatives. They all knew her, and they could be certain she would be a fair deputy for them, for she was, after all, her father's daughter. And her brother would preserve the dignity of their guild.

When it had been decided, one among them said, "Now go home and tell your wife what you have done, Gio," and there was much amused laughter.

He would tell her tonight, but not before he had spoken to Lucianna. He climbed into his litter chair, and directed it to his daughter's house. Two torchbearers ran before him, and two behind him as they hurried through the darkening streets to quickly reach her home. He climbed out of his chair and said to them, "I will not be long."

Lucianna was surprised to see her father at such an hour. She ushered him inside into the small library and invited him to sit. "What is it, Father? Is all well at home?" She handed him a small goblet.

"I have had the temerity to rearrange your life tonight, Lucianna," he began, and sipped his wine. He held up his hand quickly. "Nay, no marriage, for I respect your wishes on that, Daughter."

"Then what have you done?" she asked, smiling. As long as it was not another marriage, she was content.

"You are going to England, Lucianna," he began.

Her eyes widened in surprise, but he quickly continued.

"The earl told me before he departed that Milan was intending to set up a shop in London to display their silks so English tradesmen might order in the comfort of their own city, and not go through the trouble of traveling to Italy. It is, therefore, necessary that Florence do the same thing. The guild has chosen you, at my suggestion, to serve as our deputy in London. I thought perhaps you might enjoy being away from your mother, and her constant planning, for a while.

"I am also sending Luca with you so you may teach him the business of the silk trade. With Marco's disinterest and inability to learn, I did not consider it a bad idea for Luca to give up the military and learn our ways. That will please your mother. The earl thought it a good idea for a woman to represent us. It sets us apart from Milan. You will have far more charm than whoever speaks for them. Of course, it will be considered that your brother is in charge, but you will not allow him to abuse his authority, I suspect," her father said with a chuckle.

Lucianna gave him a mischievous smile. "No, I will not," she said, and added, "Mother does not know, does she? I do not doubt, however, that she will be glad to see Luca gone from the military."

"Nay, but when I go home, I must tell her," he replied. Then he chuckled again. "A bit of both sweet and sour for your mother to digest. She will not be happy to lose you, but she will be happy and relieved to have her precious youngest son freed of his warlike pursuits. It is Luca's happiness you and I must consider."

"There are no wars now to entertain him," Lucianna said. "I think he only chose the military because Marco was the heir, and

Giorgio had chosen the church. He is quick to learn." Then she considered England, and the Earl of Lisle. "If I go to London," she said to her father, "will it not appear as if I am chasing after Roberto?"

"I believe the Englishman is interested in having you for his wife," Giovanni Pietro d'Angelo said quietly, surprising Lucianna. "He asked me for my permission to court you, Lucianna. I explained to him that since you are a widow, the choices you made would be up to you. I do not know if he was swept away by the charm and beauty of Italy, or if upon returning home to England, he simply forgot you. But nonetheless, let us get your mother more interested in arranging Serena's life rather than rearranging yours. Unless, of course, there is someone you favor now."

"No," Lucianna told her father. "There is none here I would happily marry. Perhaps Roberto has forgotten me, but I will not know unless we have the opportunity to meet again, will I?"

"Then you will go?"

"What of your shop? Marco will simply not pay attention to the business of the silk trade. I cannot, in good conscience, leave it in his hands, Father."

"I shall go back into the shop full-time,

Daughter. And I believe I have a clever way of detaching *Signorina* Clarinda from your brother. I shall pay his wages to his wife, and instruct her to give him enough coin to walk about with his friends, but not enough to support his greedy mistress."

"He will be heartbroken," Lucianna said.

"But hopefully he will see the wench for what she really is," her father answered. "He will swear off women for the interim, and put his mind on his business before finding another mistress."

Lucianna laughed. "It is already autumn. When am I to go?"

"As quickly as possible. I want your mother to have no time to attempt to thwart me, Daughter. I am used to Orianna's bouts of pique."

"Let me call in Balia and see if she is willing to come with me."

"I believe she will be," he answered as his daughter opened the library door and called for her personal servant.

She was already seated again by the time the older woman entered the chamber. "Yes, mistress? How may I serve you?"

Lucianna quickly explained, and then finished by asking, "Will you come with me, Balia?"

"Of course I will," Balia said. "Who else

would look after you if I didn't? When do we leave?"

"As quickly as possible, to avoid familial difficulties," Lucianna told her. "How quickly can we be packed? We will take my clothing, jewelry, and bed linens. They are mine. Everything else was Alfredo's and his first wife's. I don't want it," Lucianna said. "I will lock up the house when I go. It is here if I ever come back, but if I do not, then I will sell it."

"You don't want to give it to Norberto?" her father asked.

"No. He may buy it if he so desires should I sell, but the house is part of my inheritance from Fredo. I will not just give it to his son," Lucianna said. "He has his own home, given him by his wife's parents, for she did not wish to live with her in-laws and look after them. That is why Fredo left me the house outright and not Norberto." Then she asked her father, "By what manner shall we travel?"

"I think overland to the coast facing what is called the English Channel, and then across that body of water to England itself. I will have my bankers, the Kiras, notify their London branch to see you have both a small shop and a separate house nearby that is furnished for your comfort. They will help you settle yourself. You will carry with you a letter to the English king, announcing your presence and Luca's as the representatives of the guild of Florentine silk merchants. There will be other letters for the more important of the London guilds so that your presence and authority are known to them. Ask the Kiras to suggest someone to help you in the shop. Accept their advice, but I will speak with you again before you depart. Balia, how long will it take you to make ready?" he asked.

"Six days, sir," Lucianna's serving woman said. "I will have it all packed and ready in six days."

"Excellent!" he approved. "We will not tell your mother when you are going, Lucianna. She will, therefore, have less time to meddle. As for Luca, he will meet you somewhere along the road. I am very proud of you, Daughter. This is a great challenge, but I know that you will be successful in this endeavor. You do not have to come to the shop in these last few days, for you will need time to prepare yourself, and direct Balia."

"I will come tomorrow, Father," she said. "Let me speak with Marco before you do. And he must know that Luca comes with me."

"Very well," her father said, standing. "I must go home now, and give your mother this exciting news. I hope I shall be able to gain a bit of sleep this night," he chuckled. Then, Balia escorting him, he left his daughter's house, climbed into his litter, and reluctantly directed them home to inform his wife that their third daughter was going to England.

Orianna behaved exactly as he had anticipated. "Are you mad?" she demanded. "A woman? You are sending a delicate woman to represent the silk merchants of Florence in London? I will not allow it! I will not, Gio!"

"My dear, you have no voice in this matter," he told her, infuriating her further. "This is the decision of the guild. Do you want us to lose more business than we have already lost to Milan? Besides, I will arrange to have Luca sell his commission in the army, and go with Lucianna. She will teach him our trade, and he will be saved from the military. Certainly you are pleased by that, my dear."

Orianna considered his words. Then she said, "You cannot turn my daughter, the granddaughter of a prince, into a tradeswoman."

"She enjoys it," he replied. "You would

have her sit here in Florence while you seek another husband for her, though they are only interested in her inherited wealth? No! You will not force my clever daughter into a boring and dull life because that suits you. No! She is going to London. With luck, she may attract her earl again."

"Are you foolish enough to believe that an English earl will have a tradeswoman for a wife? A mistress, perhaps, but certainly not a wife. Gio, the man is a personal friend of his king!"

"He asked my permission to direct his attentions towards Lucianna the day he had dinner with us," her husband countered.

"You never told me that!" Orianna said, very surprised.

"No, I did not. I did not want you interfering, Wife. We have had four daughters, but I claim this third daughter of ours as mine alone. You have the other three, Orianna. Lucianna is mine. Now I will not discuss this with you further. I am tired and wish only for my bed. Good night, my dear." He kissed her forehead and then left her.

Orianna was astounded by what she had learned, what he had said to her this night. Lucianna his? She thought on it and had to admit to herself that their third daughter was very much like her father. She was quiet, and thoughtful, rarely if ever revealing her private thoughts. She had been obedient in all things asked of her, even marrying without complaint a man old enough to be her grandfather.

It was only upon her husband's death that she had become independent.

Yes, Orianna realized, Lucianna was more Gio's than hers. Still, she didn't want her daughter leaving Florence unless it was in the keeping of a husband. But she knew she would not get that wish. Was her daughter pleased to have been given such a position that would take her from Florence? Yes, she probably was very delighted, and she would take the wretched Balia with her. Orianna didn't like Balia. She came from the Allibatore household and was entirely loyal to Lucianna. She would not spy on her mistress for Orianna. It was difficult to know exactly what her daughter was doing if she didn't have someone who would report to her. Who in England would, and then write to her? Orianna realized she would have to resign herself to whatever her daughter would write. If she would write. *I will have to write to her quite regularly so she will be forced to answer me back,* she realized. It was very bothersome, yet she would do it. Then she considered that Luca would be with his sister. If Lucianna was her father's daughter, her twin brother, Luca, was his mother's child. Luca would keep her informed of what was happening in England if she asked him.

The next morning, her husband ate his breakfast and then departed for his shop for the first time in several months. Orianna realized he would have to go regularly once Lucianna was no longer there. Even she was willing to admit that Marco's mind was not on their business. Gio would have to work hard to train him, but she was equally certain he already had a plan.

At the silk shop, Giovanni found Lucianna already opening up. "Good morning, Father. You actually look rested this morning."

"I said my piece. Your mother said hers, and then I told her I would not argue the point, so I went to bed," he explained. "Where is your brother, Lucianna?"

"It is Monday," she explained. "Marco does not come into the shop until after ten o'clock on Mondays."

"That will change," Master Pietro d'Angelo said grimly. "You will not yet have spoken to him, then."

She shook her head. "But I will."

When Marco finally arrived, he was surprised to find his father in the shop. He greeted them both, announcing, "I cannot remain long today, Lucianna. I am taking Clarinda to the races."

"You are a shop merchant," his father said. "You do not have time to take your mistress to the races, Marco. Do you suddenly think you are a Medici, that you may lollygag about?"

"I promised her, Father, and besides, Lucianna is always here for those seeking silks," Marco said, and she could see her father was very angry with her brother's words.

"But shortly I will not be here, Brother," she told him. "What will you do then?"

"What? Why will you not be here? I depend upon you, Lucianna. You cannot leave me."

"I have been chosen by the guild to represent them in London. A small shop is being opened in which to display the fine silks of Florence. That way the London merchants may see our wares and order directly from us, rather than travel here. The Milanese are also opening a shop."

"A woman?" Marco was surprised. "Why can they not send a man? It's unheard of for a woman to go. Tell them no!"

Lucianna laughed. "I am very honored to have been chosen, and I am excited to go,

Brother. The greatest benefit, of course, will be to get away from our mother's constant matchmaking and carping. You should also know that Luca will be leaving the military and coming with me to England to learn our trade."

"But I can't do this without you," he said, ignoring most of her words. Then he realized she had said Luca would be with her. *Luca?*

She laughed again. "You can't do it at all, Marco, but you must learn, Brother, for this is how Father earns the living for our family. He will come back into the shop and teach you while I am teaching Luca in London."

"But Clarinda . . ." he said. Luca giving up the military for silk? What was that all about? Then he considered Clarinda again.

"If she is not content to see you as other mistresses are, my son, she must learn. If she loves you, she will learn. Now, about your wages," Giovanni said.

"I will take my leave of you now," Lucianna told them. "I have much packing to do with Balia, so I will bid you both a good day." She absolutely did not want to be around when Marco learned what their father had decided. He would be furious. Helpless to change it, but furious nonetheless. She curtsied to both men, departing the silk shop quickly for the last time.

Chapter 5

It was difficult to restrain her laughter as she left the two men. She could only imagine her brother's shock to learn his wages would now be given to his wife, and that she was instructed to give him but a small portion of coin for himself. Poor Clarinda, but she was a beautiful young girl and would find another protector quickly. Marco would now be forced to keep his mind on his business.

Balia was busily packing when she arrived home. "I do not know how cold it is in this England," she said.

"Not as warm in the summer as we are, and perhaps a bit colder in the winters," Lucianna told her. "At least that is what Roberto said.

"Pack everything. What we do not need, we will store away. There are a few small bits of furniture that are mine that I would take. And I will take my own china and crystal with me, as well as my bedding and pillows. Is there anything else, Balia?"

"I do not think so, but if there is, I will pack it. Your father is supplying the wagons you will need. You will bring your litter chair?"

"Yes," Lucianna said, "but not the bearers. I will hire English bearers. My father will supply us with good horses to ride, and they will go with us to England. I must speak with the Kira banker here. Alfredo had his monies with them once he saw the Medici having their difficulties."

She left Balia to her task and went to write a missive requiring the presence of one of her bankers so she might discuss her finances and this journey to England. It was sent off that same afternoon. To her surprise, one of the Kiras arrived to speak with her the following morning. He was ushered into the library, where Lucianna was comfortable doing business.

The banker bowed. "I am Beniamino Kira, *Signora* Allibatore. I am told the silk guild is sending you to London to represent them. How may I serve you today?" He was a man of middle years. She would not have taken him for a Jew had she not known of his family. He was dressed conservatively and fashionably, as any Florentine banker would have been, with a dark robe and short hair.

"You wear my father's silk," she noted in her greeting.

"Your eye is sharp, *signora*," he replied with a small smile.

Lucianna laughed. "I am my father's daughter," she answered. Then she said, "I am going to England in a few days. I will need monies for my travels to begin with. I assume the guild has already contacted you about setting up an account for them in London. I will need to know how to access that account for their business and my own account for my personal use. Do you know with whom I will deal?"

"David Kira," the Florentine banker said. "We are a large family and have branches of our bank in most large cities now. He will attend to your needs. He has already been instructed to find you a good small shop in the right area, and a fine house in a respect- able neighborhood. We will purchase the house for you, as per your worthy father's instructions to us. You must not be at any disadvantage. David's wife is finding ser- vants for you. She is a most scrupulous woman and will see you have the best people. Her name is Yedda. Are you taking any of your own people, *signora*?"

"Only my personal serving woman," Lucianna answered him.

"Of course, of course! She will have been
with you for some time, and you are comfortable with her," he said. "Then those
escorting and driving your wagons will
return when they have seen you settled?"

"Yes," Lucianna said. "This is a new
beginning for us."

Beniamino Kira smiled. "You are a brave
young woman, if I may say it, *signora*. Yedda
will see to the servants. If you find yourself
dissatisfied, you have but to tell her. She
will help you find furnishings as well. You
may trust her."

"I am grateful to you, *Signore* Kira."

"I shall have a purse delivered to you the
afternoon before you leave. Is there any
other way I may serve you today?" he asked
her.

"This house. It must be cleaned thoroughly, the furnishings covered, the servants
paid. I will give each of them a reference.
The house should be checked once in a
while to make certain no one has broken in
or stolen anything. Only the shop and my
stepson's workshop can be available to him.
I have a single employee who now watches
over the bookstall. He is paid weekly. Will
you see to it?"

"Of course, *signora.* Everything shall be as you request," the banker told her. "Your stepson's family is not moving in here?"

"Under no circumstances. This is my house, my home, and I will eventually return to it to live out my old age," Lucianna said.

"You have no hope of this English earl, then," the banker said.

"I have no hope of anyone, *Signore* Kira, but myself. I am my own mistress now, and I will live my life to suit me alone," Lucianna said.

He nodded. "Yes, that will be best for you in a foreign place with no family to advise or counsel you." Then he arose. "If our business is now done, *signora,* I will take my leave of you."

"Yes, our business is concluded for now," she agreed. "I will escort you to the door, and I thank you for coming so promptly."

"Best to get the important business concluded early," he told her with a smile as they walked to the front door. Then, with a polite bow, he departed.

Within a few days, everything had been completed. Her possessions were all packed securely, her funds available. The servants had been paid and had their references. Her mother took several of them into her own household. Norberto's wife took the rest. Lucianna was pleased. She made a final visit to her mother the night before she was to go.

Orianna was not really resigned to her daughter's decision. "You have a home in the city. A good staff, and not one, but two small businesses to engage your time. Why do you choose to leave us to go to a foreign country? I don't understand. I am told the sun rarely shines in England. How will you tolerate that?"

"I will manage, and it is not forever, Mother. I will remain a year or two, perhaps, and then return home. By then I will have been forgotten, and can live peacefully in Florence, free from fortune hunters.

"I will be too old for you to marry off, and be glad of it. Someone must be here to care for you in your old age," Lucianna teased her mother.

Her father chuckled at that remark, but Orianna was not amused.

"You were always so obedient as a child, a girl, and a good wife," she mourned. "After Bianca and Francesca, I was so proud."

"You spoke her name," Lucianna said. "Have you forgiven Bianca, then, Mother?"

"Forgiving her has nothing to do with it," Orianna answered. "I am losing my daughter, and not to a husband, which would at least gladden my heart. I am losing you to a shop in a faraway place."

"Come and visit me, then, once you have Serena settled in marriage," Lucianna suggested. "You have never traveled far from Venice or Florence. This will be an exciting adventure for you, Mother."

"I neither need nor want an exciting adventure," Orianna grumbled. "Certainly not at my age!"

They spoke for an hour or more, but Orianna could not refrain from bemoaning Lucianna's going, and the younger woman became weary of the subject. Finally, she said, "I must go, Mother. We depart early tomorrow, and I need as much rest this evening as I can get. Traveling a long distance, I am told, is not easy." She arose.

Orianna immediately sprang up. "Be safe, my child! And write me as often as you can, Lucianna. Let me at least be comforted by your letters to me." Putting her arms about her third daughter, she hugged her hard.

Lucianna hugged her back, because she understood that her mother needed the comfort of that last embrace. And then, with her father at her elbow, she left the house of her childhood.

"Do not let them load the carts until the

first light of dawn," he advised, "and have them keep watch when it is done and they are waiting for you to come. Do you like the horses I purchased for you?

"They are sturdy beasts made for just this sort of journey. Keep them in England with you. You may be thought of as a shopkeeper, but you are the daughter of a wealthy man, and you have your own wealth. You will be shown respect once it is seen you possess your own home and animals. Insist at all times that you be treated with respect. Refuse to do business with those who do not show you respect. Many in the guild expect you to fail, being a woman, but you will not fail, Lucianna. You are a Pietro d'Angelo, and my daughter."

"You put a great deal of faith in me, Father," she replied. "But I will not fail you, I promise." As they reached her litter, she kissed him on his cheek.

"God bless you, my child," he told her when she was seated. "Godspeed!" he called after her as she was borne away.

The following day, in midmorning, the silk merchant went to Lucianna's house. It was tightly closed up. Norberto saw Giovanni Pietro d'Angelo from his upper-story workshop. Opening his window, he called down, "She was gone by the time I arrived, *signore.*

Good luck and good fortune to her."

"Thank you," Giovanni called up to him, and with a friendly wave of his hand, he walked the distance back to his shop.

Lucianna had departed even before the sun rose. The carts had been loaded when the first gray light had touched the morning skies and, already awake, Lucianna was dressed for travel. Like her sisters, she preferred riding in pants so she might ride astride. Balia was more comfortable side-saddle in her skirts. They were out through the city gates as they were opened. Lucianna was fascinated by the traffic coming into the city, merchants with goods that would be offered in the various street markets. There were so many things she had never before seen due to the secluded nature of her life, but the day was bright, warm, and sunny.

It was a journey of several very long weeks. From Florence they traveled to Pisa, then Genova, and Torino. Finally they found themselves in France. The cities they passed through were Dijon and Reims, and finally they reached Calais. Their goods were loaded onto a freight ferry that also accepted a few passengers.

Lucianna had heard that crossing the English Channel was an unpleasant experience. She and Balia were therefore delighted that the day was as sunny as when they had departed Florence, and the water as smooth as a pond. It was very unusual, the captain told her. She must be lucky. They reached a town on the other side of the channel called Folkstone, where it had already been arranged by the Kiras that they spend the night in a small convent that accepted guests.

The nuns welcomed them warmly. The Kiras had wisely been most generous to the mother superior. Their wagons were brought into the convent courtyard, keeping them safe during the night. The male drivers were offered food and the stable for their resting place. Lucianna and Balia were ushered into a small guesthouse with warm fires in both the dayroom and communal bedchamber. There were no other guests that night. Their supper was brought to them and was more than generous.

The next morning was gray, and rain threatened. The two women attended the early Mass, and although the Kiras had paid the way for them, Lucianna insisted on pressing a gold piece into the hand of the mother superior, and thanking her.

"You will be welcome anytime," the good woman said, considering all the things she might do for their flock with that gold piece that now rested in her hand. "If you are fortunate, you may reach London today."

In late afternoon, as they approached the city, David Kira rode out to meet them. "I will guide you to your new home, *signora*," he said.

"You may use English with me, Master Kira. I speak it fluently," Lucianna told him with a smile.

"I am happy to learn it, madame. It will make it easier for you to do business quickly," he told her. "I hope your trip was a pleasant one, despite its length."

"The accommodations you arranged were excellent. It was long and tiring, but at least we ate and slept well, in comfort," she told him. "Our crossing from Calais was unusually comfortable, with sun and smooth seas. The captain said I brought him good fortune," she said with a small smile.

"You were fortunate," he told her.

They were now in the city, yet outside of it. David Kira led her through several streets, finally stopping before a small stone house.

"This is the house your father bought for you. My wife, Yedda, assured me it is comfortable, though small. There is also a small garden in the rear of the building, I believe, with several fruit trees. And you have a small stable. Since it is not yet dark, I would advise your men to unload as much as they can into the house, and then put the carts still full in that stable. The others can remain outside."

"I will need servants," Lucianna said.

"Yedda has employed for you a cook, a housemaid, and a stableman. When you have decided how many others you will need, she will help you to hire them, madame."

They entered the house, and Lucianna was pleased to find the fireplaces on both floors of the building all blazing merrily. She was relieved, for the last days of their journey had been chill with autumn in full bloom now. The cook and the housemaid came forward and curtsied politely.

"I've a small hot meal, madame, if it pleases you. My name is Alvina, and the lass is Cleva." She curtsied again.

"A hot meal will be most welcome, Alvina," Lucianna said. "This is my body servant, Balia. She struggles with her English, but I know you will both help her, and try not to giggle at her errors."

Both women nodded, looking curiously at Balia.

"The stableman is Sam," David Kira said.

"He's strong, and he's reliable. My Yedda is never wrong."

"Thank you so much, David Kira," Lucianna said to him.

"I will come in midmorning tomorrow to show you the shop I have found for the Silk Merchants' Guild of Florence. And I have already begun to spread the word of its coming and your arrival. The Milanese will regret waiting until the spring to arrive. They will be most surprised to find Florence already a presence here."

"I'll look forward to seeing the shop. Can we walk?"

"Oh no, madame, you will have to ride."

"Ask your Yedda to visit me tomorrow afternoon. I can already see I will need a few more servants. Litter bearers for my litter, for one thing."

"She will come, but now I must go. I have a wife who worries a great deal. It comes from being Jewish in England. We are always being expelled, but the Kira bank has the wherewithal to thrive," he said.

"And to know who will take their bribe," Lucianna said with a smile.

David Kira chuckled. "Aye, madame, knowing who has the power — and can be bribed discreetly — is always valuable knowledge." He bowed to her. "I will come in the morning." And then he was gone.

CHAPTER 6

When he had left her, Lucianna walked slowly through her new home. To her delight, she found a small room with a blazing fireplace, lined with shelves for her books. She would need several comfortable upholstered chairs, a good straight chair, and several small tables, as well as a large rectangular table upon which to do her business accounts. The library overlooked the gardens, which were surprisingly spacious, even at the edge of the city.

"Mistress?"

She turned to see the maidservant, Cleva. "Yes?"

"Alvina apologizes, but she says you and Balia must eat in the kitchen, for there is no furniture elsewhere except your bedchamber," Cleva said in a soft, nervous voice.

"Is it nice and warm in the kitchen?" Lucianna asked, with a friendly smile.

"Oh yes, mistress! Alvina is a lover of

heat," the girl replied.

"So am I," Lucianna said. "Show me the way, Cleva!"

Balia had been upstairs inspecting the rooms there. She was just coming down, and joined them. "The bedchambers are livable if we furnish them properly. We'll need heavy draperies for the windows, for this London is cold," she said in Italian.

"Try to speak English, Balia, as I do, so the others may understand you, for it is possible they may be able to help you. Alvina has a supper for us down in her warm kitchens."

"Yes, mistress," Balia said, a bit sour at being even gently rebuked in front of an unimportant maidservant.

In the kitchens, Alvina had hot bowls of rabbit stew for them. Neither of the women had ever tasted the dish, but on this chilly, wet London night, they both voiced their approval, mopping up the rich gravy with crusty bread.

"I like your kitchen, Alvina," her new mistress told her. "It not only smells good, it's warm. I don't believe it gets this cold in Florence."

"It's the rain, mistress. Always makes it feel worse than it is," the cook said with a chuckle. "I'll try to keep your meals simple to begin with, for I suspect you are not used to our English foods. What would please you for breakfast? We find it best to begin a cold, wet day with hot food."

"Then that is how I shall begin my day, and Balia too. We also enjoy poached eggs, but what would you cook tomorrow morning?"

"I will give you a nice hot cereal to start your day, mistress, and my fresh bread with butter and jam," Alvina said.

"I suspect that will taste good after a cold night," Lucianna said.

"Oh, it really isn't cold yet," Alvina told her. "But it will get cold later on when winter finally sets in. This is just the end of the autumn."

Lucianna nodded, although she wasn't too pleased to hear it. Then she changed the subject entirely. "You will need a helper for your kitchens," she began. "And Cleva, you will need another lass to aid you. Do we have a gardener? And I will need two litter bearers. Do you think Sam can manage the stable by himself? I believe Mistress Kira will help us with that, and I will speak with Sam in the morning. Oh, what is this?" she asked as Alvina put a dish in front of her and another before Balia, who with good food was now feeling more amenable.

"Fresh apple tart," Alvina said, and then she poured a bit of heavy cream from a pitcher over their portions.

"I shall become fat as a country pig," Balia said. "You are an excellent cook and provider, Alvina."

The two English servants and Lucianna laughed, and the cook thanked Balia for her compliment. Once they had scraped up every bit of the delicious sweet, the two diners bid the cook and the maid a good night, and went upstairs.

When they were gone, Alvina said, "Well, she seems like she'll be a good mistress, and they both have good appetites."

"How can you tell just because they liked the supper that she'll be a good mistress?" Cleva asked.

"Because while she must certainly be exhausted by her travels, she did not arrive demanding and filled with complaints. She was gracious about eating in my kitchen, complimentary of the meal, and she is already considering that we will both need additional help to manage this house. Another maidservant to help you has moved you up in the ranks, Cleva. She is putting you in charge. Eventually, you will gain the position of housekeeper if you do your job well, and do not allow it to go to your head," Alvina advised. "To be the house-keeper to a wealthy woman is not a bad thing."

"I had not thought of it that way," Cleva said slowly.

"Well, my girl, you had better begin using what few wits God gave you," Alvina advised. "Go upstairs now, and make certain she is comfortable for the night. Hurry!"

Cleva hurried off upstairs and found her new mistress had already reached her bed-chamber. Knocking, she stepped quickly. "I have just come to see if everything is to your liking, mistress. Of course, we will need draperies and bed curtains made as quickly as possible, but for the next few nights I think you and Balia will be comfortable." Then she remembered her curtsy.

"I have brought my bed curtains with me and the drapes as well," Lucianna said. "You and Balia can hang them tomorrow, although I will probably have heavier ones made for the colder months. Mine will suffice for the interim, Cleva."

"There is a pitcher of water in the coals," the maidservant said.

"I must have a tub for bathing," Lucianna told the girl. "We will have to keep it in the pantry of Alvina's kitchens, for I can see the difficulty getting it filled with warm water

120

in a small house." Then she laughed. "Perhaps we should have one household manservant for the heavier chores."

" 'Twould be a great help, mistress," Cleva admitted.

"Balia, is there anything else we need for tonight? You seem to have managed getting my traveling bag upstairs, and that should do for tonight. I will want fresh clothing in the morning, however."

"I will see to it, mistress," Balia said. Then she looked at Cleva. "Thank you for coming to make certain we are settled. Good night."

"Good night, mistress," Cleva said, curtsying politely, and then left them.

"Presumptuous wench," Balia muttered.

Lucianna laughed. She had never before seen Balia so testy, and realized it was because she was unsure of herself in a new house, in a new land, and speaking a new language. "She is attempting to make a good impression on me. Certainly you can understand that? She is in a new house with a new foreign mistress and does not know what to expect of either of us."

Balia sighed, and then laughed at herself. "I must seem very fierce to the little wench," she admitted.

"It will be easier on you both eventually,

when you become used to each other and our new surroundings," Lucianna said. "Now, where are you planning to sleep?"

"There is a small chamber right next to yours, mistress. See?" She went across the room and opened a little door. "I have a bed, a chest, a chair, and there is even a tiny fireplace just big enough to take the chill out of the chamber."

"How wonderful! Now help me get ready for bed. I am exhausted, and I imagine you must be too," Lucianna said.

Both women slept deeply that night, but Balia was, as always, up before her mistress. Dressing quickly, she hurried downstairs, finding the trunks that had been brought in last evening for safety's sake. They would have to get those holding Lucianna's clothing upstairs today. Spying a chest she knew held gowns, she opened it and pulled one out.

Though she had packed each gown carefully to avoid wrinkles, there would be some. She took it down to the kitchen, hoping to find an iron.

Alvina and Cleva were sitting at the large kitchen table, eating their breakfast. Cleva jumped up on seeing Balia, but the older woman waved her back into her seat saying, "Just tell me if you have an iron in this kitchen, please?"

"I wouldn't have known what it was if Mistress Kira had not explained it to me," Alvina said. "In the pantry on a shelf. Come and have something to eat first."

Balia hesitated a moment, and then she laid the dress on a nearby chair and said, "Thank you, I will." She sat down on the table's bench.

Cleva ran to fill a bowl with hot cereal and put it with a spoon before Balia.

Balia thanked her and began to eat. To her surprise, the gray mass in the bowl was very tasty, and she took Alvina's suggestion to add some honey and heavy cream. The hot cereal filled her belly and seemed to give her energy. She ate quickly, though, as did all servants. Seeing Cleva was done, Balia instructed her to heat the iron in the fire, telling the girl how to do it. Then, finished with her own meal, she arose, took the gown from the chair, and ironed out the few wrinkles.

"Never saw anything like that," Alvina said, "but you've got the mistress's gown looking fine now."

Balia grinned. "Give her half an hour and then bring her breakfast upstairs," she said, and was gone from the kitchen and up the stairs, to find Lucianna just stirring awake.

Within the half hour the younger woman was up, washed, and dressed. She ate her breakfast quickly and commented on how good it made her feel.

Then she went downstairs just as Yedda Kira arrived.

"I have brought you some chairs," Yedda said as she came into the house, two men following her. "Where would you like them?"

Lucianna laughed, already liking the practical woman. "Follow me," she said, and led them to her library. "We can speak privately here. Just set them down by the fire," she instructed them.

"Wait by my litter," Mistress Kira said as the two men exited the room. "Ah, now, we are comfortable." She plumped herself into a chair as Lucianna did the same. "How may I help you, Mistress Pietro d' Angelo?"

"First, let me thank you for all you have done," Lucianna said. And then she went on to explain what she would need in the way of furnishings and additional servants.

"If you trust me to obtain the rest of your staff, you will have them by the evening," Yedda Kira told Lucianna. "The furnishings are another matter. Do you object to visiting a small shop with furniture that has already been used elsewhere?"

"If it suits my taste, no," Lucianna said. "The two men who carried these chairs for you, do you believe they might carry my litter so we may go together now, and quickly?"

"An excellent idea," Yedda Kira agreed.

Lucianna's litter ride through the rainy morning was quite a revelation to her. Despite the weather, the streets were crowded and noisy, every bit as much as her own city of Florence. Finally they stopped at an undistinguished shop and went in. The proprietor greeted the two women, and then left them to their business.

"But everything here seems new," Lucianna said.

"It has been nicely refurbished. Broken and cracked, it would not bring the shopkeeper what it is really worth."

They immediately found the long rectangular table Lucianna was seeking for her library, as well as several more chairs and small tables. They found a table that was just perfect for the house's small hall, along with the seating for it. There were two beds for the two other bedchambers in the house, and more tables and chairs. The shopkeeper watched with ill-concealed delight, totaling up the price he would get from the lady.

Finally, Lucianna said, "I believe that will do for now."

Yedda Kira spoke to the shopkeeper. "It must be delivered today," she said in a stern and not-to-be-trifled-with voice.

"Of course, madame, you have but to direct me," the man oozed.

"And how much will you charge for these poor pieces? My lady has just come to London and must furnish her dwelling quickly, which is why we are here. Do not attempt to overcharge her."

The shopkeeper named a price.

Yedda Kira looked at him, obviously displeased. She turned to Lucianna. "Come, my lady. There are better shops than this one that will not take advantage of two help-less women."

The shopkeeper made a more reasonable offer, and while frowning, Yedda agreed for the sake of her lady's convenience. Reaching into her purse, she drew out the required coins. Then she gave him the address. "The staff is yet small. See your goods are brought into the rooms where they belong." Then she turned. "Come, my lady. We will go to the draper's next," and she led Lucianna from the shop.

Once outside, the two women dissolved into laughter.

"Oh my, my mother would like you," Lucianna said. "You are very fierce to deal with, Mistress Kira. I would have given him what he first asked and still considered it fair."

"Believe me, he made a goodly profit on what we paid him," Yedda assured Lucianna.

They spent the remainder of the morning shopping for the household items that Lucianna would need, finally returning home to the little house that was now hers. It was there Yedda Kira took her leave.

"I must go now to choose the servants you will need," she said, not even going into the house with Lucianna. "Within a few hours you will be fully staffed."

Lucianna thanked her for the morning and went into her house, where Balia was waiting for her.

"The furnishings have arrived," she said. "I can only hope you did not pay too much for them. A new country, and new coinage, can be difficult."

"Not when you have Yedda Kira with you," Lucianna said. "My mother would fully approve of her. You should have seen how she bargained with the shopkeepers. It would have made a Florentine proud. And we will have the additional servants shortly. I have chosen fabric for the bed hangings

127

and drapes."

"You have been busy," Balia approved, "but so have I. You will find your bedchamber just as it should be."

"Where is Cleva?"

"In the kitchens with Alvina," Balia said. "Would you like me to fetch them for you?"

"Nay, let's go down to Alvina's domain. It still seems to be the warmest room in the house," Lucianna remarked.

They descended into the kitchens, where they found Alvina stirring a pot over the fireplace, and Cleva seated at the table. The younger girl jumped up, seeing her new mistress, and curtsied.

"I hear you have been busy this morning," Lucianna began. "Mistress Kira has now returned to her home and will send us a few more staff by evening. Alvina, I have asked for a helper for you, and a helper for you as well, Cleva. Sam will have a boy to aid him too, and we will gain two litter bearers. I think we will be able to manage with those few, but if not, you will tell me."

"Thank you, mistress," Alvina said, speaking for herself and Cleva. "Cleva will prepare the sleeping places for the new women and men. The boy can sleep in the stables with Sam."

"Excellent," Lucianna replied. "Have Balia bring them to me when they come." Then she turned and went back upstairs with Balia.

David Kira sent a message saying he would come on the morrow to take her to the shop they had rented for the Florentine silk merchants. Lucianna sent an answer back with his messenger saying that she would expect him at nine o'clock in the morning. The additions to her household staff arrived shortly thereafter. She spoke with each of them.

Bessie would help Alvina in her kitchens. She was an excellent baker, she told her new mistress. Alvina was very pleased to learn that.

Welsa would serve as Cleva's underhousemaid. Dunn and Gerd, two boys no older than eleven, would work in the stables for Sam. Finally, there were the two sturdy brothers, Flynt and Ford, who would serve as Lucianna's litter bearers. All were clean and polite. Once again, Yedda Kira had served her well.

The autumn afternoon slipped into evening. Lucianna ate a small meal and retired with Balia, who had spent some time in the kitchens so she might inspect these new servants. "The boys are boys," she said. "The others, respectful and polite. They are all glad for work in a respectable household, my lady."

"Good, then the household will run smoothly. When I was out this morning, I ordered liveries for the litter bearers. They are simple but will add a modicum of importance to my stature." She climbed into her bed, made up with her own fresh linens, and snuggled down.

"Do you think we will see your earl now that we are in London?" Balia wondered aloud.

Lucianna laughed. "He isn't *my* earl, Balia. I honestly hope we will see him, but perhaps he has taken a wife since his return. If he comes, I will welcome him, of course. Tomorrow I will go the the shop and see what must be done."

"Will you bring the silks you brought with you?" Balia asked.

"Nay, not until I have determined what is necessary to display them properly. Whatever I do, it must be as perfect as I can make it to attract customers for the guild. If they decide I am not doing well, they could send someone else, and I would have to return to Florence."

"You do not want to go home?" Balia was surprised.

"We have been here only briefly but,

despite the rain, I like it. London is different from Florence. Its look is unfamiliar, its smells are not the same, but I want to know more of this England."

Balia smiled. "You like it because you are more your own mistress here. You do not have your mother fussing at you to take another husband, or your father burdening you with the work that rightfully belongs to your brother Marco, or Marco whining about his adored Clarinda. Here, you are truly your own mistress."

Lucianna sat up a moment on her elbow. "I am, aren't I?" she said, smiling. "It is a little overwhelming, Balia, but I like it!"

Balia smiled back at the younger woman. "Go to sleep now, mistress. The morning will be here soon enough." Then she made certain the hearth had sufficient wood to keep the fire going and went into her own little chamber.

In the morning, Lucianna arose, ate, and dressed. She knew her litter would be waiting at the door, for Balia had spoken to the bearers the previous evening. "Good morning," she greeted the two brothers. "In a few days you will have your livery. Do you know where you are taking me?"

"Yes, mistress," one of the brothers answered. "We were told by Master Kira before we came yesterday."

"Then let us go," Lucianna said, climbing in to sit down.

The two litter bearers carried her quickly and smoothly from the residential streets into the heart of the city.

Lucianna was fascinated to see the busy streets and shops they passed. They hurried through a market that actually did remind her of Florence, with its farmers selling vegetables, late-autumn fruits, meats, chicken, milk, and other items. She saw both men and women with trays of buns and other edibles, selling their wares as they went. And there were women shopping in the markets, some servants and some ordinary housewives, seeking items for that day's dinner.

Finally, the litter was set down before a shop, and David Kira stood waiting for her. He helped her out, greeting her pleasantly. "I think you have brought some of your sunshine from Florence to us today," he said.

Lucianna laughed at the compliment. "I hadn't actually noticed; I was so busy staring at this wonderful city of yours."

David Kira nodded. "It has a bit of magic about it, doesn't it?" he said as he led her into the shop. "We will have a sign to hang above the door installed shortly."

Lucianna nodded and gazed about the room. It was rectangular and had a long counter along one wall. "It is large enough," she said. "I am concerned as to customers. How will they know I am here? I do not believe it wise to leave everything to chance, do you?"

"The merchants who purchase fine cloth have all been notified of your coming. I will be certain they know when you are ready to do business, madame."

"The space is clean and bright," Lucianna noted. "I will have the trunks with the silks brought here tomorrow. Then I will begin to see it arranged for display. This shop will be far different from what your merchants expect. There will be flowers to sweeten the air, and comfortable chairs for them to sit in while the fabric is brought to them for inspection. Have you found me a trust-worthy man to work here with me? I shall have to teach him a great deal before he can be of any real help to me," she said.

"Would you object to having one of my people working for you? I actually have a young relative who is very reliable. He learns quickly," David Kira said.

"I see no reason not to employ him," Lucianna said. "Have him here tomorrow morning, and I will begin to teach him as we unpack the trunks of material."

"His name is Baram Kira," David said. "Here are the keys to your shop, Mistress Pietro d'Angelo." He handed them to her.

Suddenly the door to her shop opened. "Welcome to London, Lucianna."

She recognized his voice immediately, and her face lit up in a smile. "Robert!" she said. "How on earth did you know I had arrived in London? Do you know my banker, David Kira?"

The earl held out his hand, much to David's surprise. It was not often a nobleman would offer his hand. "Master Kira."

"My lord." Then David turned again to Lucianna. "You will send for me if you need anything else, madame?" He made a small, polite bow and departed the shop.

"Not a Medici?" The earl was intrigued.

"My father has not kept money with their bank in several years," Lucianna said. "They had difficulties, and we found the Kiras more reliable," she explained. "How did you know I was here?"

"It is already being bandied about the court that the representative for the Florentine silk merchants' guild is a beautiful woman. The king's people always know anyone of interest or importance who comes to London."

"I would hardly consider myself either," she replied. "I just came to see my establishment today and will now return home. My father bought me a small house on a pleasant street called Ivy Lane. The Kiras have seen I was supplied with an excellent staff of servants, and Mistress Kira and I have already purchased what I needed to furnish it. I was just planning to close up now, for I am not yet ready for business."

"Will you object if I accompany you, Lucianna?"

"I am flattered," she replied. Then, leading him from the shop, she locked the door carefully and climbed into her litter with his help, although Lucianna did not really need it. "I regret I have not room for another," she told him.

"I have a horse," he told her, and then he mounted the beast.

The bearers picked up her transport, and with the earl at her side, they hurried back through the streets to Ivy Lane. To her pleasure, one of the young stable boys hurried forth to take the earl's animal as he dismounted and accompanied her into the house.

"How charming," he said.

Balia came forward, smiling. "My lord,"

she greeted him.

"Fetch the earl some wine," Lucianna said. "Come into my little library, my lord. It is the coziest room in the house."

He sat where she indicated, but he could not take his eyes from her. She was even more beautiful than he remembered, with her rich golden hair with its reddish highlights and her beautiful blue-green eyes.

"I have missed you," he said.

"Yet you did not correspond with me," she replied softly.

"There has been so much to do. I had my estates, which cannot be managed without me, so I am less in London than I would like. And when I am, my time is taken up by the king, who is yet young and must be careful from whence his guidance comes. I have no desire for power, and so I carefully blend myself into the background of the court that I not be noticed or considered a rival to any. I barely have time to eat or to sleep," he explained.

"And yet you look well rested and healthy," she murmured.

"And I still have my handsome head," he responded with a grin.

"Ah, so you think you are handsome?" she said.

"Do you not think I am?" he countered.

"You will do, my lord," Lucianna replied dryly.

Balia entered with the required wine and left quickly.

"Nonetheless, I thought of you every day," he said to her. "Did you think of me, Lucianna?"

"Now and again, my lord, but I too was consumed by my other duties, and then my father's guild decided in order to outdo the Milanese, I should come to England posthaste to represent them. There was the packing of my goods, the closing of my house, and the long trip to reach this rainy land."

"It will be brighter in the other seasons, but late autumn and winter can be rainy," he explained.

"And now I have to arrange for this shop to be properly fitted, and our silks displayed. I doubt I will have time for much else," she said.

"But you will make time for me, Lucianna, won't you?" His lips were smiling, but she saw an anxious look in his eyes that belied his confidence.

"If you will make time for me, my lord," she answered.

"Will you not call me Roberto as you once did?" he asked her.

"When we are in private as we are now, Roberto, but never in public. To do so would be considered disrespectful, and I will not appear to be some mannerless wench before your people," Lucianna said. "I am, after all, the granddaughter of a Venetian prince. I will not be disrespected for my calling and love for trade."

He heard the pride in her voice. It was a side of her he had never before seen, and while surprised by it, he liked it. "You will not be disrespected by this court," the earl told her. "The Tudors have a flimsy claim to the throne through the king's mother, Lady Margaret Beaufort, but they have firmly won the war now between the Lancasters and the Yorks. The most serious of their rivals have fled, are dead, or are in the Tower. Henry Tudor has wed Elizabeth of York, and already has a son, Prince Arthur. The queen is full with a second child, due to be born shortly. And Lady Margaret watches carefully from the sidelines for any threat to her son. I will see you meet both the queen and Lady Margaret. Become their friend, and your position will be strong within the court, if that is what you wish."

"I shall be grateful for such friendships," she told him.

"And you know you have my friendship,

Lucianna, though I want more of you eventually than just friendship."

"That is very bold, Roberto," she answered him.

"I am a bold man," he told her. Then he arose. "I must take my leave of you now, *cara.* May I visit you again soon?"

"Of course, Roberto," Lucianna said pleasantly, when what she really wanted to say was *every day.* She stood. "Let me escort you down to the door."

They walked together from her library to the front door. Once there, he took her hand and kissed it, first on the back, and then turning it over, kissed her wrist. Her knees grew weak, and it was all she could do to remain standing on her own.

"Addio, cara mia," he said. Then, releasing her hand, he departed.

As the door closed, Lucianna put her hand out to steady herself.

Balia appeared by her side. "So he has gone. Will he be back?"

"He will be back," Lucianna said with a small smile.

CHAPTER 7

Henry VII, first of the Tudors, was a careful man. His claim to the throne was fragile. The son of Edmund Tudor, who was the son of Henry V's widow, Katherine of France, he had no real claim to England but through his mother, Margaret Beaufort, who was a great-great-granddaughter of King Edward III. Margaret was the great-granddaughter of Edward III's son, John of Gaunt. Her grandfather was the first John Beaufort, Gaunt's son by his mistress and later third wife, Katherine Swynford, whose four children were legitimized. Her father, the second John Beaufort, was Duke of Somerset. Margaret was his only child, and had inherited great wealth.

Her first marriage was dissolved when she was twelve. Her second husband was Edmund Tudor, Earl of Richmond. She wed him at twelve and a half, and by the time she was fourteen was widowed, and had

delivered her husband's only child, his son
Henry, who was considered the son of an
unimportant lordling. The death of several
close male relations changed all that, and
suddenly this boy who never expected to be
important found himself the male heir to
the Lancasters.

With the Yorkists ruling, he was put in the
charge of Lord Herbert, who saw to his
education. When the Lancasters regained
authority briefly, Henry's wardship was
overseen by his uncle, Jasper Tudor, the Earl
of Pembroke. When the Yorkists managed to
regain power, Jasper took his nephew and
fled to Brittany, for the boy was now the
Lancastrian heir. For the next twelve years,
he lived under the protection of Brittany's
duke while Edward IV attempted to regain
his custody.

In England, Henry's mother worked for
his cause, and came close to losing her life
when she irritated Edward IV's brother,
Richard III, who claimed the throne on his
brother's death. Her family managed to get
her spared, although such behavior was a
trial to her third and fourth husbands. A
clever woman, she always remarried, because she knew a woman needed a man to
represent or stand behind her.

Finally, after several attempts, Henry, now

twenty-eight, won his kingship with the death of Richard III at the Battle of Bosworth. His mother became one of his closest advisers privately, never publicly. Once firmly upon the throne, Henry permitted her to sign her name as Margaret R. And to see that her son's throne was firmly protected, she arranged with Edward IV's widow the marriage between Edward's eldest daughter, Elizabeth, and her son. With the mysterious disappearance and presumed death of Elizabeth's two younger brothers, Elizabeth was now the Yorkist heiress. Lancaster and York united; the war between them was finally resolved. With the birth of Henry and Elizabeth's first son, Prince Arthur, the succession was secured.

Robert Minton, Earl of Lisle, was the king's own age. His family had supported the Lancasters quietly, and his father, Richard Minton, had managed to secure a place for his only son in Henry VII's train when he escaped to Brittany. He didn't know what would come of it, but he advised the young Robert to try to make friends with the boy who would be king.

"Do not be like the others, seeking his friendship for what you may gain for yourself or your family. Seek that friendship just so you two may become friends, and if you obtain it, maintain it. One day it may prove invaluable to you," Richard Minton said. "Leave power to the others. It will, in the end, mean more to this lad who will be our king one day, my son, to have a friend in you."

The boy had followed his father's advice and found it correct. Henry of Lancaster had been besieged by the other boys in his train, but Robert Minton simply became his best friend. Once, when they were in their late teens, Henry had asked him why he did not seek for himself as the others did.

"My lord, I have all that I need in this life. A title, wealth, an estate, and most important of all, your friendship. One day, as you will, I will choose a wife and have heirs. What more could I possibly want?"

Henry Lancaster had laughed. "I think you are cleverer than all the others put together, Rob," he told his friend. "I have written to my mother about you, and she has said so. My mother is a wise woman."

The friendship had grown, and never again did the king question Robert Minton's motives. Robert was the friend who did discreet errands for his king such as going to Florence to obtain silks for his young queen, who loved beautiful things. While not generous by nature with others, Henry was very generous with his wife, and Elizabeth never tried his nature, understanding what it was like to grow up without quite enough coin. And Henry let his wife follow the generous example of his beloved mother, who was adding colleges to the university at Cambridge, was a patron of the arts, and was most benevolent to the church and to others who needed her aid.

Robert Minton had never shown any interest in a woman, but now that Lucianna was in England, he could no longer hide his interest.

He knew eventually he would request permission of the king's mother to bring Lucianna to meet her. It would prove interesting, for while Margaret Beaufort valued her position and heritage, she was not a snob by nature. And she was curious about a woman from a foreign country who had been given a position of importance from an important guild.

Lucianna's shop was now open to the London cloth merchants seeking fine silks to offer their own customers, who were from the nobility. Hearing of Lucianna's beauty, however, certain young lords had taken to visiting the shop in an effort to make her acquaintance. She was charming but laughed at them, and sent them away each day. They would return the next day, good-natured for the most part, and once again attempt an aquaintance.

It was sometimes difficult to do business with the legitimate merchants. Lucianna was finally forced to hire two burly fellows whose job it was to see that their mistress's admirers did not impede the business she had come to England to do. Not all of the young men were discouraged, and some waited in the street for her to go home. As she did not wish her dwelling known if she could avoid it, Lucianna took to exiting from the rear alley of her business and leaving her assistant, Baram Kira, to lock up.

"I have refused some very generous bribes to reveal your secrets," he told her seriously one day.

Lucianna laughed. "I imagine that you have," she said, "but it is very irritating to be importuned so by these men."

"Their motives are not . . ." Baram trailed off, searching a moment for the right words. "They are not pure where you are concerned. I have told Mistress Yedda of these men, and she says you are managing the situation very well."

"You must understand," Lucianna explained to him, "until I was thirteen, I never left my father's house. When I reached that age, my mother began to take me with her across the piazza each day to Mass. In my oldest sister's day, the young men would come to the square just to see her cross it when she went to Mass. It did not please my mother at all.

"I never met anyone outside of my family in those years. It was our parents and siblings, the servants, and, if I was considered old enough to be put on display with my brother and little sister, an occasional visitor. When I was old enough to marry, then I was allowed with my mother, or a servant, to visit a market or shop. I was taken by my parents to the Medici household for receptions so I might be seen by families with eligible sons. But, alas, my dower had shrunk in the poor economy, and while my two elder sisters, who had very large dowers, were sought after, I was not, even though my sister Francesca is the ruling duchess of a small principality. People still whisper about my eldest sister's runaway marriage to a Turkish prince."

"But you did wed, didn't you?" he asked her.

"Yes, to a kind old man who sought a companion in his last years. He left me a wealthy woman in my own right," Lucianna told him.

"Ah," Baram said. "And a wealthy woman is a sought-after woman. Is that not so, mistress?"

"Indeed," Lucianna agreed. "I wanted no man in Florence, for most sought me for that wealth. For the interim, I prefer to remain my own mistress, which I realize is shocking to most."

"I think you very wise," Baram said, nodding.

At that moment, the door opened, and one of her guards stuck his head through. "Mistress, there is some lord out here who says you are friends, and you will let him in. He says his name is Robert Minton, Earl of Lisle. Shall I allow him to pass?"

"Yes, and always," Lucianna answered him, smoothing imagined wrinkles from her gown as she went forward to greet her visitor.

He came past her burly guard, smiling. "So it has come to this, my lady of Florence? You must post guards at the door of your shop?"

"Before I did," she told him as he kissed her hand, "I had a shop full of young courtiers impeding my business. How bold you English are, Robert. The legitimate merchants couldn't get in. The guild will

147

not be pleased should they learn the interest these young men have in me prevents me from doing what I was sent here to do."

"Your beauty draws them," he said.

"Surely there are prettier women in England, and the true motive of these men is seduction, nothing more," Lucianna said candidly. "You know that as well as I do. I represent the Arte di Por Santa Maria, the Silk Merchants' Guild of Florence. I will not bring shame upon them with lascivious behavior. Believe me, when the Milanese representative of their silk merchants arrives, he will be quick to report any unseemly behavior believed on my part back to both Milan and Florence."

"I will see these fellows no longer disturb you," he told her.

Then he walked to the door of the shop and stepped outside past her guards. The young courtiers lingering in the street could not help but stop and look at the Earl of Lisle; most of them recognized him. "I am the Earl of Lisle as many of you here know. Looking about, I know most of you.

"Cease disturbing this street with your foolish behavior over a pretty woman. Do not come back here again. Your quest to meet with Mistress Pietro d'Angelo is futile. She will not receive you. She is a respectable woman. Get you gone now!"

They stared at him silently for a long moment, and then one bolder than the others spoke up. "Why should we?" he demanded.

A slow, amused smile lit Robert Minton's face. "Because," he said, "I am the Earl of Lisle and your elder, and I outrank you. But most important, you audacious gamecock, because from the moment I met Mistress Pietro d'Angelo in Florence some months ago, I determined to make her mine. Are you foolish enough to believe you can come up against me, and win, Sir Edmund?"

The young man bowed in a half-polite, half-reluctant manner. "I give over, Lord Lisle," he said, "and wish you good fortune with the lovely lady."

Robert Minton returned the bow courteously and turned to the others. "And the rest of you?" he asked.

But they were already withdrawing down the small street. He returned to the shop past the two now-admiring guards at the door.

"So, from the moment you met me, you decided to make me yours," Lucianna said. She didn't know whether to be amused or offended. "You are a very bold man, Robert."

"You knew it," he answered quietly. "Do

not demur. You are too intelligent a woman, Lucianna."

"Aye, I knew it," she told him. "The difficulty, however, is that I do not know if I mean to be any man's. I will certainly be no plaything, my lord. And I do not believe my birth is enough for a man of your stature. So, for now, might you be content just to be my friend?"

"For now," he agreed. "Remember that I spoke with your father, Lucianna. And yes, my ancestors hold a higher rank than did yours, but I will not allow our ancestors to dictate our fates. This age of Tudor is a new age. I don't want a plaything. I want a wife."

He was blunt, she thought. "I am not quite ready to rewed, though your *offer* is gracious."

"I have not offered yet," he told her. "When I do, I shall get down on my knee and request your hand properly, Lucianna, as a gentleman should do. I simply want you to understand that I do not mean to take you as a mistress."

She had the good grace to blush at his gentle rebuke. "I understand now," she told him, then added wickedly, "You wish to prevent others from pressing their suits, respectable or not, until you have made up your mind about me. Is that correct, my lord?"

Instead of protesting her suggestion, he answered her wickedly. "Aye, my lady, that is just what I mean to do. You are clever to have divined it."

"Oh, you are so difficult!" she told him, irritated.

He laughed at her. "I am merely giving you back what you have given me, Lucianna. If you mean to outwit me, you must do better."

She wanted to shriek at such boldness, but instead she gave him a small smile. "Oh, I shall, my lord. You may trust that I shall."

"Good!" he said, approving of her words. "If you didn't, I should be disappointed," the earl told her. "Will you allow me to escort you home?" he asked politely.

She hesitated, wanting to say no just to punish him, but instead she said, "Yes, you may." Then she turned to her assistant. "Baram, please close up the shop for the day. It is already dark outside. See the guards have torches to light my bearers' way. I believe the master of the cloth merchants will visit us on the morrow. Do we have enough wine?"

"Yes, mistress," Baram answered. Then he hurried off to see to the torches so they might leave. He would report this little interlude between Lucianna and the earl to Yedda, who would be interested to know, if she did not already know.

"Is that why you came?" Lucianna asked the earl. "To escort me home this afternoon?"

"Yes, and so we might eat and talk together. I have been so busy at court with the king's business, I have had no time to visit with you. I have missed you, Lucianna."

"And I, you, to be honest," she told him. "Other than my servants, and Baram, I have no one with whom to talk in the evenings. Sometimes I am lonely, but other times I am not."

"I have the privilege of being considered a friend by the king's mother, Lady Margaret," he said. "She is curious to meet you, for I do not believe she has ever met anyone from Florence. And an independent woman who manages a commercial venture is very intriguing to her. Would you come with me one afternoon and meet her? Perhaps we will celebrate a small holiday with her, as December is almost upon us now," he suggested.

"When I write to my mother that I have met the king of England's mother, she will be beside herself with delight. She was not happy that I agreed to come to England," Lucianna explained.

"Mistress, the bearers are ready," Baram announced, having come to tell them. "Good night, then."

"Good night," they both told him, and went outside to where her litter awaited, along with Robert's horse and the two guards. They set off through the darkening streets. Some shops were still lit, which brightened the streets until they reached the more residential area, and then Lucianna was doubly glad of her torches, for the streets were very dark, it seemed. She did not like coming home in darkness. She must remember to leave her shop earlier so they might travel in the light.

They had not spoken during their journey. It was better not to be distracted by a conversation. It was better to keep one's thoughts on the journey itself. To Lucianna's relief, they reached her house quickly tonight. It seemed her people were eager to escape any difficulties too.

Balia had been watching for them and flung open the front door as the earl dismounted and helped Lucianna from her litter chair.

"Good! Good! You are safely home. I worry when it gets dark so early, mistress."

"I think I shall come early until the light begins to return," Lucianna agreed.

"Baram sent a boy to say the earl would be with you and remaining for the meal," Balia said. "The food is hot and ready, if you will go into the hall."

"Make certain the earl's horse is stabled and fed," Lucianna said.

"It will be done. Sam isn't about to allow a fine animal to remain in the streets," Balia replied, but she hurried off to be certain it was being done.

They walked into the little hall of the house. The large fireplace blazed, and the small size of the room allowed it to feel warm. A tapestry hung on the wall behind the high board. There were two high-backed tapestried chairs on either side of the hearth. But other than the high board and its seating, there was little else in the hall. They sat as Balia had directed them, and immediately her servants brought in the food. They ate, for they were hungry. Lucianna had had no food since her morning meal, and men, she knew, were always hungry.

Alvina had cooked a fine capon stuffed with bread, celery, and onions. First, however, there was fish, bought fresh this morning from a fishmonger by the river that her cook favored. There was a small vessel filled with a rabbit stew with carrots and onions, along with fresh warm bread, butter, and cheese. It was far more than Lucianna usually saw on her table in the evenings when she was alone. She was surprised it was ready so quickly, but Alvina had a magic about her. She could do amazing things, Lucianna had discovered, in a very short time.

Robert Minton ate heartily with a good appetite. He did not speak, concentrating all his attention upon the food. It was obvious that he was very hungry.

"Do they not feed you at court?" she finally asked him when she had finished her own plate.

"Except at state dinners, courtiers eat when they can, especially if, like me, they have other duties. The king, his mother, and the queen often eat together. They are served by their courtiers, who are served by the servants, but courtiers do not eat. Unless you are invited to eat with the king or his family, you do not," he explained. "I think I ate last night, but I don't really remember."

Lucianna was horrified. "That is awful!" she said. "You must come and eat more evening meals with me then, Robert."

"I will come when I can get away, and I thank you for your kind invitation, Luci-anna." He reached for the bread, butter, and cheese.

"Perhaps I should marry you right away," she said. "Then we could go to your home where I might see you eat regular meals daily."

He laughed. "So my well-being concerns you, does it?"

She considered his words and then said, "I suppose it does. I have been taught that the purpose of marriage is children, after all. If you are not strong enough to mount me, we will never have them. So you must be fed daily, and well." She blushed at her own words.

Reaching out, the earl took her hand, which directed her to look into his face. "Lucianna, never fear I should be too weak to mount you," he said, and the smoulder-ing look in his eyes caused her blush to deepen. She tried to pull her hand away, but he would not let her go. He began to nibble upon each finger, his teeth gently grazing them.

The sudden intimacy between them was startling.

"If you are still hungry," she half whis-pered, "I'm certain Alvina has made us a

156

sweet. Bessie, her helper, is quite expert at sweets."

"You are enough sweet for me," he told her in a thick voice. He tightened his grip upon her hand, pulling her from her chair and into his lap. Releasing her hand, he kissed her, his mouth covering hers, and taking complete possession of it.

When Lucianna had a moment to breathe again, she could only say, "Oh my!" And then she felt his hand caressing her breasts through the heavy silk of her gown. "Robert!"

"I can't not touch you, *amore mia*. You are simply too tempting."

"But I've never before had my breasts touched," she half whispered. "It is strange to me."

"Your husband did not touch your breasts? How could he resist you, Lucianna? You are delicious," the earl told her.

"The purpose of our marriage was not conjugal, but companionable," she reminded him.

He considered her words carefully. "Are you telling me that even on your wedding night, there was no coming together?"

"Oh no! Alfredo had his own bedchamber, and I had mine," and as she spoke, it suddenly dawned upon Lucianna what she was telling him in the most discreet, but direct way.

"You really are a virgin?" He said it softly, low. The implications of it were astounding. She had told him before, yet until this moment, he had not considered the true impact of it. If she was still a virgin, then no man had ever possessed her, and no man ever would but him, he determined.

"Yes." She said it low.

"Sweetheart, sweetheart," he groaned.

"It displeases you?" Why was he acting so oddly?

"Displeases me? Nay! How could such a thing displease any man? You have simply burnished your perfection with this unexpected gift. Nay, I am more than pleased to know you are untouched."

"Why? You seemed to desire me before you knew it?" she said.

"I did, but it pleases my vanity to learn now that no man has ever had you, and no man ever will but me!" Then he was kissing her again, and Lucianna let herself be swept away by the passion of it until she realized they were still in the hall. She struggled from his embrace and his lap, jumping up and saying, "My lord! This is too public a place for such delights."

His cock was swollen and tight against his

garments. Propriety was the last thing on his mind right now, but when he looked up into her concerned little face, he had to laugh. Struggling to his feet he said, "You find my kisses delightful?"

Now she blushed even more deeply. "I did not say that!"

"You said the hall was too public a place for such delights. What else could you have meant?" he teased wickedly. "I find your kisses a delight as well, Lucianna." His eyes were twinkling at her.

She was beginning to regain a hold of herself again. "I meant any intimacies between us should not be public for any to observe," Lucianna told him.

"I agree," he said. "So where shall we retreat to, sweetheart, for I admit I do not feel ready yet to stop kissing you."

"You are . . ." she began, and he finished the sentence for her.

"So bold," he said. "I know. It is the English way." He grinned. "Are not Florentine gentlemen enamored of certain ladies eager to kiss them and cuddle them?"

"I don't know," she admitted. "My experience has not been great. An elderly husband who quickly kissed me on the lips once at our marriage, and never again touched his lips to mine. Females of my station do not kiss gentlemen at random. And certainly not if they are not married to them," Luci-anna explained. "That is what a man's mistress is for, my lord. His pleasure. His wife is for giving him children, should he want children, and for keeping his house in order. Nothing more."

"But she can also be for his pleasure and delight," the earl told her, much to Luci-anna's surprise.

Then she recalled that her mother would occasionally spend the night in her father's bedchamber, and in the morning they would both be smiling. But while she had seen her parents share a quick kiss now and again, she did not ever remember them in a passionate embrace publicly.

"Do the English treat their wives so formally, my lord?"

"Sometimes, and sometimes not," he told her. "My wife will always know that she is loved, for I shall not hesitate to kiss her regularly in public and in private."

"My lady, my lord." Balia was suddenly by their side. "I think the earl must remain the night," the serving woman said. "The weather has turned most foul outside. It is raining heavily, and the winds are fierce. It is not a night for riding within the city."

The two women saw him consider, and

then he said, "I will not despoil your reputation, Lucianna. If I remain and it becomes known . . ." He left it for her to decide.

"If the weather is that dreadful, then I would prefer you remain," she said. "Remember that I am a widow. Whatever anyone else may believe or choose to think, it is not as bad as it would be if I were a maiden with my virginity to protect, my lord. Yes. Remain."

"I'll see a room is prepared for the earl," Balia said.

"As far away from your mistress as possible," the earl suggested.

"I will sleep upon the trundle in her room tonight," Balia told him. "Unless, of course . . ."

But Lucianna quickly said, "No, that will be enough to preserve my reputation from any who would think otherwise, Balia."

"Yes, my lady," and Balia hurried off to direct Cleva and Welsa.

"You are generous, and I thank you," he said. "At home, if I ride in a heavy rain, I can return home to a hot tub, warm clothes, and my bed. Here at court, I have not those luxuries and would sleep wet."

"Court hardly sounds like the place for a simple lordling," Lucianna observed.

"It isn't," he said. "Those few who are

always by the king and queen have small accommodations where such things are available. If not, they sleep where they can find a place that is dry and warm. Some of the more important nobles attending the king have homes of their own in London, and travel with their own pavilions and servants. The rest of us do the best we can. I do not have a home in London."

"You may stay in my house, my lord, whenever you are in the city," Lucianna offered. "If the meal is over, you can always go to the kitchen, and Alvina or Bessie will feed you."

He was astounded by the generous offer. "I do not believe your most proper mother would approve of such an arrangement," he said.

Lucianna did not demur. "No," she agreed, "she would not, but this is London, not Florence, and we are friends."

"Ah," he said with a smile, "you have decided we are friends?"

Lucianna smiled, unphased by him now. "Yes, I believe we are friends, my lord."

"We are friends," he agreed. "It is a good way for us to begin."

CHAPTER 8

He was gone by the time Lucianna came down to go to her shop the next morning. He had obviously departed early, for the servants had not seen him go. She was touched that he had a care for her reputation. Without the gaggle of young men in the street, her shop was now open to the various cloth merchants in London. Several came each day to inspect the quality of the Florentine silks. She was even given some orders, which she dispatched to Florence via pigeon.

Her days fell into a regular pattern. November ended, and December passed. It had been a very lonely holiday season. She and Balia celebrated together, and Lucianna saw that each of her English servants was given a small gift including sweets and nuts, which were a real treat for them. They were at first surprised by her generosity, and then grateful for it. She told them when God had gifted them with his only son, it set an example for them to gift others on that feast day. She did not see Robert Minton until the middle of January.

When he finally came to her home one Sunday afternoon, he looked exhausted, and Lucianna could not help but comment upon it.

The king's forte, it seemed, was finance, and Henry knew a rich king was a powerful king. He had spent little time with the court enjoying the Christmas season with his wife, infant son, and mother. Instead, he had closeted himself with Robert Minton to discuss new ways of raising revenue. Robert, it seemed, was his sounding board before he would bring his thoughts to the public.

"He has decided to manage everything himself, for he believes the Exchequer has been careless. They had little to do, as his treasury was empty when he became king, but he now checks his accounts daily, and then has a group of accountants double-check him. He will be raising taxes, expanding trade, whatever he must do to fill his treasury."

"And so you sat and listened to him, advised him," Lucianna said.

"I do little but agree," the earl admitted.

"He has been considering this for weeks now and knows what he means to do. But first he would say it aloud to me to see if I can offer any strong objection to his ideas before he tells the Lord Chancellor and others.

"I did suggest we needed a standing army to protect England. It would thwart challengers to the throne, for the king is not yet entirely secure. He actually agreed. Said he would choose several of the more martial of his lords to do so, as well as build a navy for England. I pointed out we must control our seas if we are to discourage foreign invasion."

"All very wise," Lucianna said, "but that should not account for the exhaustion I see upon your face, my lord."

"I had to go home to my estates briefly, for I had not been there in months. I am the local magistrate, among other things. My bailiff and my steward can do only so much without my authority. Hereford is some distance from London, so they cannot send to ask my permission or opinion on every little issue that nonetheless requires my approval or disapproval. I rode alone, stopping only long enough to rest my horse in the dark hours. More times than not, we were in the open at night."

"And you hurried back the same way so as not to leave the king without your counsel for too long?" Lucianna finished for him as she sat him down by the hearth in her little hall. Then she put a goblet of strong red wine in his hand. "Can you remain?"

He drank deeply, and then sitting back, sighed deeply. "Aye. May I take advantage of your kind offer from the last time we were together? To sleep here tonight?"

"I told you, my lord, that you might make free to consider my little home yours when you are in London," Lucianna said quietly. "I do not make offers lightly, Robert. Where is this Hereford of yours?"

She sat down opposite him, hands folded neatly in her lap.

"North and west. It borders Wales, which pleases the king. He is not ashamed of his Welsh heritage. Most of those surrounding him are English, but like the Tudors, my family is mixed with English and French," the earl explained to her.

"I understand," she said. She wondered if she was gushing. She could not say it to him, of course, but she had missed his company. She had missed him. But despite his past kisses, she did not really understand his attentions. He suggested marriage, and yet Lucianna was not a fool. Would an

English nobleman of an old family want a merchant's daughter, a shopkeeper, for a wife? Lucianna somehow could not believe it.

The color was beginning to come back into his face. "Lady Margaret would very much like to meet you," he told her. "She has requested I bring you to her midmorning tomorrow. You must send to Baram to open the shop and manage your business. I believe he is capable, is he not?"

"He is," Lucianna agreed. "I will send one of my lads in the morning with a message for him to do so. Why does Lady Margaret wish to meet me? I am just a shopkeeper."

"Do not be modest, Lucianna," he said to her. "You are far more than *just* a shopkeeper. The king's mother is curious to learn if you can be of any use to her, or to the young queen. She asks to meet no one without a purpose, but I would have no idea what, for she does not often share her thoughts with anyone, wisely keeping her own counsel."

"I have never been to any royal court, Robert. What should I wear to meet a king's mother?" she asked him.

He chuckled. It was such a feminine question. "I would imagine your best day gown would suffice. This is not a formal occasion."

"Will the young queen be there?" Lucianna wondered aloud. "When I write to my mother, she would be thrilled to learn I had met a queen."

"I have no idea. Lady Margaret wants to meet you first, I would guess. She will take your measure, ask questions, and then if she likes you, she will probably invite the queen to join you. It is her usual way," he explained. "She is a very wise and clever woman, else she could not have made her son a king, or survived the Yorkists, considering her activities during their reign. She was always carefully manuvering to see that Henry was in an advantageous position when the time came."

"She was a good and dutiful mother," Lucianna said. "Much like my own mother. Orianna has always been involved in her children's lives. Now she concentrates more on the boys, for my eldest brother, Marco, while sweet in nature, cannot seem to grasp being an adult. I can only imagine the misery he is in without his mistress. Giorgio, of course, makes her the proudest, being in Rome."

"And your twin brother?"

Lucianna laughed. "Luca was always the

soldier," she said.

The servants began bringing in a hot meal, and his hostess saw him to the high board, where she filled his plate not once, but twice.

"You are not eating," he observed.

"I ate earlier. It suits my disposition," Lucianna told him.

"You keep country hours, up with the sun, and to bed soon after it sets," he said with a smile as he helped himself to some cheese.

"Shopkeepers are little different from country folk," she agreed.

After his meal, they sat again by the fire, talking quietly for a time. He told her of his home in Hereford. "It is pure country, green and lush. The Mintons have held it for several hundred years, and the earldom since the time of Henry the Fifth. One of my ancestors married an heiress whose family name was Lisle. When Henry the Fifth offered an earldom to him, he asked it bear the name of Lisle in her honor, for he loved her dearly."

"How lovely, and how very romantic," Lucianna exclaimed.

"I never actually considered it that way," the earl said. "I suppose I am not a particularly romantic fellow."

Lucianna did not know if she agreed with

his assessment, but she decided that would be a good time to end the evening, which she did.

In the morning, she awoke to find her tub already filled and awaiting her. Yawning, she exclaimed her surprise.

"You'll not go dirty to meet the king's mother," Balia said sternly.

Lucianna laughed, thinking her mother would approve her tiring woman's words. Getting up, she stripped her chemise off and climbed into the tub. Balia saw her scrubbed, and washed the golden hair with its reddish highlights. Once out of the tub, she was dried and seated by the fire while her hair was first toweled and then brushed dry. A clean long-sleeved *camicia* was followed by an underskirt, and finally a gown of dark green velvet with a small V-neckline. The neckline was embroidered with wide green and copper-colored braid that ran down the front of the gown and about the hem. The turned-back sleeves were also quite wide and trimmed with the same braid. A belt of the same material hung at hip length. It was an elegant and flattering gown. Lucianna wore it on the days she knew she would be receiving an important buyer. Today, she would wear a soft hood with a veil.

She had eaten a small meal of hot oats and watered wine while Balia had brushed her hair dry. Although the king's mother had requested her presence this morning, who knew when she would next see food again that day? If she was indeed the king's silent adviser, Lady Margaret might have much more to do than chatter with a Florentine shopkeeper this day. Lucianna had heard that she would probably wait before she actually was ushered into that august lady's presence.

Balia now slipped a pair of low-heeled leather boots on her feet. "These will serve you better today than fancy slippers. With all this rain, these English streets are muddy."

Lucianna nodded, agreeing. Besides, she knew no one would look at her feet. They would be far more interested in the jewelry she was wearing. About her neck was a short gold chain from which hung a small gold crucifix. She slipped several different rings on her fingers.

Standing, Lucianna now viewed herself in the beautiful full-length mirror she had brought with her from Florence. It had been a gift from her grandfather in Venice upon her marriage, and she treasured it. She smiled, pleased by what she saw. Yes, she would do her family and Florence proud this day.

Balia chuckled at the look of satisfaction upon her mistress's face.

"Yes, you are beautiful, and the king's mother will not find you wanting, my lady. Now hurry, for the earl is waiting for you."

Downstairs, Robert Minton's eyes showed his pleasure in her appearance. Balia gave him time for a good look, and then she silently placed a dark green wool cape lined in warm marten about Lucianna's shoulders, handing her a pair of dark leather gloves lined in silk. Outside, the horses awaited them, for they would ride to Lady Margaret Beaufort's house.

It was cold, and there was no sun, but there was also no wind. They rode through the busy streets, keeping to the center and listening for the warning cry of "Ware!" as an occasional night jar was emptied from above. It was not a great distance to Lady Margaret's house, and upon arriving, their horses were taken, and they were shown inside.

Lucianna shivered as they were taken to a small antechamber to await their summoning. "I cannot quite get used to this damp cold," she said, rubbing her gloved hands together and holding them over the small fire available to them.

"It is not as damp in the country," he answered her. "It is cold in Hereford, but not dank as it is here in the city. It is the river, and the nearness of the sea, of course." He drew a small straight-backed chair next to the fireplace. "Sit down," he said.

She accepted his invitation, and after a few minutes the heat of the flames in the small hearth began to warm her. Her shoulders relaxed, and she pulled off her gloves, tucking them in an inside pocket of the fur-lined cape. "Ah, this is better," she told him.

The door opened and a black-robed priest entered the room. "Good morning, Robert," he said, and he smiled at Lucianna, who had risen out of respect. "This will be Mistress Pietro d'Angelo," he remarked, with another smile. "She has sent me to fetch you. I am Father John Fisher, Lady Margaret's confessor. You need not come, Robert, but are free to wait for Mistress Pietro d'Angelo."

The earl quickly removed Lucianna's cape and gave her a small smile. "I'll find you when you are ready to depart," he promised.

Lucianna followed the priest, who swiftly led her from the antechamber down a hallway, opening a door at its end to usher

173

her inside. There were two or three ladies seated within the chamber, who smiled at her in a friendly fashion. Then the door to another room opened, and a tall woman emerged as the others came to their feet, curtsying.

She had a face that was long rather than round. Her eyes were round and dark blue, with elegantly arched brows above them. Her nose was long and extremely aristocratic. Her mouth was neat and small. She was garbed in a beautiful, elegant dark gown, her only jewelry being a simple, heavy, red-gold cross. Upon her head she wore a silk veil such as a lady would wear in her home. "Good morrow, Mistress Pietro d'Angelo," she greeted Lucianna as she seated herself in a tall-backed upholstered chair. "Please," she invited, "come and sit by me." She indicated an upholstered stool by her chair. "Thank you, Father."

The priest nodded, and departed the chamber.

Lucianna curtsied first, and then sat as she had been directed, saying, "Thank you, madame."

"Robert tells me you are quite fluent in the English language. I am impressed, for it is a difficult language to learn. There will be times, however, when I will speak to you in

Italian because I do not want our conversation overheard. I believe my Italian to be fairly acceptable." The last sentence was spoken in Lucianna's own language. "Yes?"

"Indeed, madame, yes," the younger woman said politely.

"Tell me how you like London. Is it very different from your Florence?" Lady Margaret inquired.

"I like London very much, but then I have been a city dweller my whole life, but for a few months in the summer when we went to my parents' villa in the Tuscan hills," Lucianna explained. "Both cities are old and busy, but we have gates to certain roads. I have seen no such gates in London."

"You are a widow." It was a statement.

"Yes. My husband was many years my senior. He was a kind man, and I was fond of him. I like to believe I made his last years a comfort. I am told it is so, but I think a woman is always concerned as to whether she is doing her best by her lord."

"A good woman is," Lady Margaret responded, her voice approving. The girl seemed intelligent and kind. She would not have been as concerned as she was in Lucianna's character, but Robert Minton had hinted to her of his interest in the Florentine girl.

Indeed, she seemed more girl than woman. "Tell me about your shop. I understand the silk merchants' guild in Florence sent you to represent them. Why a woman? Is not such an undertaking more a man's task?"

"Milan seems to believe so," Lucianna said, "but in Florence our guild is more enlightened."

"And cleverer," Lady Margaret noted, with a small smile.

"My father is head of our guild. I was sent because I knew the business of silk, and it was believed a woman could present it better. I can, too. Now that we have managed to keep the street upon which my shop is located free of young men coming to see the phenomenon I seem to be, my sales have become quite brisk."

"The Milanese will give you some competition when they arrive," Lady Margaret noted.

"Their silk is inferior to ours, as a discerning eye will quickly discover. That is why the silks His Majesty sent the Earl of Lisle to purchase came from our shops, and not Milan's," Lucianna said proudly. "My father personally traded with the China folk in his younger days. Only when he married my mother did he cease his travels and send a representative."

"Does your mother come from a silk family?" the older woman asked Lucianna.

"Oh no! My mother is a daughter of Prince Alessandro Venier, a Venetian. She was very outspoken as a girl, and to add to that, her dower portion was small. While her older sisters had married into Venice society, none sought her. My father had frequently sailed east from Venice. He admired her beauty and spirit. When he learned that she had no hope of marrying because of what were considered her flaws, he was daring enough to offer for her. He says he fully expected Prince Venier to throw him into a canal for his boldness," Lucianna said with a small smile. "Instead, my grandfather accepted his offer, with the condition he cease traveling, and my parents were married."

"Was your mother happy to finally be wed?"

Now Lucianna laughed. "No. She fancied herself in love with another, and she decided Florence was gloomy compared to Venice. Nonetheless, she made my father an excellent wife, for she understands her duty. I am one of seven siblings, and our mother has had a strong hand in raising us."

"Are you said to be like her?" Lady Margaret asked candidly.

"I don't believe so. My sister Francesca is more like her. She was wed to the Duke of Terreno Boscoso. He was murdered by a servant in the pay of the French, but Francesca saw this traitor executed, and now rules the duchy while her son grows into manhood."

"Ah, now there is a woman I can understand," Lady Margaret said. "My son was born to a deceased Lancaster lord, and I had to see him protected, for he was in line for the throne — especially once the two little Yorkist princes disappeared and King Richard's only son was killed in battle. So your sister protecting her son's inheritance is most understandable."

The two women spoke a while longer before Lady Margaret said, "I have kept you too long from your place of business, Mistress Pietro d'Angelo." She stood, and Lucianna did too. "Thank you so much for coming and satisfying an old woman's curiosity."

"Why, my lady," Lucianna said ingenuously, "you are not old."

"You are kind, my dear, to say so," Lady Margaret answered her. "Lady Mary, please help my guest find the earl."

Lucianna curtsied deeply and then was

ushered out by Lady Mary, who said, once they were free of being heard, "You could not have said a kinder thing to her, Mistress Pietro d'Angelo. She is not really old, of course, but she worries about not being here to help the king. She is a very good mother."

"Indeed, I could see her concern for the king," Lucianna responded.

Lady Mary brought Lucianna back to the same antechamber. "You wait here, my dear. I will find the earl for you." With a polite curtsy, the two women parted.

Lucianna sat down to wait for Robert. It had been a very interesting meeting, and she would write to her mother in great detail about it. She knew how much Orianna would enjoy learning everything her daughter could tell her about the king of England's mother — and how very much Orianna would enjoy bragging about her daughter's small adventure. She imagined it was difficult for Orianna to deal with the gossip that was certain to be circulating about her third daughter's travels and business in England. It had been difficult for her mother to accept an elderly bookseller as a son-in-law when she had always hoped to make great and grand marriages for her girls. Hopefully, Lucianna thought with a smile, she would gain her heart's desire with the baby of the family.

The door to the room opened, and the earl stepped in. "Did you enjoy meeting Lady Margaret?" he asked her. "She is a most fascinating woman to my mind."

"I found her charming," Lucianna said. "And most gracious to me. She did not appear to be a king's mother in attitude."

"She is too wise for that," Robert noted. "Here is your cloak." He carefully put it about her shoulders.

"It is warm!" Lucianna exclaimed, surprised.

"It's been toasted by one of the kitchen fires," he told her, with a smile. "Where do you wish to go? To your shop, or your home?"

"Where will you go after you deliver me?" Lucianna asked as she carefully fastened her cloak.

He looked surprised by her query. "I hadn't considered it," he said. "I did not know how long Lady Margaret would keep you, and so I planned nothing else for this day."

"Let us go home," Lucianna said. "I am certain Baram can manage the shop for today. Will you play chess with me? I will feed you dinner." She smiled at him as she drew on her gloves.

180

He was both surprised and delighted by her invitation. "Yes," he said to her. "I should like that, Lucianna."

They departed Lady Margaret's house and rode back through the narrow streets, which became less busy as they reached the area where Lucianna's house was located. Her stable boys came quickly to take the horses and bring them to the shelter of the stables.

Balia hurried downstairs, having seen them coming from the upper story. "Well?" she asked. "What is she like? Did she like you?"

"The king's mother was a lovely lady, and yes, she was most welcoming and kind to me. I enjoyed my visit with her. Now the earl will be remaining for dinner, so tell Alvina. We'll be in my library as it's warmer than the hall, I am certain."

Balia hurried off with a nod as Lucianna and the earl settled themselves in her library. They seated themselves by the hearth, setting the game table between them. Lucianna opened her box of chess pieces, and he was surprised by the beauty of them. The black were carved from ebony. Both the king and the queen wore tiny silver crowns, the bishop a silver mitre, and the knights silver helmets. The white were ivory with gold décor.

"I always play the white," Lucianna told him as she set her pieces upon the elegant wood board.

"Then, of necessity," he said with a chuckle, "the black is mine."

They were evenly matched in skills and played several games. The earl won a few, and Lucianna won the others. They enjoyed playing with each other, for both were clever and enjoyed outwitting the other. He felt no necessity to play down to her, nor did she feel any reason to overplay him. And as they played, they spoke to each other.

"Come the springtime, I hope you will allow me to take you to visit my estates in Hereford," he said to her.

"Do you mean to spend the winter here in London, then?" she asked him, curious. "Do you always spend the cold months here?"

"I rarely spend the winters in London, but this year I am here for the king. Once he dismisses me, I will return to Hereford. I believe he is becoming comfortable enough to speak with his queen on certain matters on which he would normally speak with me. As she was raised in a royal court, her instincts are very good. Her mother is no fool, although she would meddle if she could."

"Then one day you will return to your Hereford for good," Lucianna said. "I hope it will not be soon, my lord."

"I will not return to Hereford for good until I am able to take you with me for good," Robert Minton shocked her by saying.

The pawn in her fingers fell to the board. She could not have heard him right. "What a charming thing to say, my lord, but alas I have a duty to my guild." There. That would give him a way to explain himself easily.

"Lucianna," he said quietly, taking her now-empty hand in his. "I asked your father's permission to court you with marriage in mind should we find that we suit each other. I have been trying to do it ever since you arrived in London several months ago."

"I am a shopkeeper," she said. "The widow of a shopkeeper. Lords do not wed with shopkeepers."

"Lords wed with whomever they choose to wed," he countered. "You are your father's daughter. The child of a wealthy silk merchant, the granddaughter of a Venetian prince. But if you were no more than a milkmaid, and I loved you, I would want you for my wife, Lucianna."

"You would be the laughingstock of the court," she said to him.

"I have little to do with the court. I am nothing more than the king's true friend," Robert Minton insisted. "Lady Margaret knows my intentions towards you. Why do you think she wanted to meet you? She wanted to be certain that I was not being foolish. She now tells me I am not, and that you will make me a fine wife, Lucianna."

"You spoke to her after I was dismissed from her presence?"

"I did," he replied.

"I have a duty to my guild, Robert. Do you think because I am a woman that my duty is any less than a man's duty?"

"I have spoken too soon, and I never meant to press you, Lucianna. You need more time to know me better."

"You have surprised me, I will admit," she told him. "And do not think, I beg you, that I am not both flattered and honored by your desire, for I am, but I am not quite ready to marry again. My family took care of me all my life until I wed Alfredo. Then it was I who took care of him, and myself. I like being in charge of myself, Robert. I wonder if you can understand that, my lord."

"I honestly don't, but I love you, and so I

respect your feelings on this matter. Understand that I will continue to pursue you, *amore mia.*"

"I have not said I would refuse your offer, my lord." She smiled at him. "I have simply stated I am not ready to be a wife again."

Balia came to tell them that the meal was ready and being brought into the hall. They ate, but their conversation was sparse.

Afterwards, he took his leave of her, and Lucianna went to write to her mother. She would tell her about the king's mother, but not about the earl's proposal of marriage. She was not ready to deal with Orianna, even long distance, about such a thing. And what if her mother decided that she must come to England to encourage her daughter to another marriage? Marriage for Orianna was important, but not in the same way as it was for her third daughter. Lucianna needed time to consider what being married to a man like the Earl of Lisle would be like.

She suddenly realized that, like her sisters before her, love was the paramount thing. For Orianna, there had been no such option. There had only been a husband socially beneath her, and exile to another city.

Would marriage to Robert Minton be filled with his love for her, or his duty to

King Henry and her duty to his estates and any children they would have? This had not been something she needed to consider when she wed Alfredo Allibatore, but she certainly needed to consider it now.

CHAPTER 9

Henry Tudor's throne was not quite secure. In the months preceding Lucianna's arrival in England, it had been threatened by a Yorkist pretender claiming to be the young Earl of Warwick, son of Edward IV's late brother, the Duke of Clarence. It was said that Warwick had escaped from the Tower where Henry had installed him after winning the Battle of Bosworth against Richard III.

That this boy was an imposter was accepted by many Yorkists, yet they still supported him. He was crowned in Ireland as Edward VI. His armies then made their way into the heart of England before being defeated at the Battle of Stoke. Those managing this young pretender were killed in the battle, and Lambert Simnel, for that was his real name, received clemency from King Henry, and was put to work as a turnspit in the royal kitchens.

Robert Minton related all of this to Lucianna.

"The Medici would have publicly tortured such an imposter," Lucianna replied. "Then they would have executed him for all to see as a warning to others."

"I thought you said the Medici do not rule Florence," he said.

"Legally they do not, but their wealth and position of power give those who do not know better the impression that they do, which is why when someone desires a favor of Florence, they go first to the Medici."

He laughed. "It is clever."

Lucianna then told him, "The Medici like the power, but they do not want the responsibility, for if it were officially theirs, they would not have time for all their amusements. So they eschew any claim of governing, and instead hold festivals for the people with much food and fountains of wine that seem to flow endlessly."

"Such behavior can work for a city," Robert told her, "but not an entire country, I fear."

Thinking about it, Lucianna had to agree, especially knowing now what she had learned about England.

Late winter begat early spring, and the representative from the silk merchants' guild in Milan arrived, setting up his own shop. He was surprised by the brisk business being done by Florence, and by the lovely Lucianna. He had heard they had sent a woman, and found it amusing until he discovered that she had taught the London merchants the difference between fine silks and those of lesser quality. His shop did some trade once the local cloth merchants had investigated his premises. Only those seeking to sell silk cloth to customers with less coin to spend came to buy from him. The Milanese representative wrote home, complaining to his guild that he must have better-quality materials if he was to compete with the Florentine woman. April passed.

In May, the Earl of Lisle invited Lucianna to visit his estates in Hereford with him. She accepted, leaving Baram Kira in charge of the shop while she was gone. "There are several orders and new inventory arriving from Florence shortly," she told him. "You know what to do."

"I do, mistress," he assured her.

Having come to know Baram Kira over the past few months, Lucianna was confident that she could trust him, and so she left London on a bright sunny morning in the company of the Earl of Lisle for Hereford. She knew her mother would be shocked, but she was becoming more English in her ways, and liked the freedom their women seemed to have. She would write to Orianna when she returned. By then, her description of the earl's estates would fascinate her mother so much that the fact Lucianna went with only Balia as her chaperone would not trouble her as much.

They traveled for several days. Nightly refuge was found at inns chosen in advance by the earl. As they grew farther and farther from London, Balia complained to her mistress.

"I have never been in such a wild place before. Where are these estates of his? At the edge of the world?"

"Hush!" Lucianna cautioned. "He has said they are a distance from London, and it would seem he does not lie. I am as curious as you are as to where we are going."

The next day they rode along the river the earl told them was called the Wye. "My estates border it and are near the border with Wales. It is not far now. We should be there by midafternoon." Then he added, "The stone cairn we just passed marks the borders of my lands."

"Does this cairn signify anything else

other than a border marker?" Lucianna asked him.

"It is probably a grave marker as well," he said.

The track they now followed went through lush greenery populated by cattle. It seemed to Lucianna that it was a very large herd.

Seeing her unspoken interest, Robert Minton said, "I raise cattle and feed for them. I also have a fine apple orchard that produces some of the finest cider in the county."

"I have never tasted this cider," Lucianna said.

"It's made with apples," he explained to her, "and is very favored here in Hereford."

"Your people do not drink wine?" She was surprised. In Florence, both rich and poor drank wine.

"Wine is expensive in a simple place like this. Cider is not. I allow my cottagers to take the apples I do not use and make their own if they so choose," he said.

Lucianna was fascinated. She had always assumed everyone in the world drank wine. Water was not safe, as a rule.

Finally, as he had predicted, they reached his home. It was a large manor house of wood and brick, known as Wye Court. It sat on the banks of the river Wye in a small hollow between the hills.

"The hills to the west are in Wales," he told her. "These lands were given to my family by the first Norman king, William, although the Welsh claimed it. The first house was burned to the ground about two hundred years ago by a lightning strike. We rebuilt it, and the family's heir married the Welsh daughter of a nearby neighbor, thereby assuring us of the friendship of the Welsh ever since. Now and again, we marry into a Welsh family, but I shall marry you when you agree."

Balia's ears perked up at this bit of knowledge. She wondered if her mistress had passed this bit of information on to her mother, but suspected she had not, else Orianna would be in England inspecting the suitability of the earl, and seeing to her daughter's quick acceptance. Though he was a foreigner, he was noble. A nobleman was indeed an acceptable mate for Orianna's daughter.

They stopped their horses before the house, and servants hurried out to aid them. Lucianna was very impressed by the warm greeting the earl was given by his servants. She was less pleased when he said to them, "I hope to make this lady my wife one day, so be on your best behavior."

"You had no right to say such a thing," Lucianna complained to him afterwards. "I have not said I would wed you, my lord."

"You will," he said with a grin, "and I am willing to give you your way in the matter until you are ready to accept the responsibility of being my wife, Lucianna. I am patient."

"You will have to be!" she told him sharply.

"Are you aware of how charming you are when you are indignant, *cara mia*?"

"You are impossible! I should demand you return me to London immediately, my lord," she said, trying to sound as if she meant it. But the truth was Lucianna had already fallen in love with Wye Court, and the countryside surrounding it. It was different from anything else she had ever known. Her father's Tuscan villa was little more than a large family farmhouse, but Wye Court was more of an elegant country home. She liked it. It felt comfortable, even from the outside.

Inside, it was, she found, even more comfortable. The rooms were large, the furniture substantial. The walls were paneled in warm wood, and hung with either tapestries or paintings. The large windows were hung with draperies. It had the feel of a home. Even Lady Margaret's house had not had that particular feeling. Lucianna was immediately at ease, to her surprise.

"Let Argel show you your rooms," the earl said. "I must speak with my steward now and learn what has been happening since I have been away."

Argel curtsied politely to Lucianna. "I am the earl's housekeeper, and I hope you will be comfortable in the rooms I have chosen for you and your servant." She led them upstairs, down a hallway, finally stopping before a door. Opening it, she entered, ushering Lucianna and Balia inside.

Ever mindful of her mistress's comfort, Balia took a quick look about her and then went to inspect the bedchamber. It was a lovely, small apartment. Pleased, she said to Argel, "Thank you for choosing such comfortable quarters for my mistress."

"The earl has never before brought a lady to Wye Court," Argel said. Then, unable to control her curiosity, she asked Lucianna, "Are you really going to wed my master, my lady?"

"So he says, and he assures me he had received my father's permission while he was in Florence. I know a good daughter would accept her parent's decision in such a matter, but my father said nought to me. I am a widow, so I must assume my father is leaving the final decision in this matter to me," Lucianna told the housekeeper. To her surprise, the woman laughed.

"You are one of those shocking women who claim to think for themselves," she said, chuckling. "I hope you will wed him, my lady. He needs a strong wife, not one of those mild-as-milk court lasses." Then, with a curtsy, she left the two women, saying, "I will send a maidservant when it is time for the meal. Your baggage will be brought shortly."

"You could do a lot worse," Balia said bluntly. "He has charm, and a fine house for a wife."

"And I should never have to go back to Florence, and my mother's meddling," Lucianna said candidly. "But, I would love him before I wed him."

"Mistress, you know better. Marriage is for stature and wealth. Do not be foolish like your sisters were," Balia advised, as she knew Orianna would want her to advise Lucianna.

"My sisters, for all the difficulties they caused, were happy — are happy. Bianca loved her prince enough to give up her family. Her love was strong and certain. And Francesca fell in love with her duke, so much so that she has resisted our mother's pleas to remarry."

"Your sister Francesca has a duchy to rule for her son until he comes of age," Balia reminded Lucianna. "And as for Bianca, who knows if she remains happy with her prince? But having cast the die, she must live with her decision now."

"I believe she is still happy," Lucianna said. "If she were not, she would return home despite the shame that would be heaped upon her."

"He cannot take his eyes from you, or perhaps you haven't noticed?" the serving woman said.

"I have noticed," Lucianna admitted. "Such scrutiny makes me uncomfortable, I fear. It is as if he is looking for some flaw in my person but cannot find it, so he continues his surveillance of me."

Balia laughed. "He will find no fault in you because he doesn't want to find a fault. The man is already in love, mistress. Why must you discourage him?"

There was no chance for Lucianna to answer her companion, for a knock came upon the door, and several menservants entered, carrying their luggage. Balia quickly directed them as to where to place the trunks. Lucianna stood before the afternoon fire, warming her hands, for they were chilly. It might almost be summer, but it was still chilly here in the country.

"We'll want water for a bath up here," Balia said to the man who looked in charge.

"Will ye now, my pretty?" he responded boldly.

"Yes!" Balia answered him, standing her ground and looking him directly in the eye. "My mistress has been a-horse for days, and she does not wish to greet the earl later stinking of the road."

"Well now, that being the case, I expect we could get a bit of water up here," the serving man answered. "My name is Fflam."

"Is it? Well, Fflam, I will be grateful if you will see to the bathwater for my lady. My name is Balia."

He gave her a small nod of his head, and then with a wave of his hand he signaled the others to leave the apartment. "We'll be back," he said to her with a grin.

"Now to find the tub," Balia said once the men had departed. "I think you should bathe here before this fire." She began opening cupboards and peering inside until she found a round oak tub. Pulling it out, the two women set it in front of the hearth. "You go wait in the bedchamber," Balia instructed Lucianna. "When they have filled the tub up, I will call you, mistress."

Lucianna did as her serving woman had suggested, taking the opportunity while she waited to pull off her boots and her garments.

When Balia finally called her, Lucianna stepped naked into the dayroom and settled herself in the surprisingly hot water. Balia quickly scrubbed her golden red hair with the fresh water before she allowed her mistress to wash herself.

As the tub was not a large one, Lucianna washed quickly, and then climbed from the water to be wrapped in two warmed towels Balia had hung before the fire. When she shivered, Balia quickly dried her and saw her garbed in a fresh *camicia,* and a warm houserobe before she began to brush dry Lucianna's now-damp hair. Once finished, she insisted her mistress get into the bed, tucking her beneath a down coverlet for extra warmth.

"Now you nap until I call you," Balia said. "I will go and learn from Argel when the meal will be served so you will not be tardy." She hurried from the bedchamber, closing the door behind her.

To Lucianna's surprise, she fell asleep, awakening at the touch of her servant's hand upon her shoulder. "I could remain here forever," she told Balia.

"But you won't," her servant said. "The supper will be served shortly, and you must be dressed."

"What will I wear?" Lucianna asked. "A country supper cannot be too formal."

"A simple gown such as you would wear during the day will do, mistress. I asked Argel. Get up now. I have already taken a gown from our luggage, and seen to any wrinkles."

It did not take long to dress Lucianna in a simple medium blue gown. Then Balia set to work doing her mistress's hair. She brushed it thoroughly and then plaited it into a single thick braid. The serving woman lastly slipped a pair of simple house slippers on her mistress's feet. "You're ready," she told her.

Lucianna went down to the hall, and a servant met her at the foot of the stairs. It was not a grand hall, but medium in size, with windows on either side and two large hearths that were now blazing. The earl came to meet her, and brought her to the high board, where he seated her in the chair reserved for the mistress of the house. He then sat next to her.

"Are you pleased with your quarters? Argel told me that Balia considered it suitable."

"I am most comfortable," she admitted. "I hope your steward had only good news for you, my lord."

"He did. We have had at least half a dozen calves born this spring, and three more of my heifers will deliver shortly. A healthy herd must be constantly replaced."

"And your orchards?"

"Still blooming, and giving every evidence of a good crop come the autumn," he told her.

"Yours is a prosperous estate, then," she said.

"Aye, but it is also well cared for; herds and apples do not flourish without constant attention."

"How long will we remain?" she inquired. They had already been gone from London for several days, and she found now that they had arrived, she was concerned for her shop.

"We will remain as long as it takes me to convince you to agree to be my wife, Lucianna," he surprised her by saying. "I want you to see and learn what your life as my countess would be like."

"My lord! You cannot be serious! 'Tis not fair of you. I have a great responsibility to the Arte di Por Santa Maria here in England. Do you think my responsibilities are any less than yours because you are a man, a noble? They are not! Besides, you do not love me. Why tarnish your reputation marrying a foreign shopkeeper when I am certain the king's mother would choose you a proper bride if you asked it of her?"

"Not love you? Of course I love you!"

"You have only said it once!" she shot back.

"I thought that you understood it," he replied. "I do not introduce every girl I meet to Lady Margaret. I have never before brought any female to Wye Court. Of course I love you, *cara mia.*"

"How could I understand or know such things if you did not tell me?" Lucianna said. He loved her! He actually loved her. She had not ever been loved by a man before. Alfredo, of course, had been fond of her the way one would be fond of a young relation. But he had not loved her as a man loves a woman. How could her father have known if she didn't? And was this why he had managed to send her to England? In hopes that the earl would declare himself?

"Do you love me?" he asked her. "Not that it matters, for I will have you anyway, Lucianna. The thought of any other man marrying you is, for me, untenable."

"Oh my," Lucianna said, very surprised by all of this. "I must think," she said. "My responsibilities . . ."

"Marry me," he repeated. "We will remain in London until your guild sends another representative, but then I would come home to Hereford. Would such an arrangement please you?"

Lucianna nodded. He loved her! And she had loved him from the moment he had walked into her little bookshop. Yet she had never dared to hope he would return her affections seriously. So she had pushed her tender emotions aside while accepting his friendship, but now . . . could she marry him? Never return to Florence again? Never see her family again? Yes! Yes she could! This was the way of all women — to marry and form a new family.

"Will you let me tend to the shop until the guild sends another?" she asked him.

He nodded in the affirmative.

Lucianna took a long deep breath. "Then I will marry you," she told him. "I too love you, and I have since we first met."

"Here," he said. "Here at Wye Court. To-morrow."

Lucianna laughed. "Here," she agreed. "And before we return to London, but give me a few days to accustom myself to the idea, my lord, if you will."

He caught her hand and kissed it fervently. "Very well, I will restrain my eagerness. The contracts must be drawn up first. Tomorrow you will meet Father Paul, the estate priest. He will do them for us."

"My property remains mine," she said quickly.

"I agree," he replied. He was not going to argue with her over the inheritance she received from her first husband.

They finished their meal, and then before he might protest, Lucianna excused herself and hurried upstairs to her apartment, where Balia was awaiting her. "Did you eat?" she asked her serving woman.

"Aye, in the kitchens," Balia said. "Why did you not remain in the hall with the earl? You have returned from your meal quickly."

"I have agreed to marry him, Balia. Before we return to London," Lucianna said without preamble to her companion.

"Santa Anna!" Balia said, crossing herself. "Did he admit his love for you, mistress?" Then she grew serious. "But what of your mother? She will be overjoyed you are wedding a noble, but furious she cannot be with you."

"She was with me when I was wed to Alfredo Allibatore," Lucianna said. "I believe my father was aware that Robert loved me, which is why I was sent to England. He hoped for this very outcome."

"Aye, your father is a quiet man, my lady, but he is clever. Still, what of your responsibility to the guild?"

"I shall return to London to send to Florence for a replacement, and once he has been sent, I shall return here to Hereford. Will you dislike it too greatly if we spend our lives in the countryside, Balia?"

"This is a pleasant place, mistress, and my position as personal servant to the countess will assure me of a proper ranking among the other servants here. Nay, where you go, I go," Balia said to Lucianna.

Lucianna found Balia's declaration a relief. It was one thing to never go back to Florence again, but to lose her only contact with her previous life would have been difficult indeed. "Thank you," she said to Balia. "I am comforted to know you will remain with me."

"What of the London house?" Balia wondered aloud.

"I will permit the new representative to live there," Lucianna said. "And, I will charge the guild for his board."

"Ah," Balia said, "there is your mother

speaking."

"Why should the guild get for free what my father paid for?" Lucianna answered her. "I have done excellent business for them and kept Milan's silk merchants in their place as well. Let them send someone else who will do the same."

She slept restlessly, surprised she could even catch a few minutes of sleep, considering what had happened. She loved him, but was she doing the right thing marrying a foreign nobleman in a foreign land without her mother? Yet her father approved, and Lucianna realized that, like her two older sisters before her, she had done her duty by her family first. This time was for her — and for Robert.

Up early the next morning, she bathed and dressed carefully before going to the hall to break her fast. The earl was awaiting her, and his eyes lit with pleasure as she entered the hall.

He came quickly towards her. Smiling, and taking her hand in his, he said, "We will go to Mass in the chapel, *amore mia.* The priest is awaiting us. I have already spoken briefly with him, but we will speak at length afterwards." Then he led her to a small chapel within the house itself.

The chapel had two long stained-glass

windows. Lucianna had never before seen such windows other than in a large church. The walls were paneled, but there were several beautiful small paintings of saints, including one she recognized as Santa Anna with the girl Mary. Lucianna felt it was a sign that she was meant to be here. The altar was simple, fashioned of wood with a lace-edged white cloth, golden candlesticks, and a cross upon it. Her mother would surely be impressed that her new home had its own chapel.

Father Paul spoke the words of the morning prayer, aided by a young boy. The Mass was soon concluded, and several of the servants, including Balia, hurried out, leaving the priest to the lord and the lady. Father Paul was a large, tall man who looked one directly in the eye.

"So," he said to Lucianna, "you wish to wed with my lord earl?"

"Nay, good Father, 'tis he who wishes to wed with me. As my father has given him permission to do so, as a good daughter, I must obey my parent's wishes," Lucianna replied.

The priest was surprised by her candid words, and then he burst out laughing. "Ah, Robbie, you've not chosen a meek one, have you?"

Robert Minton chuckled. "Nay, I have not," he said. "Will she not make a fine mistress for Wye Court?" He grinned and put an arm about Lucianna's shoulders.

"She will indeed," the priest agreed. "Come! We will go to the hall and discuss the terms of the marriage agreement. Toby!" he called to the altar boy. "Bring parchment, a quill, and ink."

"Yes, Father Paul," the boy said, and ran off to do as he had been bid.

"You are a brave lass," the priest said to Lucianna, "to leave your homeland and come to England to wed this man."

"But I did not come to wed him," Lucianna told him. "My father is the head of the Arte di Por Santa Maria, the Silk Merchants' Guild of Florence. He sent me to England to open a shop where I might display our fine silks. This way your cloth merchants do not have to go to Florence, but they can choose what they want in London. I met Robert when he came to Florence last year to purchase silk for Queen Elizabeth."

"Ah," the priest said. "I understand now. Your family obviously approves of my lord, else they should not have encouraged a liaison between you. Did your mother not wish you to remain in Florence?"

"My mother is the daughter of a Venetian prince," Lucianna explained. "She wanted her daughters to wed men of wealth and position. One of my sisters is the Duchess of Terreno Boscoso."

"You have just one sister?" he inquired of her.

"Nay, but because the eldest of us ran off with a Turkish prince, we rarely speak of her," Lucianna said. "And there is still one more at home to be matched. My first husband was Florentine."

"You are a widow, then," the priest noted.

"I am," Lucianna replied, crossing herself.

He nodded. "Then I can understand your family placing their trust in you, my daughter," he said. Then he sniffed. "Do I smell bacon?" he said. "My weakness is bacon."

The earl chuckled. "And cook does know it," he said. "Come! Let us break our fast, and then get down to business. I would be wed to this woman as soon as possible."

The priest raised an eyebrow. "Such unseemly haste, my son," he chided. He looked to Lucianna. "And you, mistress?"

"I did not come to Wye Court with the intention of wedding this man," Lucianna told the priest, "but I do love him, and if he is willing to make a silk merchant's daughter his wife, I will not say nay. But a few days to prepare would be welcome. And I would send for my brother Luca, who is in London. If sent for today, he can be here quickly."

Father Paul nodded. "So be it, then. I will marry you in five days' time, not a moment before, and her brother must be here to approve it."

The earl looked disappointed, but he nodded in agreement, seeing that Lucianna was pleased. "You are a stubborn woman," he said to her. "But I will have you anyway."

She laughed at him. "The dish is sweeter for the anticipation, my lord," she replied to him.

Now it was the priest's turn to laugh. "Ah, Robbie, you have picked yourself a good and practical woman. May God bless you both."

Then, seeing a small platter of bacon set directly before him, Father Paul quickly mumbled the blessing and set to work breaking his fast, a pleased smile upon his face.

CHAPTER 10

Before Robert Minton might even announce it to his servants, they all knew of his impending union. It was obvious when a messenger was sent off posthaste to London to fetch Mistress Pietro d'Angelo's brother that a marriage was to be celebrated. Argel came to ask if they should prepare for guests, but her master told her no. Their marriage would be celebrated in private, surrounded by the folk of Wye Court.

"Have you no family you would have come?" Lucianna asked.

"My parents were both only children," he explained. "I'm certain there is someone who can claim a blood tie with me somewhere, but if there is, I know them not. The king is my closest friend. As boys, we had much time together in Brittany, but now he has little time for anything other than ruling England. That is as it should be."

"I have a large family," she told him. "Not

just my brothers and sisters, but my mother's family in Venice. Her sisters always felt sorry for her because she was wed to a Florentine merchant, whereas they were married into noble Venetian families. Of course we were richer, but my mother was always generous to them, despite their looking down on her position as my father's wife."

"They were glad to accept her generosity, I am certain," Robert said with a knowing smile.

Lucianna laughed. "Aye, they were, and they always behaved as if it were their due to do so. I remember one aunt who came with my cousin so they might receive the finest silk from my father for the girl's wedding gown. My aunt would not trust us to send the best. She must come and see which was the more expensive. Bianca and Francesca were gone by then, and my aunt remarked that it was a shame I was not as beautiful as my eldest sister, for I would not find a titled husband. Gentlemen of wealth and position want extraordinary beauties for brides, she told my mother, who could not deny it, as they were then considering a marriage for me with my first husband. I recall my mother telling me to say nothing about the bookseller. She always became extremely aware of her position as Prince Venier's daughter when she was with her siblings."

"Your mother will be pleased, then, that you are marrying a rich, titled man," the earl remarked.

"Are you rich?" she asked. "Having my own wealth, I was not considering yours," Lucianna told him candidly.

"It is wise not to brag of wealth," he told her.

"In Florence, everyone knew Alfredo had left me almost everything," she said. "Families with wealth always want more, and they obtain more by wedding their sons to young women with large dower portions."

He thought about it for a moment, and then said, "I suppose it is that way everywhere, but I neither need nor want your wealth. I want you, Lucianna, *amore mia.*"

She believed him. When their marriage contract had been drawn up, Father Paul was somewhat shocked, and he protested at the earl's insistence that Lucianna's possessions remain hers alone. Robert Minton had no claim upon them, nor would he take advantage of the traditional way of doing things. He knew that Luca would approve the arrangement. It would assure him the earl was not marrying his sister for her wealth.

The priest insisted that whatever Lucianna brought to the marriage should become his, even as she would become his, but Robert Minton refused. "Make certain this contract reads that what she brings to the marriage remains hers alone," he said.

Lucianna knew her mother would be very shocked by this, but she also knew that if accident or war cost her her husband, she did not wish to be at the mercy of whoever would gain the earldom. She wanted to be able to control her own fate. So the marriage contract was drawn up as she and the earl desired.

"We shall be married in five days," she told Balia. "We but wait for my brother to come from London."

"Your mother will be disturbed not to be able to be here and direct it all," Balia said, with a chuckle. "I think you are like her in that you would have your own way in this matter."

Lucianna laughed. "I suppose I am, but I know my father would be very pleased to know that I have engineered the marriage contract to say that my wealth remains with me."

"Will you sell the house in Florence?" Balia asked her.

"Eventually," she said, "but not quite yet. To sell it means to cut all my ties with Florence, and I am not yet ready to do so."

Balia nodded. Then she said, "What are you to wear, mistress, on your wedding day? You have no wedding gown."

"There must be something among the gowns we brought that will do for a widow," Lucianna said. "Let us look now."

As they laid the gowns out, Balia suddenly crowed with delight. "Here is that new gown you have not yet worn," she said, drawing forth one of pale blue-green silk brocade. "It is perfect for you, and most flattering," she noted.

"Ah, yes! I remember seeing the fabric among my father's samples, and had the gown made just before we left Florence. Why have I never worn it, Balia?"

"It was not warm enough for winter wear," her serving woman said. "When I was packing for you, I remembered it, and thought it would be perfect for a late-spring day."

"I recall my mother thought the fabric especially beautiful and unique. She will be pleased I wore it on my wedding day. Robert will not wait for her to come from Florence. It would take too long."

"Best you wed him quickly before another lass lays eyes on him and snatches him up."

Lucianna laughed again. "You are as bad as my mother," she teased Balia. "But at least Luca will be here to represent the family."

The next few days were busy ones for the servants, although the bride-to-be spent much of her time riding with the earl about the estate.

She saw how proud he was to declare to each cottage that the lady with him would be his wife in another four days, in another two days, tomorrow. He declared a holiday for the estate folk.

Lucianna was amazed at the size of the earl's holding. His lands seemed to stretch on forever. She wondered if the Medici, for all their wealth, had so much land. She doubted it. They were not much for the countryside, but true city folk.

Luca arrived from London, surprised to have been sent for, as no explanation had been given him, although Baram Kira had smiled and nodded when told he would be responsible for the shop for the next few days. Unlike the young Florentine, Baram saw the earl's deep interest in Lucianna, and he rightly guessed marriage was in the offing.

The earl's cook came to her, asking how many guests would be coming and what her ladyship would like for the meal.

"The earl has said we will have a morning wedding, but there will be no guests to my knowledge, other than my brother and Father Paul. I understand he has no family left," Lucianna told her. "What would you suggest for a wedding breakfast?"

"Eggs poached in marsala wine, rashers of bacon, and I shall bake a special cake for the occasion, my lady."

"I think since the earl has declared a holiday, we might feed everyone on tables outside? What think you? Is such hospitality allowed? I know so few of your English customs," Lucianna said.

"I wouldn't have enough eggs to feed them, my lady, but yes, the estate folk would appreciate a meal. What say you to ham, fresh bread, and cheese, along with several casks of ale? They would enjoy that, I know," the cook told her.

"Then do so. And while I would have you bake a small cake for us, bake a large one so each of the cottagers may have a bit of sweet," Lucianna instructed the cook.

" 'Tis most generous, my lady. A cake with raisins will please all." And with a curtsy, she left her new mistress.

Lucianna knew how to direct a small household, but the earl's staff was even larger than her mother's. She realized that she would be expected to manage the servants, to choose menus, to oversee it all. She wondered to herself if she was capable, but if not, she would have to learn quickly. They did not celebrate as many saints' days and holidays here in England as they did in Florence. She must learn when and how. But who was to teach her? Her knowledge of English customs was meager, and she could not shame Robert by running an inefficient household. There would be none but cottagers at their wedding, but that would all change once her earl had a wife.

Luca was concerned and did not hesitate to voice his doubts. "Are you certain you are doing the right thing marrying this foreigner? Why does he insist on such a hurry? Why cannot he wait for our parents to come from Florence?"

"Have you never been in love?" Lucianna asked him.

Luca looked at his twin sister as if she were a madwoman. "In love? Love is for dreamers, Sister. I always thought you a practical woman, like our mother. Besides, love is nothing more than romantic lust, Lucianna."

She laughed at him. "Our mother loved the wrong man, a married man, before Grandfather saw her wed to our father for expediency's sake. My marriage to Alfredo was a similar union."

"Mother has been a good wife to Father, as you were to the bookseller. This union seems hurried to me. I cannot help but wonder why, Lucianna. I am a cautious man."

"When did my brother, the soldier, become cautious?" she mocked him. "There is nothing unseemly in my impending union to Roberto. He loves me. He lusts after me. As for me, Brother mine, I feel the same way. Our parents will be pleased with this union. Our mother, because I have wed a noble, a close friend of a king. Our father, because I have kept my fortune to myself." Reaching out, she patted her brother's hand. "I am happy, Luca. For the first time in my life I am truly happy for the choices I have made. They are mine alone. No one made them for me. I did not make them because they were expected of me. I made them because it pleased me. Be happy for me."

He sighed. "I was sent to watch over you," he said. "I wonder if our parents will consider I did a good job."

Lucianna laughed softly at him. "When will you learn to please yourself, Luca, and not our parents? You are a man now."

Her brother made a face at himself. "How did you become the wiser of us?" he asked her, and she smiled lovingly at him.

Tomorrow was her wedding day, and she realized that her affianced husband had hardly touched or kissed her in the past few weeks. He knew she was a virgin, so she could take hope that he would be gentle with her. For the first time in her life, Lucianna felt shy.

When Balia brought up the subject of the wedding night, Lucianna put her off saying, "I am twenty-two and know what is expected of me."

Balia dropped the subject. She wondered if Lucianna did indeed know, for she knew Alfredo Allibatore had never coupled with the girl. Had her mother spoken to her? Or had Orianna found it unnecessary, knowing the celibate marriage her daughter was entering into six years ago? She would pray for her mistress. It was the best she could do. The earl, however, seemed a kind man.

Lucianna took the time to bathe on her wedding day, arising very early to find a tub of hot water already before her dayroom hearth. Balia took her time, not rushing her mistress, for she could see that Lucianna was nervous. The serving woman washed the long gold-red hair using a soap that was scented with the fragrance of the night lily. It was Lucianna's personal favorite, and Balia thought the familiar smell of it would be comforting to her. Afterwards, she brushed the lovely soft hair until it was dry.

"What style have you decided upon?" Lucianna asked.

"You will wear it unbound, as you should," Balia said sternly. "You are a virgin, my lady."

"But what will people think?" Lucianna said, concerned.

"I will see the house servants understand your first marriage was to an elderly gentleman who was not able to perform his duties, and that you are therefore untouched."

"I do not know if . . ." Lucianna began, for she doubted that even Luca knew, but Balia was going to have her own way in this matter.

"Your mother would be pleased I maintained proper tradition, my lady. I will hear no more about it." Balia's voice was determined.

The serving woman dressed her mistress in the blue-green gown. It had a modest V-neckline, and about the neck, running down the gown itself, was beautiful gold-and-blue embroidery that also edged the hemline. A low hip belt of the same fabric fell from her waistline. The sleeves were narrow to the elbow, then widened into large embroidered cuffs dripping fine Venetian lace.

"Oh, my lady," Balia said, stepping back a pace. "I only wish your mother could see you in this gown on this day. You are every bit a beautiful bride. You must wear no jewelry to take away from your perfection." She wiped her eyes, and then said, "This is what Master Alfredo would have wanted for you. A good husband, and the prospect of a happy marriage."

Lucianna smiled softly. "Aye," she said. "I know he would bless this second union I am about to make. He was a good man."

There was a knock upon the dayroom door, and Argel stuck her head in. "Oh good," she said, "you are ready. "The master is as jumpy as a boy about to get his first kiss," she said with a chuckle. "Ah, my lady, you look beautiful. Your brother awaits to escort you."

"Has the priest arrived?" Lucianna asked.

"Aye," the housekeeper said. Then she added, " 'Twas most generous of you to include the servants and cottagers. We are all honored to share in this day with you."

Lucianna nodded. "You are now all my English family, and I am grateful for it," she replied.

Luca was waiting in the corridor when Lucianna stepped from her chamber. "Santa Anna!" he exclaimed, "How beautiful you are, Sister." He escorted her down to the hall where the earl was awaiting her. The bridegroom was garbed simply so as not to take the glory from her. His hose were silk. The length of his sea blue doublet, which he wore over a white cotton shirt, was short, but his deeper blue coat was trimmed with fur. About his neck, he wore a large gold pendant.

"Good morning, my lord," Lucianna greeted him. "How handsome you look. I have never seen you garbed quite so elegantly."

"I might return the compliment, madame. You are even more beautiful today than I have ever seen you," he answered. "It is said, of course, that all brides are beautiful," he told her, and smiled.

Luca harrumphed audibly.

Lucianna ignored her brother. "I am pleased that my garb meets with your approval, my lord," she said, curtsying.

"I suspect," he told her as he took her

from her brother, and whispered in her ear, "that you are even more beautiful without it."

She felt the warmth in her cheeks. "So bold," she murmured back to him, but she smiled as, much to her surprise, he escorted her to the courtyard. "Where are we going?" she asked him.

"To the village church," he told her. "We will walk the distance so our cottagers may get a better glimpse of you. You have invited them to share in our day, Lucianna. I am pleased you did so, and would have them share it all from beginning to end."

"I had not considered walking," she responded. "I hope it is not too distant, for my pretty silk slippers are not fit for long walks."

"Not far," he promised as they began a walk down the hill upon which Wye Court was set. Luca walked behind them.

The day was glorious, with a flawless sky and bright sunshine. The narrow little road from the manor house was lined with cottagers.

Recognizing a few faces, she directed smiles at them, to their delight. And he had not prevaricated. The village church was just a few steps from the base of the hill, and it was filled with Wye Court's servants, and certain of those considered the more important of the villagers.

Together, bride and groom walked up the aisle to the waiting priest. Lucianna had not felt particularly like a bride when she had wed Alfredo Allibatore, but today she felt every bit the bride. And she found she did regret the absence of her parents. But even if they had traveled at top speed, it would have taken more than a month for them to reach England.

Besides, her mother did not travel quickly and must have several trunks with her to assure a wardrobe she could tolerate. No. It was better this way, with only her brother to give her away. And who knew if Balia wasn't correct, and some lass, neighbor, or someone from among the queen's ladies was waiting to snatch Robert up? But they could not. He was hers now. She smiled as she gave Father Paul the proper answers to the vows he asked of her.

And then it was over. Robert Minton took Lucianna in his strong arms and kissed her most thoroughly, to the delight of those in attendance. Lucianna blushed, hearing someone among the crowd say, "We'll have an heir before very long now, won't we?" And those in the little church who had heard the remark nodded in the affirmative.

But Luca scowled, for such candid chatter was unseemly, he thought to himself, but then these English were plainspoken.

Outside, they found someone had brought their horses down so they might ride them back up to the house. The earl lifted his new wife carefully into her saddle, and their eyes caught briefly. He said nothing, and neither did Lucianna. She must keep calm, she reminded herself, until after the feasting was over. Lucianna saw the servants running ahead of them so they would be ready to give service.

They rode slowly through the crowd of estate folk, smiling. The earl greeted many by name and laughed at their bawdy humor, answering them back in friendly fashion. Lucianna saw how well he treated these people. They were his, barely out of serf-dom, but he treated them with respect and kindness.

"They love you," Lucianna noted.

"I have grown up with many of them. My father was a good lord. I hope I am too," he answered her.

"Those treated with respect more often than not give better service," she replied. "My father said it often."

The morning slipped into afternoon. With late spring, the day would be a long one. By midafternoon, all had been fed, and some of the casks of ale were empty, the remainder running low. The tables that had been set in front of the river were slowly emptying as the estate folk departed for their homes while it remained light. Even the hall began to empty of the more favored of the Wye Court folk. Luca had disappeared with a very pretty village girl.

"Has it been a happy day for you, *amore mia*?" Robert asked her, tipping her face up to his.

"It has," Lucianna told him. "I never expected such a fine second wedding day, my lord."

"Your first was not?" He was surprised.

"Alfredo had been most direct with me. Our marriage was not a romantic liaison. He wanted a pretty wife to care for him in his old age. My parents obliged him out of desperation. We wed in my family's church, and I was gowned as befitted a bride. But my family invited few guests, angry that those families who had sought after Bianca and Francesca had not wanted me. Our wedding supper was small."

"You consider this a *romantic liaison*?" he asked, having heard little of what she said after those two words.

"I love you," Lucianna said simply. "You

226

have said that you love me, *amore mio.* Is that not romantic?"

He pulled her into his lap from her chair at the high board where she had been seated next to him. "Yes! It is romantic," he agreed, "but there is more to romance than mere words."

"I know," she told him, blushing. "I know what I must do, and what is expected of me."

"No woman ever really knows that first time, Lucianna, and it will be your first time," he said softly in her ear as he cupped a breast in his palm. "The first time, I have been told, can be heaven or hell."

"Who told you such a thing?" Lucianna said to him.

"The venerable Lady Margaret. She lectured both her son, the king, and me on the matter when we were lads. She said milkmaid or lady, a woman in a man's bed must be treated with kindness no matter her rank. I don't know if the king listened, but I did."

"Have you had many women in your bed?" she inquired of him. She was, after all, his wife now, and she should know just how experienced he was. But from the fingers teasing her breast through the cloth of her gown, she suspected his expertise was more than sufficient.

He laughed. "I have had enough women to satisfy my manly appetites, but now I have you. I shall have no others."

"Do not promise such a thing, my lord," Lucianna surprised him by saying. "All men of wealth and stature have mistresses. It is expected of them. As long as you love and respect me as your wife, I will not complain. Wise women do not."

"Perhaps in your Florence, this is so. And certainly even here in England some men keep mistresses. But there is no shame put on a man who doesn't and is faithful," he explained.

"Do you have any bastards?" she asked, again startling him.

"No! Certainly not to my knowledge." And then he laughed. "I wonder how many other brides have discussed such a thing on their wedding day, madame. We are obviously well matched, as you, it would seem, are as bold as I am, sweetheart."

Lucianna giggled. "My poor mother would be horrified with such a discussion as we are having. But what if I don't please you, my lord? If you vow to be faithful and I disappoint, I will relieve you of your foolish promise, Robert."

He gave her breast a little squeeze. "We cannot determine that, madame, until I have bedded you," the earl told her. He tipped her from his lap. "Go upstairs, and prepare yourself for me."

His words gave her pause for thought. Not even turning back as she slipped from his lap, Lucianna departed the hall, and as she reached the stairs, Balia joined her.

"You will not be sleeping in your old chamber now that you are the earl's wife," she explained. "There is a suite for the earl and his countess to cohabit. Argel and I have spent the afternoon preparing it for you. It is a lovely apartment, my lady. I hope you will be very happy there." Then the serving woman led her mistress upstairs to her new quarters, which were indeed lovely. "Now that you are his wife," Balia said, "you must choose a lass I may teach to help me with your care. I will remain her senior, but you must have two serving women, my lady. 'Tis expected of a lord's wife."

"How will you know who to choose?" Lucianna said.

"Argel has a niece, Mali. I have spoken with her, and she seems a nice lass, my lady. I have asked her to help me disrobe you. This will give you the opportunity to see if you like her."

"Very well," Lucianna replied. "I expect if she pleased you, she will please me too."

Mali was awaiting them in the new countess's apartment. She curtsied deeply as Lucianna entered the rooms. She could not have been older than thirteen, Lucianna thought, greeting her. She had a plain, freckled face, and, smiling shyly at her new mistress, she revealed a row of surprisingly perfect front teeth. Her dark brown hair was pulled back, but even so, several recalcitrant strands insisted on sticking out. Aware of them, Mali was forever attempting to put them in order.

Her brown eyes were full of eagerness to please.

Balia began instructing the girl in simple tasks. "Take off my lady's slippers and stockings," she instructed her. "Put them aside, and I will show you afterwards where they belong."

Shyly, Mali set to work to complete her task.

"It was a beautiful day," Balia remarked. "Your mother would have enjoyed it."

"Perhaps, but she would have been surprised by all the estate workers asked to join in the festivities," Lucianna said.

Balia laughed. "I suppose that is true," she agreed. "She would have been filling your ears with her plans on how to improve everything here, and would have even offered to remain to help you do it."

"My father might have let her, and then hurried home to Florence by himself," Lucianna said. "I think it better my mother was not here today. I do not know if Robert could have borne a year with her, for she would have remained here at least that long. Luca will go back to London shortly, though he will still share the London house."

"What of your youngest sister?" Balia asked. "Would your mother have left her behind? I don't believe she would have."

"No, she would not have, but at least I would have had Serena here to amuse me. Perhaps she might have found an English husband too," Lucianna said thoughtfully.

Mali listened to all this conversation, for it had been spoken in English, and not that funny foreign tongue they sometimes used when they were together. She wondered if she might learn it, but then decided no. There was too much she had to master first to be a good maidservant to her ladyship. Even being second in the new countess's personal household gave her a certain ranking among the other servants, which she had to admit she would enjoy. Especially with those two boisterous housemaids who had come into service with her from the village. They were noisy lasses, always giggling together and flirting. One of them had gone off this evening with the mistress's brother. Mali knew it was her quiet demeanor that had recommended her to Balia.

"Where shall I put her ladyship's shoes?" Mali asked the older woman. She knew that the stockings would go into the laundry.

"You will find racks for them in the wardrobe chamber," Balia told her. "Then come back, and help me with these skirts."

Mali did as she was bid, hurrying to put the shoes away.

"She seems biddable," Lucianna remarked in Italian.

"She is," Balia answered her in the same tongue. "She is a quiet maid who keeps her own counsel. I did not want a chatterbox or gossip like so many of these other English girls are. And she is clever enough to learn all she must learn quickly. These English winters are difficult. What if I grew ill? You must have someone to care for you besides me. Especially now that you hold rank, my lady. Your husband should appear stingy if you did not have at least two personal servants."

"Like the king, except with his mother and his wife," Lucianna said, with a smile. Then she switched back to English. "Robert is everything that is good and kind. I am fortunate."

"So is he!" Balia replied, with a smile. "Ah, Mali, here you are. Let us get these skirts off my lady. We will need to brush them before they can be stored away."

Lucianna was soon divested of her wedding finery. She bathed, lightly smiling as Balia instructed Mali to refill the pitcher and see it placed in the hearth to keep warm in the night. The bride noted that her new serving girl shyly kept her eyes from her mistress's nakedness.

Well, Mali would get used to it in time, Lucianna decided as Balia slipped a silk sleep chemise over her.

"See to the bed, lass!" Balia instructed her junior, indicating that Mali should turn back the coverlet so Lucianna might enter the bed. When it had been done, they helped her settle herself. Then both women curtsied and, bidding their mistress good night, left her.

Lucianna sat quite still. The room was very, very quiet. A small fire burned in the hearth. It was the bedchamber's only light. One of the bedchamber windows was open a bit, and she heard a night bird begin to sing. The birdsong seemed different here. Her ear was cocked for the sound of his footstep in the hall. When would he come?

Her second marriage, her first wedding night, Lucianna thought. What would it be like? What would he be like as a lover? Her mother always had said even an inexperienced woman could tell the difference between a good lover and a poor one. Was that really so, or was it something Orianna had said to reassure her daughters?

She heard a soft click, and he stepped into the chamber through a small door in the wall she had not even noticed, but then she had had no time at all to inspect these new rooms. An involuntary sound of surprise excaped her.

"You did not know there was an entry between our bedchambers?" he said. "I am sorry to have startled you."

"I had no time to seriously view these new rooms," she told him. "Balia and her new assistant were in too great a hurry to ready me for bed. Tomorrow I shall walk about and see if there are any more surprises for me." She saw he was wearing a nightshirt.

"I must thank them," he teased her gently. Knowing her history, he realized how tense she must be right now. However, he also realized it would do no good to encourage her fear by delaying the inevitable. He pulled the coverlet back and climbed into the bed next to her.

Lucianna stiffened. She didn't want to, but she could not help it.

"You must not be wary of me, *amore mia*," he said quietly. "I am not here to hurt you, and you well know it."

"Do not, I beg you, make me feel any more foolish than I do," Lucianna said to him. "Passion is not something I am familiar with, Robert. I have never known it, though I am twenty-two."

"Yet your kisses tell me there is passion in you," he responded, and as if to demonstrate, he gave her a long, deep kiss to which Lucianna eagerly responded. "See," he said as he released her lips.

"Yes," she agreed, "but then tell me why I feel like such a foolish maid when I am a woman long grown?"

"Yet still a maid," he said softly. "I think it will be easier between us once your virginity is gone," he told her.

"Then, my lord, you must relieve me of that impediment so we may be ourselves again," Lucianna said to him.

Robert Minton laughed. "In time, my pet, in time." His arms wrapped about her. "Just let me hold you, for the week has been a long and exciting one for us both. Now that you are my sweet wife, we will spend the summer months learning to know each other better, and enjoying the joys that both passion and Wye Court can offer us."

His words were soothing and comforting to her. Now that the initial moment was over, she was beginning to seriously realize what she had done. She had wed a man who was really barely known to her. She had allowed him to sweep her away to the countryside, and cajole her into a marriage. He did not need her fortune. He might have asked the king's mother to choose a wife for him, thereby binding him closer to the Tudors. Instead, he had picked the daughter of a Florentine silk merchant to be his countess, and permitted nothing to stand in his way to have her.

It was flattering, and yet she worried. Her husband seemed an honest man. He claimed he loved her. Love was not a word Lucianna really understood. Love, to her small knowledge, always seemed to lead to tragedy or unhappiness of some kind. Her oldest sister, Bianca, had given up everything for what was called love. She had deserted her family, her church, her city, without a moment's hesitation to go to a man who already had two wives. Was she truly happy?

And what of her second sister, Francesca, who had first given her girlish heart to a

Venetian gentleman who married another. And then that sister had the good fortune to find brief happiness as the Duke of Terreno Boscoso's duchess. Until a traitorous servant had murdered Francesca's husband and left her alone to raise their children. She had obviously had enough of marriage, for she refused to take another husband.

Lucianna, the third daughter, had been obedient to her family's wishes and had wed an elderly man. Alfredo had been her friend, but never her lover, for he simply had not the stamina for it. Once widowed, she had never discussed it with anyone, even her mother. Only Robert, for she had not hesitated to tell him her whole story. He had not made a jest of her late husband's inabilities, but had simply accepted them. Nor had he attempted to take advantage of her position to seduce her.

He had instead offered his friendship to her when she arrived in England. Introduced her to the king's mother. Declared his love to her. Swept her away to Hereford, and convinced her to wed him. Her question to him broke the silence of their bedchamber. "Why have you wed me, my lord, when you could have made a more advantageous match for yourself?"

"Because I love you," he said simply. "I realize love does not play a part in many marriages, but I love you and wanted you as my wife."

"I do not understand this word in either your tongue or mine," Lucianna told him.

Raising himself up on an elbow, the earl looked down into his bride's lovely face. "The mere idea of anyone else claiming you for himself, touching you in an intimate manner, taking you to his bed, can send me into a black rage, Lucianna. From the first moment I set my eyes upon you, I knew that you were mine, and I, yours. Are you then already unhappy to have agreed to be my wife?" His look was very concerned.

"Nay, my lord," Lucianna quickly assured him, reaching up to stroke his handsome face. "It is a good union between us. We are friends, which I have always believed a necessity in a marriage. Each of us has our own fortune. I know you did not wed me for my wealth, which reassures me that you do care for me and will respect me."

"But you do not love me yet," he said.

"I care for you, aye, I do!" she told him earnestly. "I just do not truly understand love."

"Then I shall have to teach you," he said

with the confidence of a man — a man in love.

Chapter 11

His sensuous mouth was suddenly possessing her own in a deep and passionate kiss. Lucianna wondered if toes actually could curl as she experienced the kiss throughout her entire body. She tingled with the sensation of both his lips and his hard body against her. When he released her briefly, Lucianna pulled her sleep chemise off even as he drew his own up, and, taking both garments, he tossed them to the floor.

She felt a blush warming her cheeks as his blue eyes devoured her naked body.

"God!" he groaned, "You are so very beautiful, my love." He reached out to caress her gently, and his touch sent a thrill through her.

"How does a man in love feel?" she asked him, honestly curious.

"Like this," he said, kissing her again, slowly, deeply.

She felt the emotion filling him, the rising

need for her as he began to caress her tenderly, but Lucianna pulled away from him. "Is it more than just desire to couple with me, Robert? Is love just passion? Or can it be something else? Remember, there are those who will say, and rightly so, that you have wed beneath you, my lord." She saw him swallow hard as he struggled to control the lustful emotions that had begun to fill him. What was the matter with her that she was, at this point, asking him to justify himself?

"Stop talking, woman," he said fiercely. "You are more skittish than a new colt." He tried to kiss her again. "I adore the very ground you tread, and I do not give a damn that anyone will dare to say I married beneath my station. I love you, Lucianna! And I would make love to you if you would but let me."

The mixture of frustration, caring, and impatience was so plain on his face that Lucianna could not help but laugh. "I'm sorry," she said. "I do not understand why it is I need so much reassurance, my lord."

His hand caressed her red-gold head. He kissed her forehead gently and smiled into her eyes. "Because for all your experience in your father and brother's world, and despite your previous marriage, you are still a girl, a virgin, and I have overwhelmed you by hurrying you into marriage, Lucianna. But I could not bear the thought of not having you, my beautiful love." His lips lingered on hers in a kiss that gave truth to his words.

Lucianna slipped her arms about his neck. "My mother will hold Luca responsible for allowing this marriage without her," she said. "He was supposed to *protect* me. My father, however, will not be unhappy."

"We did not run away," he said, enjoying the sensation of her body against his. "I just did not share my plans with anyone, but then I did not share them with you either. Your father suspected I wanted to wed you. Would your mother have preferred it if I took you as my mistress? I think not. I suspect she will not be unhappy to have her daughter a countess, even if I am an Englishman." His kiss touched her slender throat.

"Make love to me, Roberto," she said softly in her Italian tongue. His smile sent her heart soaring. He did love her. She could see it in his blue eyes. She was his wife, his mate until death parted them. And knowing that, Lucianna suddenly realized she was not unhappy or unsure any longer. He was hers, and she, his. As his hand caressed her, she felt herself thrill to his touch. The feeling was gentle, and yet at the same time possessive. She had never imagined such a sensation.

When she had instructed him in her native tongue, it had sent a thrill of excitement through him. It told him, as nothing else could have, that she was ready to be his wife in every way. Her body was exquisite.

It was slender where it should be, and fuller in equal proportion. He could feel his own heart beating wildly with the excitement he felt.

Her skin was like her finest silk, soft and wonderfully smooth. The very sensation of it beneath his fingers set him aflame with his need to complete his possession, but with supreme self-control he proceeded slowly. He was aware that removing a female's virginity could be both pleasant and difficult at the same time. There was no easy way.

Her lovely round breasts were so tempting. A hand fondled them slowly, enjoying the enticing feel of the alluring flesh. She murmured a sound of pleasure that encouraged him further. Lowering his head, he licked at a nipple several times before taking it into his mouth and suckling upon it. Lucianna groaned low but made no move to stop him.

His mouth on her was arousing. She shivered with the deliciousness of it. The sensations arousing her now moved lower, first to her belly, making it quiver nervously, and then lower to that secret place between her thighs. Then suddenly his other hand moved to cup her there. Lucianna gasped with surprise and tried to pull away. Was she ready for such intimacy?

"Nah, *amore mia,* let me touch you there," he murmured in her ear, kissing when his words ceased.

Lucianna said nothing but ceased her retreat. He was her husband. Her body was now his. He would not harm her. A single finger gently stroked several times between her nether lips before pushing between them and finding the most sensitive portion of her flesh. She wanted to resist, but the finger rubbing that nub took away all her resistance. Lucianna found she did not want him to cease. Her body, seemingly of its own volition, rose up to meet that probing finger as he pushed it gently into her body.

It was very much as he had expected. She was wet and ready for him, but she was also very tight. He considered the size of his own manhood, and as he withdrew the one finger, reinserted two and then after a brief time, three fingers that moved slowly, carefully within her.

By the time the three fingers had entered her, Lucianna was growing quite excited with a feeling she had never experienced. She heard herself moan but one word. *"More!"* When his big body covered her, she could scarcely contain her excitement. Then she felt his manhood beginning to enter her body. She gasped with surprise. It was nothing at all like his fingers. He was hard, and it was demanding of her as slowly he pushed forward until he almost filled her sensitive sheath. "Santa Anna," she whispered, "it is so large."

"Yet it fits you well," he groaned, moving slightly on her.

"Oh!" she exclaimed. "Am I a woman then, Roberto?"

"Not quite," he told her. "Your virginity is tightly lodged, *mia amore.* When you are ready, I will have it of you." *Jesú!* He was dying to have all of her, but she must be more than willing. She must be eager.

He moved gently within her, stroking her excitement.

The sensation of him was wonderful, Lucianna thought, but there was more. Much more. And she wanted it. She wanted it *now.* Instinct instructed her. Wrapping her legs about his torso, she whispered fiercely into his ear, "*Sí*, Roberto! Now! Take me now!"

He thrust hard through the shield of her virginity, wincing at her cry of pain, and now fully lodged, caressing her, soothing her as he began to fuck her slowly at first, increasing his tempo as he felt her eager response. Her nails dug into his shoulders. Her gasps of open pleasure excited him wildly. Then suddenly he could not hold himself back a moment longer. His boiling tribute flooded her.

Lucianna sobbed, but her cries were ones of happiness. She was his wife in all ways now. Perhaps this first coupling would give them a child, but there would be many more such nights if she could have her way, and she would.

He rolled off her onto his back, gasping with his release and his pleasure. It had been a magnificent coupling, and unlike anything he had ever experienced before. It was his love for her, he knew, that made it so. How different passion was with a woman you loved as opposed to just a woman willing to share her body. He had promised her he would take no mistress, and now he knew he never could after this night. "I love you, Lucianna, my beautiful Florentine wife. I love you!" he declared to her as he turned to look down into her face.

"Can we do it again?" she asked him ingenuously, smiling up at him. "It won't hurt even a little the second time, will it?"

Robert Minton laughed aloud. "No, sweetheart, it won't hurt after this first time. And yes, with a little time to recover my strength, we will most certainly do it again."

They were late to arise come the morning, but finally Balia decided that enough was enough and came to see them roused. The happiness on Lucianna's beautiful face both relieved and pleased her. Her mistress had survived the taking of her virginity in good spirits.

She wondered how long it would be before Lucianna would quicken with a child. "Master Luca has been asking after you all morning," she told her mistress.

"My impatient brother has never had a wedding night," Lucianna said, smiling.

The earl chuckled. "I saw him go off with that new housemaid. One can hope he hasn't gotten a bastard on the saucy wench."

"He should go back to London now that he has seen our marriage celebrated," Lucianna decided. "I know he would enjoy spending more time here in the country away from the shop, but he must return to take on this new responsibility. I am content here, unless you go back to London and wish me with you."

"You may need to oversee the shop until you are certain Luca is ready to take it over for your father's guild," the earl said.

"Baram Kira knows as much as I do," Lucianna replied. "He was far quicker to learn than my brother. Poor Luca. He is really a soldier at heart. He has given up his dream because our elder brother cannot seem to manage what my father, and his father, built up. With Giorgio in Rome, poor Luca is the only son remaining to keep the Pietro d'Angelos' silk business viable. My father cannot manage the Florence shop forever. Luca will have to return to do that, and I shall recommend to the guild that they take Baram Kira into their employ to manage this shop in London for them. It has done well, and the Milanese have not."

"The Milanese hire no English, nor does the man they sent make any effort to encourage the London cloth merchants to friendship as you did."

"With your help," Lucianna reminded her husband.

He smiled in acknowledgment. "If you had not been successful, you would have had to return to Florence," he reminded her. "I did what I had to keep you here."

"And now I shall never return to Florence, except possibly to visit my parents with you," she said softly. "I have chosen a future in England with you."

He grinned. "So you have, madame. So you have."

"Who knows of our marriage?"

"I told Lady Margaret I would do my best to win you over," he admitted.

"The king does not know?" she asked.

Robert Minton shook his head. "Nay," was all he said.

"Oh, Robert! You must tell him yourself, and quickly, before he learns of it from another. He trusts you, and what if he had another lady in mind for your wife? A lady who would have been of use to his family, and therefore to you."

"Henry Tudor wed who he wanted to wed. I have but done the same," Robert Minton answered her.

"Henry Tudor married the last king's niece, the daughter of the king previous to him. She was England's heiress. He has united two warring factions by that marriage, which is, praise God, a happy one if the gossip be true. How many years have the Lancasters and the Yorks quarreled over England's throne? Wars like that are detrimental to a society, as any scholar of history can tell you."

"You are a scholar of history, then?" he teased her.

"My father educated his daughters as well as his sons, even as I shall do," Lucianna said proudly. "I do not want you to lose favor with your king, Robert. You must tell him of our marriage face-to-face."

The earl sighed. She was right, and he knew it. "I will go to London with your brother. But I will return quickly. I do not intend our time together to be interrupted now that you are mine."

She nodded, pleased that he had taken the first wifely advice she had given him. "When will you leave?" she asked him.

"Today," he said firmly. He climbed naked from their bed, and Lucianna swallowed her giggles at Balia's surprise. Especially when he turned to her serving woman and said, "Go and tell Master Luca to be ready to depart within the hour."

"I'll see him before he goes," Lucianna quickly put in, knowing her brother would not go until he was certain all was well with his twin.

"Right away, my lord," Balia answered, forgetting to curtsy as she almost ran from the chamber.

Now Lucianna did laugh. "Oh, Robert,

how you shocked her. She is not used to seeing a naked man."

"She'll get use to it," he said dryly. Then he added, "I'll go and dress. I'm certain Fflam is waiting for me patiently." He disappeared through the almost-hidden door in the wall through which he had entered the previous evening.

Lucianna reached for her sleep chemise, which lay on the floor near the bed. Slipping it on, she waited for Balia to return, but it was Mali who came first, carrying a tray.

"Balia thought you might be hungry," the girl said.

"I am," Lucianna admitted. "What have you brought me?"

"Some nice hot oats with honey and cream, new-baked bread, butter, jam, and a bit of watered wine," Mali replied, speaking slowly so as not to forget the contents of the tray.

"It all sounds wonderful!" Lucianna told her, smiling.

"Will you eat in your bed, my lady, or shall I set it upon a table?"

"This morning I shall spoil myself and eat in my bed," Lucianna told her. "I saw my mother do it now and again, especially when she had been out late at some festival or entertainment. I always thought it quite luxurious, and have wondered if the food tasted better eaten in bed. What do you think, Mali?"

Mali giggled. "I wouldn't know, my lady. In our cottage if you weren't at the table for a meal, you didn't eat. Unless you were working in the fields, of course." She brought the tray to the bed, setting it carefully on her mistress's lap.

Lucianna smiled at the girl. She suspected that Mali was going to become an excellent helper for her Balia. She began to eat even as Balia hurried back into the bedchamber. The older woman immediately began instructing Mali what to get out for her mistress to wear this day.

"Master Luca will be ready when the earl is," she said to Lucianna. "I can certainly tell you I was surprised when he jumped from the bed, my lady. I will admit it startled me at first, but it was certainly a fine sight."

Lucianna giggled. "He says you'll get used to him."

"I believe I will," Balia cackled with a wide grin. "I'm just glad our young Mali wasn't with me earlier. She is yet too young to see such a fine sight as his lordship presents."

"I've seen my brothers naked when they

swim," Mali volunteered. "Are not all men the same?" But she blushed at the boldness of her query.

"Some are better than others," Balia said frankly, "and while we should not speak of such things, I think my lady will forgive me if I say the master's accomplishments are the best I've ever seen." She chortled.

"Having seen my brothers swimming in the summers too, I should probably have to agree," Lucianna said with a smile.

"Agree upon what?" the earl asked, stepping back into the bedchamber, and the three women burst into giggles.

"Nothing to concern you, my lord," his countess answered. "Just women's chatter." She saw he was already dressed for travel. "Have you eaten?" she asked him. "Balia, do not let the earl go off without some food in his belly."

He came to the bed, and, bending down, gave her a long kiss. "I could send the king a message with your brother," he said.

"Nay, this is news you must deliver in person, my lord," she advised him quietly. "Have we not previously discussed it?"

"We are but wed a day," he grumbled.

"And with God's blessing we will have many more days together," she told him, feeding him a piece of her bacon.

"You are a determined wench," he said with a small smile.

"I am," Lucianna agreed. "Now go and eat something before you spend the entire day in travel, for I know you will only stop to rest the horses until you reach London."

"And if the king is not in London, I shall have to find him wherever he is, won't I?"

"You will," Lucianna told him. "If the king or his mother had a noble bride in mind for you, you must allay any irritation they may feel. You cannot lose their favor, my lord. Even if you prefer living on your estates as opposed to living at court, you cannot destroy the long friendship you have had with Henry Tudor and his mother."

"Lady Margaret knows my feelings for you, sweetheart," he said.

"Ah, but did she know you would carry me off and wed me?" Lucianna asked him. "I believe she thought you would make me your mistress, Robert, not your wife."

"I wanted no other," he told her.

"Nor did I," Lucianna said, frankly, "but a marriage between an English earl and a Florentine silk merchant's daughter can hardly have been expected by your peers. I shall have to prove myself worthy of you to all, Robert."

"You need prove nothing!" he insisted, but

Lucianna smiled. She knew better, even if her husband didn't.

A knock came on the bedchamber door, and Mali hurried to open it, curtsying as she saw her mistress's brother there.

"May I come in?" Luca asked, and seeing his twin nod, he stepped into the chamber. "I have come to say good-bye, Sister."

The earl arose. "I will go and eat," he told his wife. Catching her hand up, he kissed it slowly, his eyes meeting hers. "I shall be gone no longer than I must, madame," he told her. Then turning, he departed.

"You look as though you have survived your wedding night," Luca said frankly in their native tongue.

"I have," Lucianna answered him.

"You will not come back to the shop now, will you?" He looked worried, but the query was straightforward.

"Nay, I cannot now. I am the Countess of Lisle, and a countess does not serve in a shop. Luca, you must trust Baram Kira. He has learned far quicker than you have and will be of great help to you. The Kiras are to be trusted. This endeavor of the guild's must continue to thrive. The Milanese are about to give up and depart. Give them no advantage, I beg you. You are a proud man, and turning yourself into a merchant when your heart lies in soldiering is difficult, I know, but Father needs you. 'Tis you, and not our older brother, Marco, who will keep our family's business from failing."

"You place a great deal of responsibility upon me," Luca said.

His sister smiled. "I know," she agreed, "but you are far more disciplined than Marco. You can do it, and once Father sees that, he will feel secure in turning everything over to you. Marco will be relieved that the responsibility is yours."

"I cannot manage our family's business from London, Sister," Luca said to her. "And to be frank with you, I do not like this dank English weather. I would be home in our sunny Florence."

"You will be," Lucianna promised, "and soon."

"And you will remain behind in this England," Luca said.

"Happily, I will." She smiled. "I am with the man I love, Brother. You must find a good wife when you return home. You have but to tell our mother, and she will gladly help you."

He laughed. "Well," he said, "though you have escaped our mother's clutches by coming to England and wedding your earl, she cannot complain. You willingly, and without any drama, wed your first husband for her sake. She could not know that he would leave you everything, making you an independent woman."

Lucianna laughed now too. "No, she never imagined such a thing." Then, pausing, she considered a way in which she might help her twin. "Luca, would you like my house in Florence? You do not have to live at home if you do not wish it."

" 'Tis generous of you, Sister," he replied, "but Mama has never kept track of her sons' comings and goings. We were not as confined as our sisters. I am happy to live at home until I wed. I may even live there with my bride for a time. Many sons do. Even Marco did at first, if you remember."

"I remember Marco's wife did not like it, which is why her father bought them a house," Lucianna replied. "I will give you a key to my house so you may always have an escape, should you need it."

"You are generous as always, Sister," Luca said. Then he kissed her cheek. "I will not return to Florence without seeing you," he promised her. Then bowing, he left the bed-chamber.

"You did not tell him to eat," Balia said, chuckling.

"He had already eaten, I am certain,"

Lucianna said. "Luca is not one to miss a meal."

"Will you be arising, my lady?" Balia asked.

"I will," Lucianna said. "I am sure there is much for me to do, and Argel will tell me. Wives cannot be idle, Balia. Even noble wives."

She was right. By the time she reached the hall, her husband and her brother had already departed for London. Argel greeted her and outlined the duties expected of the Countess of Lisle. They were much as she had expected. The household was hers to direct. She must plan meals with the cook. Ride out with the bailiff to visit the sick. Appear at Mass daily to set a good example. And while her husband was away, she must settle any disputes that could not await his return.

She had ridden the estate several times with Robert. Today she decided she would take Worrell, the bailiff, and ride out herself so the villagers and the cottagers might become accustomed to their new lady. The day was fair, and Lucianna was glad for the travelers' sakes. Worrell was respectful of his new lady and impressed that she would seek to ride out with him. She was a foreigner and, he knew, not of noble family. Still, she was polite to him, asked good questions, and even solicited his advice. "She is not puffed up at all," he told those who would listen that evening. "The lady may not be one of us, but I believe she will make our lord a good wife."

"They say she has a great fortune," one woman said.

"I would not know that," Worrell replied a bit stiffly. "I do know she was kind to Mary by the river, who has just been widowed. Asked if there was anything she needed for herself or the young ones. This lady of ours has a kind heart."

Having gained the bailiff's approval, Lucianna discovered the Wye Court folk were suddenly more friendly. It made her feel more at home, even with Robert away. She wondered how long it had taken her husband to reach London, but she knew he had ridden quickly. And he had, surprised that Luca had so easily kept up with him, and told him so.

"I am a soldier at heart," Luca said, grinning. "If the horses hold out, then so can I, my lord." Luca left his new brother-in-law at the silk shop, where he discovered Baram Kira busily taking orders from a line of merchants for the silks they wished to sell come the autumn months.

Luca realized then and there that it was Baram Kira who would manage this shop once he had returned to Florence. He felt any small resentment for the young man fading away with the knowledge that the London shop would be in excellent hands. Selling his family's silk was his business now. He could approach the task like a good tactician to gain the best results, as he had done as a soldier.

It was not a difficult undertaking, unlike Robert Minton's duty, which was to tell his king of his marriage.

To the earl's relief, Henry Tudor was in London, although he was soon to depart to reassure the countryside that, despite the continued Yorkist plots, the Tudors were on the throne to stay.

"Where have you been?" the king wanted to know when the earl was ushered into the royal presence.

"At Wye Court," Robert answered. "I took Lucianna and her brother with me, my lord."

"Ah, the beautiful Florentine silk merchant. Have you finally managed to make her your mistress?" The king grinned mischievously.

"I made her my wife, my lord," the earl answered the king.

Henry Tudor's face registered surprise. "You wed her? Why?"

His companion laughed softly. "Because I love her, my lord. A most unusual turn of events, is it not? I have left my bride after only one night in her bed to come and tell you, my lord. She insisted that I do. I would have waited otherwise."

"She did not insist *before* the marriage, I note," the king replied.

Robert Minton was surprised by the king's words and realized he must protect Lucianna from any suspicions. "But she did, my lord," he lied. "She pointed out the unsuitability of a marriage between us several times, for I have sought her hand for some months." That at least was the truth.

"Yet she wed you nonetheless," the king replied thoughtfully. "Have you told my mother? I think she may have had a bride in mind for you, although she has not spoken of it to me, but you know you are her favorite, Rob. Now that I am wed, surely you would have realized she would want you married too."

"I am not of royal blood, my lord. I am not interested in gaining power through you. I am a simple country lordling. I love Lucianna, and she is the perfect wife for me. I am flattered you believe your own

261

mother, with all her duties, would want to choose a wife for me, but the Lady Margaret never said so to me. I chose my own wife as simple country men do. I would have your blessing, my lord, but if you cannot give it, it will not change my love or my loyalty for you, my lord. I respect you far too much."

"She is beautiful," the king said. "And you will be envied by those who thought to make her their mistress, Rob."

"Aye, she is beautiful, and just the thought of any other having her caused me to wed her quickly, my lord," Robert Minton answered.

The king suddenly laughed. "I have always envied you the ability to act as you see fit. I cannot do that. I have been taught to be cautious, and kings cannot just do as they please. My mother will be disappointed, but she will forgive you, even as I do. Be happy in your marriage, Rob. Your wife will always be welcome at my court. Now go and make your peace with the Lady Margaret, my friend."

"I am grateful, my lord, for your kindness, as Lucianna will be," the earl told the king. He bowed, and departed the royal presence.

Making peace with the dowager, however, was a bit more complex. Lady Margaret

Beaufort had indeed had a young woman in mind for her son's dear friend. She had foolishly told the girl's parents she would make her an earl's wife. Fortunately, Lady Margaret had not said which earl, but now she must find another unwed title.

"You might have at least discussed this with me before you acted, Robert," she said to him. Her tone was disapproving. "Would she have not settled for being your mistress?"

"No, she would not, nor did I suggest it, madame, for I have too much respect for Lucianna and for her family," the earl answered candidly.

"A silk merchant's daughter," Lady Margaret said.

"With a grandfather who is a Venetian prince," the earl reminded the king's mother. "My mother-in-law is a very proud woman. She would not tolerate it should Lucianna have become my mistress. She has already lost her eldest daughter to the Turks. To lose Lucianna would have been too painful for her, and she would have considered her lost under such dishonorable circumstances."

Lady Margaret looked sharply at the earl. "I was not aware that you had an acquaintance with your wife's mother," she said.

"And there are more Venetian princes than stars in the sky."

"I have been entertained in the Pietro d'Angelos' palazzo in Florence," he told the king's mother. "My mother-in-law is much like you in character, Lady Margaret. She is devout and deeply devoted to her children and their welfare."

"Indeed," the king's mother said, but a small smile played at the corners of her lips. "And is my son content with your actions, Robert?"

"He has accepted it, and said my wife is welcome at court," the earl told her with a small smile. She was going to forgive him.

"Where am I to find another young man with a title for my young lady-in-waiting?" she complained to the earl.

"Whoever you find, madame, he will be far more suitable for her than I would have been," the earl said.

"You love her," the king's mother said.

"Aye, I love my Lucianna," he admitted. "Madness to love one's wife, I know, but I cannot help myself."

"Well, at least she is wealthy, if the rumors speak truth," Lady Margaret said practically. "Is she?"

"She is, madame," the earl answered. He did not bother to mention that Lucianna's wealth would remain hers alone. Lady Margaret would be horrified.

"And she has a house here in London," the king's mother continued. "Wealth and a small property. It could be worse, Robert. I am relieved that it is not."

He caught up her two beautiful, beringed, graceful hands. "Am I forgiven then?" he asked her, kissing those hands.

Lady Margaret chuckled. "Even my own son cannot get around me, Robert. Few people can, and yet you always do. Yes! You are forgiven for wedding your Florentine silk merchant. I will welcome her to court and to my house, even as my son has. She is a clever young woman. I enjoyed her company."

He thanked the king's mother, and then set off to Lucianna's house to spend the night. In the morning, he would begin his return journey to Wye Court, and rejoin his bride. A summer of love lay ahead for them. The king would shortly go off on his progress, but the Earl of Lisle would not go with him this year. Robert Minton would remain home to husband his lands and enjoy his beautiful wife.

Three days later, he stopped atop a hill overlooking his estates. A soft rain was falling, but the land around him was green with healthy growth, and the blue river flowed peacefully below. He actually sighed with happiness. Lucianna would be awaiting him in the hall, he knew. His horse was eager for home too and needed little encouragement to move forward. Together, man and beast rode eagerly down the hill to Wye Court.

CHAPTER 12

Lucianna flung herself into her husband's arms, kissing him passionately. "You are home!" she cried softly. Then in more practical tones she asked, "Is the horse alive?"

"He rested well each night," the earl told her.

"You found the king?"

"We are forgiven, but far more easily by the king than by Lady Margaret, who thought to match me eventually with one of her young ladies-in-waiting," he told her. "How could we have known that?"

"Oh dear! I should not like to make an enemy of Lady Margaret," Lucianna fretted.

"You have not. As she pointed out, she has never been able to refuse me my way." Robert chuckled. "Would that you were as easily convinced by my charms."

Lucianna laughed. "When I feel myself

weakening, I think of what my mother would do," she teased him.

. Now it was the earl who laughed, and he told her what he had said to Lady Margaret about Orianna Pietro d'Angelo.

Lucianna was thoughtful, and then said, "I agree. They are much alike in temperament, but I find Lady Margaret more thoughtful than my mother, who will have her way no matter what others think."

"Lady Margaret is much the same, my love, but she is more skillful at managing herself," he explained. "I remember when the king and I were boys, and the Yorkists threatened him. He was not born to be king, you know. There were several heirs ahead of him, but the constant warring between Lancaster and York took the others. Suddenly, young Henry Tudor found himself his family's chief heir. Realizing it, the Yorkists took him under their *protection.* But then the house of York began to lose its heirs, and before anyone else saw it, Lady Margaret realized the danger her son faced from ambitious men. She managed to get him to safety in Brittany, choosing several of us to go with him so he would not lose sight of who he was, and what lay ahead for him. We spent our later boyhood there."

"What of the king's father?" Lucianna asked.

"His father, Edmund Tudor, was killed three months before he was born. Lady Margaret was just thirteen at the time. She was an orphaned heiress, and put herself in her brother-in-law's care at his castle of Pembroke, which he held as constable for the Lancasters.

"The Yorkists captured Pembroke when the king was just four years old.

"His custody was sold to Lord Herbert for a thousand pounds. He meant him as an eventual husband for his daughter, Maud. The Herberts were good foster parents. The king was raised at Pembroke, and at their castle of Raglan. As their future son-in-law, he was considered part of the family. He was well educated, even as his own mother would have seen it done. The Herberts are decent folk."

"Did Lady Margaret not remain with her child?" Lucianna asked. She was curious about this now-powerful woman.

"Nay. She was married to a second husband, Henry Stafford, who died, and then she wed Lord Stanley," he told her.

"I cannot imagine leaving my child to others," Lucianna said.

"Lady Margaret needed a protector,"

Robert explained, "a husband disposed to the Lancasters. Without one of her own choosing, she and her son were vulnerable. The political situation was constantly changing then. When the king was almost fourteen, old King Henry the Sixth was restored to his throne. Jasper Tudor regained custody of his nephew. He was sent off to Eton briefly to study. That was where we first met. But early the following year, he and Jasper Tudor returned to Wales. Once again, war between Lancaster and York erupted. I was with Henry Tudor then as his companion. The battles went badly for the sixth Henry, and we were forced to race to Pembroke for our safety.

"Of course we were besieged there, but with the help of friends, we were able to escape. We reached Tenby and sailed for France, but a storm forced us to land in Brittany. There, Duke François gave us his protection. We remained there for the next thirteen years. Because I was not particularly known as the king's companion, I was able to move back and forth between Brittany, France, and England, carrying messages to our supporters and to Lady Margaret.

"King Edward attempted several times to gain custody of what he called 'the last of

Henry's imps,' but both the French king and Duke François protected him. Then King Edward caught a severe chill and died. Who knows how long he would have reigned had he not grown ill. He was not an old man. His brother, Richard, took the king-ship of England when Edward's two young sons disappeared. Henry Tudor's adherents say Richard murdered them, but I have never believed it. Richard loved his many nieces and nephews."

"Who then could have killed those in-nocents?" Lucianna asked. "If indeed they were murdered."

"I believe some misguided follower of the Tudors saw to the disappearance of the two princes. No bodies were ever found," the earl told his wife. "The rumors, however, were enough to weaken Richard's hold on the throne. The Lancaster supporters took the opportunity to rise up against him. Henry Tudor took that moment to return to England, where he was greeted like a savior. A battle at Bosworth decided the matter once and for all. Richard was killed, and the Lancasters were once again England's rul-ers."

"Were there no Yorkist claimants to Rich-ard's throne?" she asked, curious.

"One, Edward, Earl of Warwick, son of

King Richard's other deceased brother, the Duke of Clarence. Richard's own son had been killed fighting for his father. Henry ordered Warwick arrested and imprisoned in the Tower even before he reached London. We came into the city to be greeted by the mayor and the aldermen. They escorted us to St. Paul's Cathedral, where King Henry Tudor deposited his battle standards upon the high altar. We won at Bosworth on the twenty-second of August, and at the end of October, King Henry was crowned at Westminster.

"Henry had been betrothed for several years to King Edward's eldest daughter, Elizabeth, who was now the Yorkist heiress. A match arranged between Lady Margaret and King Edward's queen, Elizabeth Woodville, a duplicitous woman, I might add. The king is most patient with her, though it is not always easy.

"Parliament met in November, requesting that the marriage take place and pronouncing that the heirs of such a lawful union would inherit. Since bride and groom were distantly related, it was necessary for the pope to give his permission. He did so speedily. The king set the wedding date for mid-January. He understood by marrying Elizabeth he was uniting the houses of

Lancaster and York. There would be no further cause for widespread and partisan rebellion.

"Although there are still some diehard York loyalists who dislike what has happened, and will probably support any pretenders until they are shown for what they really are, England is now at peace, and hopefully will remain so," the earl concluded.

"Did the king not reward his chief supporters for their faithfulness?" Lucianna wanted to know. The Medici would have.

"Indeed he did. His uncle Jasper became Duke of Bedford. He was also given a sister of Elizabeth Woodville to wife. His stepfather, Lord Stanley, was created Earl of Derby. There were others restored to their lands, given lands, and some given titles," Robert told her.

"And you?" Lucianna queried bluntly. "What reward were you given for your loyalty?"

"There was nothing I wanted when asked. I have a title, lands, and enough wealth to suit me. The king insisted, however, that I must have something. Finally, it was the Lady Margaret who came up with the perfect reward. I will always, no matter what, be granted access to the king's person when I so desire it. There are many who would kill for such access if such an act made it possible," he explained with a small smile. "Unfortunately, it is mine alone. I could be a powerful man if I chose to remain at court. I do not for many reasons, but knowing I have the privilege is enough to keep me away. My loyalty was not given for any reward I might gain. It was given in honest friendship."

"Yes," Lucianna said. "I can understand that. You would be constantly importuned by those wishing to gain access to the king."

He nodded. "One day I may need the king's ear for myself, or for my family's benefit. I do not wish to wear out my welcome with him, nor do I want to tire his patience with me. Henry Tudor has little time for fools."

"How clever of Lady Margaret to consider such a prize. She knows you will not take advantage, but at the same time she satisfied her son's need to reward you for your good service," Lucianna noted. "She is indeed a lady to be admired, my lord."

"She is," he said with a smile. "Now, madame, tell me how all went while I made my brief visit to London."

"Worrell and I rode out every day," Lucianna said, "to make certain the fields were being kept properly, to see if any repairs were necessary to the cottages. All is in good order, my lord. Now you tell me of my brother, and my guild's London enterprise."

"Your brother and I parted ways when we reached the city," he explained. "There was no need for me to go to his shop, as you were no longer there. I believe you may trust Baram Kira to see nothing goes wrong, my love."

Lucianna was disturbed by his words. Her brother had not her experience in the silk trade. He was a headstrong man, and she worried he would spend more time seeking out the pleasures London had to offer now that she was not there to monitor his behavior. Her only hope lay in Baram Kira. She could not allow her marriage to cause her to forget her duty to the Arte di Por Santa Maria of Florence.

"You are my countess now," the earl said, seeing the concern in her eyes.

"Luca is not fully competent yet to manage the shop, nor has my father's guild appointed him to do so," Lucianna explained. "Baram Kira understands more than Luca does."

"Your brother is a soldier at heart. He has left his passion because of his loyalty to your father," the earl said, "but his heart is elsewhere, Lucianna."

"I do not regret our marriage, my lord," she told him, "but it was hastily done, and without my parents' formal permission. I cannot simply abdicate my other responsibilities like some moonstruck maiden. I must make arrangements for my guild."

"You are a widow and did not need your parents' formal permission," he reminded her.

"I am a widow, but young enough yet that my mother would have arranged another match for me had I allowed it," she said. "And what of my guild, Robert? I cannot simply abdicate my responsibilities to them without giving them notice."

"Write to your parents, and share the news of our marriage with them," he suggested. The Arte di Por Santa Maria was another matter. "Let your father, who is his guild's master, decide how to manage their London shop. He surely understands, as I know your mother does, that a nobleman's wife does not engage in trade."

"I was a silk merchant before I was your wife," she replied quietly. "Certainly, when you pursued me so hotly, you understood that, my lord of Lisle." Then Lucianna softened her stance. "Our marriage was celebrated in such haste that I had no time to make arrangements for my guild's shop, Robert. I will do it as discreetly as possible, but I must do it. Your wedding band upon my finger cannot absolve me of my other responsibilities."

"You cannot go to London," he said stubbornly.

"I will do as much as I can from here, but it will take time for the Arte di Por Santa Maria to tell me their wishes," she explained. "In the meantime, I will rely upon the Kiras to aid me."

"But you will not go to London," he repeated.

"Only with you, my lord, if we decide to visit the court," she promised him with a small smile. She did not need to go to London right now, Lucianna considered, but eventually she would. Still, there was no use arguing with her new husband over it now.

"The king will shortly go on his summer progress, but he will not go far from London this year, and the queen will remain at Westminster Palace, as she is with child. As I generally eschew the court, we are free to remain here on our own estate. Write your letters, and I will see them sent by the fastest messengers. Now, come and kiss me again, Wife. I have missed your company."

Men! Lucianna thought as she kissed him again. They were all so alike, but she had learned long ago by observing her mother that while men seemed to need their way all the time, there were ways of getting around them if a woman was clever. She had not had to employ such tactics with Alfredo, for he had always been content to let her have her own way. She had never been unreasonable, but she had also never known if Alfredo's kindness towards her had come from his trust in her or his fear she would leave him. But Roberto was a stronger, younger man. It was unlikely he feared anything.

And it was then that Lucianna realized how little she and Roberto actually knew about each other. They had indeed married in haste. But were not all married couples usually strangers when they wed? Melting into his embrace, she allowed his deep and passionate kisses to still her thoughts. They were wed, and she did not want to quarrel with him.

"Stop thinking!" he commanded her.

Lucianna laughed. "Stop attempting to read my thoughts," she teased him. "You cannot."

"One day I will," he promised her.

"Perhaps," she said with a smile. Then she slipped from his embrace. "I must write to my mother now, and to my father as well if these messages are to go off first thing tomorrow morning. And there is Luca to instruct from here, and the Kiras."

"Go," he said. He was pleased she understood him, and would not attempt to go to London.

Lucianna smiled up at him, and, turning, left him. Men could be so simple, she thought. She could see he was content that she would obey his directive like a good wife. Yet her responsibilities to her father's guild could not be ignored. She wrote first to David Kira in London, telling him of her marriage and informing him that her personal wealth would, according to her marriage contract, remain hers.

"How clever she is," Yedda Kira said to her husband when he told her of the missive he had received from the new Countess of Lisle. "She has his title and has managed to keep what is her own."

"Yes," David Kira agreed. "A strong woman and an astute one as well. She wants me to tell our cousin, Baram, that she has written to Florence to advise her father to send for her brother so he may now learn from him while advancing Baram to be in charge of the London shop permanently."

Yedda clapped her hands in delight. "This

is such an opportunity for him," she said, pleased.

In Florence, Giovanni Pietro d'Angelo read his third daughter's letter to him, well pleased. He had always prided himself on being able to understand other people, and he had not been wrong about the Earl of Lisle. Robert Minton had fallen in love with Lucianna here in Florence, and it was not just a passing fancy. He had suspected if the young couple had the opportunity to be together more, the earl would make Lucianna his wife.

Orianna was not as pleased. "She has wed without her parents. What will this English king, and his mother our daughter so admires, think of such rash behavior?" she fretted.

"She is a nobleman's wife, my dear," her husband answered. "Is that not what you wanted for our daughters? Wealth and titles?"

"And where has my pride gotten me?" Orianna surprised him by replying. "We cannot acknowledge Bianca's liaison, nor ever know the granddaughter she gave us. Francesca is widowed after all the difficulty we had in getting her to wed her duke. She will never marry again, she says, and I must believe her, for she has a will of iron. And now this third daughter has wed without us in a foreign land. I am surely cursed, Gio."

"We can visit England next year," he promised her, "and do not forget we still have our fourth daughter to match."

"I despair of Serena," Orianna told him. "She is almost eighteen, and past her prime for a husband. She will not be biddable as Lucianna was when we accepted the bookseller as a husband for her. But at least Luca will be coming home if you accept Lucianna's advice."

"I do," he said. "Marco tries, but his heart is not in silk. It is not in anything that I can see. I thought when you forgave him, it would encourage him to be the young man he once was. Lucianna says that Luca is slow to learn, but he has learned enough for me to teach him the rest of what he must know to take over the family enterprise. I will send for our youngest son immediately."

When Lucianna wrote to her twin brother what she had written to their father, he was, to her surprise, not pleased. Leaving Baram Kira with the shop, he came to Wye Court to speak with his sister.

"I like London," he said. "I am content to remain here for the time being. I have begun

281

to make friends," Luca told Lucianna.

"You have learned much from me," she said, "but you are not really ready to manage a shop on your own, Brother."

"Let us not pretend, Sister," he replied. "We both know when you are not there it is Baram Kira who manages our silk trade."

"Aye, it is," she agreed pleasantly, "and that is why you need to return to Florence so Father may teach you further. Our father grows older, and Marco will never take over our family's enterprise from him. He doesn't care, and he cannot understand that without a thriving business, our family cannot survive. It will take several weeks for my letter to reach Father in Florence. Then it will take several weeks for him to reply, Luca. You probably have the summer before you must return to Florence. You cannot shirk your duty to the family."

"I know," he admitted. "Like you, I was enjoying my freedom. You know as well as I do that when I return home, they will have found a wife for me. I will be married, and my life set into the pattern of a silk merchant. I realize I have no choice, but I had hoped . . ." His voice trailed off.

Lucianna felt sudden pity for this twin brother who had wanted nothing more in his life than a career as a military man. "You have the summer," she reminded him once again. "Let Baram run the shop, and enjoy your friends while you can. It will not be so bad in Florence, and a pretty wife should ease your time."

"*If* she is pretty, but our parents will wisely seek a girl with the largest dower portion. It is my experience the larger the dower, the uglier the bride," he said gloomily.

Lucianna laughed at this, but he was probably correct. "Well," she said cheerfully, "then you will pick an extraordinarily pretty mistress, and be the envy of all."

Now it was Luca's turn to laugh. "You have always had the gift of taking a bad situation and somehow making it better, Sister." He remained at Wye Court for several days before returning to London.

"Now, perhaps," the earl said as his brother-in-law rode off, "I may be alone with my bride."

"Now?" she teased him mischievously, giving him a quick kiss.

"Nay, damn it! This morning I must listen to complaints, sort out disagreements, and sit in judgment of those accused of minor misdemeanors. I do this once a month. It will last much of the day."

"Then go and be a good lord. We have the

evening ahead of us, do we not?" she answered.

The evening could not come quickly enough, Robert Minton thought. He had discovered he could not get enough of his beautiful wife. As for Lucianna, she was an eager student of his tutoring, and he smiled to himself, remembering their nights together. It seemed that the day would never end. He noticed that the warmer weather seemed to bring more complaints and disagreements between neighbors. There was a charge of theft to judge, but upon hearing the complaint, the earl realized it was simply just another misunderstanding between two neighbors.

One man, who had promised two sheep to his neighbor's son in exchange for marrying his daughter, had not delivered the dower portion, and the bride was now with child. The bridegroom was threatening to return her unless her dower was paid. The families brought the matter to Father Paul, who brought it to the earl.

"Why haven't you given your daughter's dower to her husband?" the earl asked the bride's father.

"I promised him two ewes, but one of the ewes he chose is with lamb now. I asked him to choose another ewe, but he would not. The creature is big, and may birth twins, my lord. He will gain four sheep for my daughter instead of two. It is not fair," the bride's father protested. "My daughter is not worth four sheep."

The earl turned to the bridegroom. "Why did you choose that particular ewe that you cannot pick another?"

"She looked healthy, my lord," was his answer.

"Are any of your sheep unhealthy?" the earl asked the bride's father. He wondered why the bride wasn't worth four sheep, but that was not the difficulty. The girl's sire was accusing her husband of theft.

"I possess a small flock of six, my lord. All are healthy."

"Withdraw the charge of theft against your son-in-law," the earl ordered the man. Then he turned to the bridegroom. "And Father Paul will choose a second sheep for you," he said to the younger man. "The ewe with her lambs remains with your wife's father. You were promised two sheep, not three or four."

"If he will accept what is due him, I will gladly withdraw the charges, my lord."

Later that evening, Robert Minton told Lucianna the story of his day, and she laughed. "I was surprised when the farmer said his daughter wasn't worth more than two sheep," he said.

"Have you seen the lass?" his wife asked.

"Nay," the earl admitted.

"Now, when I ride out, I shall have to see who she is," Lucianna said, "or if her sire is merely mean and beggarly. What an unkind thing to say about his child, even if it were true."

"You are worth more than two sheep," the earl said to his wife.

"And how many sheep would you have offered my father for me?" Lucianna asked him, chuckling.

"There aren't enough sheep in the wide world," he responded with a grin.

"Oh, wicked man!" Lucianna said. "You have sought to flatter me beyond reason."

"And have I?" he queried her.

"Perhaps," she replied.

Robert Minton laughed. "Will you never give me the advantage, *amore mia*?"

"Why, my lord, you are a man. Do not men always have the advantage?" she said innocently.

He laughed again. "You are too quick-witted by far, my Florentine wife. I believe if I chose to join the court, you would quickly gain a reputation that now is only attributed to the king's mother." He pulled her into his arms.

Lucianna slipped her arms about his neck. "I don't want to live at the court," she said. "I would have little patience with the many ladies who would look down on me."

"You are the Countess of Lisle," he said. "No one would dare look down on the Countess of Lisle."

"I am a silk merchant's daughter who has married above her station, and worse, engaged in public trade," she reminded him.

"Then how fortuitous that we both prefer living in the country," he remarked, and he began to kiss her.

She loved his kisses. They were slow and deep, and she found herself tingling with every one. This was marriage as she had always imagined it would be. Though she remained silent, Lucianna knew that she had fallen deeply in love with her husband. She wondered if all women were as fortunate as she suddenly realized she was. She hoped Bianca was, and that Francesca had been. She hoped Serena would find the same happiness one day as they had, she thought, as her husband began to make love to her.

His hands caressed her gently as he pushed her chemise up from her. "You are so beautiful," he told her as he bent to kiss her nipples.

She ran her hands through his dark hair, caressing the nape of his neck. "I have fallen in love with you, my lord," she murmured to him.

"You fell in love with me months ago. You are just now willing to admit it, *amore mia,*" he replied.

"You are so vain," she told him.

"We are so fortunate in each other, Lucianna," he said softly.

"I know," she said, smiling up at him.

Gathering her up, he carried her to their bed and laid her down. Then, stripping off his nightshirt, he joined her, pulling her back into his arms. Lucianna melted against him with a passionate sigh of delight. Their need for each other was great. Within moments of more kisses and caresses, their bodies were joined, his sheath buried deep within her.

Lucianna cried out in pleasure with his entry. She loved being filled by him. It made her feel complete, and until he had first had her, she had never realized the pure enjoyment the joining of a man and a woman provided. "I love you!" she repeated.

He groaned, and answered her, "As I do you, *amore mia!*" Then he began to move upon her, pushing them both towards an utter and complete pleasure that finally left them both exhausted and totally content.

CHAPTER 13

Baram Kira was very pleased as he read Lucianna's missive to him. Her brother would go home to Florence by autumn, and Baram would be in charge of the shop. She had recommended him to her father, and the head of the Florentine silk merchants' guild would certainly take his daughter's suggestion. Baram had, at last, a future and could consider taking a wife.

One thing, however, disturbed Baram Kira. He did not like the men that Luca Pietro d'Angelo had chosen to befriend. The local gossip, to which he was quite privy, told him that they were troublemakers. Luca was a foreigner, a soldier at heart. He did not understand these Englishmen who spoke disrespectfully of King Henry. And when Luca began to share their thoughts, Baram Kira became worried.

"He has no real claim to the throne," Luca said. "He is a usurper."

"Nay," Baram told the young Florentine. "His claim is weaker than the Duke of Clarence's son, it is true, but his claim is through his mother, who was a great-granddaughter of King Edward the Third's third son, John of Gaunt, and his third wife, Kathryn Swynford. Gaunt's eldest son was King Henry the Fourth. The king's grandmother was a French princess, wed to King Henry the Fifth."

"Indeed," Luca said. "How is it you know this?"

"I am English," was the reply.

"You are a Jew," Luca answered.

"But an *English* Jew," Baram Kira told Luca.

"And obviously an adherent of the Lancasters," Luca noted.

"The Kiras are loyalists," Baram Kira said. "It is not wise for a Jew to take sides. We are simply loyal to whoever is in power."

"But if you could pull down a usurper from the throne, wouldn't you want to do it?" Luca queried his companion.

"My task is to be the best representative in London that the Florentine silk merchants' guild can have," Baram answered him. "Your sister tells me when you are returned to your own city, this shop will be my responsibility, Luca Pietro d'Angelo. I

291

would do your father's guild little good to become involved in treason. It would but taint his family, and his guild. Perhaps you will do well to follow my lead in these matters. My people have survived these centuries by being prudent and not involving themselves in matters of no concern to them."

Luca was surprised to be chided in such a manner. What would Baram Kira, a Jew, know of politics, the right of things? He did, however, mention what he had learned to his friends when they met later at a nearby inn. He did not, however, say from where he had obtained his information.

"Both York and Lancaster have legitimate claims to the throne," he was told. "But York is a stronger claim. If it were not, would this man who styles himself King Henry the Seventh have imprisoned the Duke of Clarence's son? This Welshman must be pulled down and a proper English king crowned."

Luca considered this strategy and decided that such a statement was probably true. It was what a good soldier would have done. But he was curious as to why these men he had met just recently would attempt to involve him in their plot. His question was answered without his even asking as the ringleader continued.

"We need a man experienced in the military with no loyalties to either side to approve our plans," the man said. "You are a foreigner, and I am told you were a soldier once. Is that so?"

"It is," Luca answered him. This was a fact he would have ascertained before involving a stranger he met at an inn in a possibly treasonous plot. He wondered just how clever these men were, or if this talk of pulling down a king was just talk.

"We need to get the young Earl of Warwick released from the Tower," the man went on. "We know not how to accomplish such a task, but I suspect you would know how to help a man escape such a confinement. Help us in our endeavor, and you will be rewarded."

Luca did not bother telling this conspirator that gold was the least of his worries. The man was obviously a fool, but if Luca learned more of this plot, and revealed it to his new brother-in-law, would it not increase his sister's status as the earl's wife? And would not King Henry be grateful? This English king was beginning to accept trading partners, the first English king to do so. If he saw the loyalty of the Florentines, would he not consider them as worthy trading partners? And would the Medici not be well pleased by such a turn of events?

"I know little of this Tower of London other than it is considered a most worthy fortress," he said slowly. Best to let them tell him.

"One of our men is a guard there," the ringleader said.

"And he knows where your duke is housed?" Luca asked.

"Aye! He has made us a drawing of it."

"I will have to study it for several days to consider the quickest, easiest way both in and out of this prison," Luca told him.

"We will bring it to you. Tell us where you live," the man said.

"Nay. Bring it to the shop of the Florentine silk merchants' guild, and leave it with my assistant if I am not there." He smiled. "I have just taken a mistress and must spend more time with her. You will not see me here for a time. I will inform you when I have a plan for you."

The ringleader nodded. "Very well," he said. Then he sidled away from the table where Luca sat drinking.

A fool, Luca decided. What kind of successful conspirator confided his treason to a stranger? The answer was obvious. The man actually did need his help, but he also needed someone who could be blamed if his plot failed, thus diverting attention from himself. That was cleverer than Luca would have given him credit for, which led him to consider who among the nobility was contemplating treason. If he could learn that, it would be even better.

Luca did not return to that particular inn, and several days later Baram Kira handed him a packet. "This came for you late yesterday," he said.

Luca took it from the young man. "It will be a diagram of the Tower," he said. "I am privy to a plot against the king."

Baram Kira was horrified. He wanted to ask Luca Pietro d'Angelo if he had suddenly gone mad. He said nothing, allowing his look to say what he would not.

"I am no traitor to your king," Luca quickly reassured him, seeing the expression on Baram Kira's face. "I have been approached by them. I am pretending to involve myself in this plot. When I learn who is truly behind it, I will inform the earl so he may warn the king."

"Why would you even consider such a thing?" Baram finally asked, horrified. "If it is believed you are involved in any way, it will reflect badly upon your sister and her husband, Luca Pietro d'Angelo. There are those who would happily discredit Robert Minton for their own gain. It would bring suspicion and shame upon Florence."

"I did not approach these men. They came to me, offered me gold for my aid. They know little about me other than I am a foreigner and soldier. If their plot goes awry, they think to blame me."

"They think to involve your brother-in-law," Baram said astutely. "You must have nothing more to do with these men, and report them to the king's people at once!"

"Not until I can learn who is behind these clumsy fools who would involve a stranger in their plots," Luca said.

Baram Kira went to the head of his house in London, the banker David Kira, who was astounded that Luca would involve himself with such men. "I thought the countess's brother wiser than that," he said.

"What shall I do?" Baram said. "If he is found out, no matter his good intentions, the earl and his wife could be considered disloyal."

"Not necessarily, considering Robert Minton's history with the king," David responded. "Still, the earl should be told before this can go any further. I will send to him, Baram. I am glad that you came to me. Your future is at stake as well."

Several days later, the Earl of Lisle received a messenger from London. He read the missive that the man had brought, swore softly, and then said to Lucianna, "Was your brother always such a damned fool, *amore mia*?" Then he handed the letter from David Kira to her.

Lucianna quickly read the parchment. She grew pale with concern for her twin. "I cannot believe Luca has been so foolish," she finally said. "Why would he even consider such a thing? Why did he not simply send these men away?"

"In his heart, he is still a soldier," the earl noted astutely. "This has given him the opportunity to plan a campaign, a strategy. I suspect he misses that."

Lucianna sighed. "You are right," she said, "but my brother can no longer allow himself to think like a soldier. He is a silk merchant now. He endangers you, Roberto, my family, our city itself."

"He cannot see that," the earl explained to his wife. "He sees himself using his military background to bring these traitors to justice, and improving my reputation with the king."

"You are the king's friend," Lucianna said. "You need no help from my brother to gain favor."

"Nay, I do not," he agreed. "But now I must go to London to put a stop to Luca's foolishness."

"I am going with you," she said.

His instinct was to say no. He was more than able to manage his well-meaning brother-in-law. But he also understood that Luca's behavior had distressed his wife. She would not be content unless she had her say in the matter. "We must ride quickly, and without the usual accoutrements a lady travels with, Lucianna," he told her.

"I have clothing in London," she told him, "and I am perfectly capable of dressing myself. Balia will remain here. She will be most distressed when I tell her of Luca's behavior."

"It is too late to leave today. We will go come morning. I have already sent Kira's messenger ahead, telling him I am coming."

"Oh, Roberto, I am so ashamed of my brother's behavior!"

And Lucianna was — ashamed and angry. How could her brother be so witless? She was going to ask him when they next met.

Balia was very upset to learn of the contents of David Kira's letter to the earl. "How could he compromise you in such a fashion? Well, my lady, soon he will be sent back to Florence. For your safety, I should not wait for your father's permission. I should send him as quickly as possible," the tiring woman told her mistress.

"I think you are probably right," Lucianna agreed. "His mind is not yet engaged in the business of the silk trade. Heaven only knows what chaos his well-meaning behavior will cause next. Back in Florence, our father will see he becomes more engaged in business. He is more than capable of it, Balia. Yes! My brother must leave England as quickly as passage can be arranged for him."

The earl agreed with his wife. When told, the king would be irritated, but before knowledge of Luca Pietro d'Angelo's foolishness became known to the court, he would agree with Robert that the young man must return home immediately. This would also allay Henry Tudor's natural suspicions.

They started for London the following morning. Arriving several days later, Robert saw his wife to the silk shop, waiting outside for her while she dealt with her brother. Entering the shop, she was relieved to find it empty but for her brother and Baram Kira. Her former assistant bowed respectfully, and Lucianna smiled. "Good morning, Brother. Baram, you may leave us, for I wish to speak with Master Luca privily."

He bowed again, saying, "Yes, my lady," and disappeared into the back room of the shop to busy himself sorting the new examples of silk that had only yesterday arrived from Florence.

"I did not expect to see you here again," Luca said. "I realize you do not yet think me competent to manage without you, but I can, Sister."

"*My lady,* Luca Pietro d'Angelo. I am the Countess of Lisle, and you will address me respectfully and properly in a public place. This shop is a public place," Lucianna said angrily. "How dare you endanger my husband with your foolishness? When you were approached by traitors, you should have reported the fools immediately, or at the very least written to Roberto for his advice. But no! You must involve yourself in a treasonous plot that could destroy the friendship my husband and the king share."

"I but sought to learn who was behind this plot," Luca said, attempting to explain to his sister. "The fools who approached me were not capable of such guile, *my lady.*"

"And did you learn the identity of that man, Luca?"

"Not yet," he admitted.

"Not ever!" she almost shouted at him. "You will go home to Florence, Luca Pietro

300

d'Angelo. We will arrange passage for you as quickly as we can. Your behavior will not tarnish our family, Florence, or the Mintons. But first, you will be taken to King Henry, and you will tell him exactly what you know, Luca Pietro d'Angelo. You will admit your foolishness. You will admit everything. You will beg his pardon. I can only hope that my husband's long friendship with this king will not be damaged by what you have done."

"How did you learn of this?" Luca wanted to know. He glanced towards the rear of the shop. "Baram Kira told you, didn't he? How eager the Jew is to have control of this shop," he snarled.

"Baram Kira?" Lucianna feigned surprise, and then said with complete honesty, "No, Baram Kira did not expose you to us, Luca Pietro d'Angelo. Do you think my husband is not without resources? That he has no friends looking after his interests? How we learned of your stupidity is not important. Roberto is waiting for you outside. He will accompany you to the king, where you will confess your well-meaning foolishness to him, and beg for his forgiveness."

"I have done nothing wrong," Luca said stubbornly. "I have only attempted to unmask a plot against this king. Had I been successful, your husband's loyalty would have been even more appreciated."

"Henry Tudor is a suspicious man by nature, and by virtue of the life he has endured along the road to his kingship," Lucianna told her brother. She could see that Luca was beginning to realize the seriousness of his actions. "There are very few, if any, in whom he confides. The only person in the world he trusts completely is his mother, Lady Margaret. His wife, whom my husband tells me the king has come to love, does not enjoy that level of his confidence.

"The king's confidence in Roberto is based on his complete honesty. His ability to not take sides in any matter where factions quarrel among themselves. My husband has always spoken the truth to the king, and there have been times when the truth was not what the king wanted to hear, but he listened because it was Roberto speaking to him, not someone attempting to gain his way or curry favor with the king. You will now have jeopardized that trust, Luca. Go now. Roberto awaits you outside. You will ride my horse. You will not return to this shop again.

"If the king does not clap you in the Tower, you will depart England as quickly as we can arrange it. You will carry a letter to our father from me. I will not expose your stupidity to him, Brother, for we have always kept each other's secrets. I will tell him since Baram Kira is more than capable of managing the shop, you decided to return home as quickly as possible to be of help to our father, and learn from him what I could not teach you," Lucianna told him.

He did not argue with her. As she had scolded him, Luca Pietro d'Angelo was suddenly made fully aware of his own ignorance of English politics. Well, he couldn't say that Baram Kira hadn't warned him. The Jew had probably gone directly to his banker cousin, and it had been David Kira who had written to his brother-in-law, exposing him for a fool. Raising his sister's hand to his lips, he kissed it.

"Signora la contessa," he said, and then turning, departed the silk shop.

As soon as the door closed behind him, Baram Kira came from the back room. "I have sorted the new silks by color, madame," he said politely.

She knew he had heard every word spoken between the siblings. But she wondered how well he understood the Italian language, for she had upbraided her twin in their native tongue as it was easier for her to say what

303

she must to him, and Luca had responded in kind. She did not ask her assistant, however, for it really didn't matter.

"My brother will not be returning to this shop, Master Kira," she said. "You will be responsible for it now. I cannot, given my rank, engage in my father's trade any longer, but you are free to correspond with me should you need my advice or further guidance. Please accept my thanks and those of my husband for advising us of my brother's well-meaning, but unwise, actions. I know it is you who spoke with David Kira, who wrote to notify us."

"I hope Master Luca will not be imprisoned," Baram said. "That was not my intention, my lady."

"A brief stay in a dank cell might do him some good, although I doubt it. Nay, I imagine the king will agree with my husband that Luca meant no harm, but now there will always be a small worm of distrust for us in the king's heart. I am sorry that my kinsman will be responsible for it," Lucianna said regretfully. "I know that I can rely upon your discretion, Master Kira. We will not speak of this again."

Baram Kira bowed. "I will endeavor to do my best for you, my lady," he promised her.

"I will return now to my house," Lucianna

told him.

"You will walk?" She had always had a litter or had ridden her horse.

Lucianna laughed. "I am capable of walking home, Baram. Please tell his lordship when he returns. The day is fair, and the streets busy."

He bowed again. "I will thank you then, my lady, and bid you a good day," the new shopkeeper said.

"Good day, Master Kira," she answered, and departed the silk shop. The day was pleasant and warm. Lucianna walked quickly, aware of everything and everyone about her. The garments she wore were not lavish, and she attracted no undue attention. Soon the busy streets were left behind for the quieter paths, but the now-empty way left her nervous. She was relieved to reach her house, where the door opened to her knock.

"My lady!" Cleva, the young housekeeper, was surprised to see her. She quickly curtsied and stepped aside. "We did not know you were in London, my lady."

"The earl had a matter of urgent business, and I came with him. Of course I went to the shop first," Lucianna explained, smiling. She had elevated Cleva's status before leaving London to visit Wye Court.

"May I ask how long you are staying?" Cleva said. "I must tell Alvina in the kitchens. Preparing meals for only Master Pietro d'Angelo does not require as much food, but with two hungry men in the house, Bessie will have to be sent immediately to market, my lady."

"I am not certain, a few days, no more," Lucianna said. "I did not even bring Balia." She smiled at Cleva. "I will retire to my room to rest now, for the earl would travel quickly."

"Of course, my lady."

Cleva hurried off to speak with Alvina, the cook, while Lucianna climbed the stairs to her old bedchamber. Fortunately, there had been no damage. Surely the king would forgive Luca. His actions, misguided as they were, had caused no real harm. The king would see the conspirators rounded up and imprisoned. And his jailors would have their own means of learning the identity of the man behind the plot. Her husband's reputation with Henry Tudor could be salvaged.

She wondered if he and Luca would be admitted to the king's presence today, or if it would take several days to see him.

As he rode through London, Robert Minton was beginning to consider the same thing. Men, even close friends, could not simply appear upon the royal doorstep for a visit. He thought that perhaps he would be wiser to seek Lady Margaret's advice in this uncomfortable matter of his brother-in-law.

"This is not the way to the king's residence," Luca said to him.

And Robert Minton suddenly realized he had directed his horse's steps towards Lady Margaret Beaufort's home. "Nay, it isn't. I must speak with the king's mother first in this matter. She will advise me on how to approach the king and inform him of your actions, without getting you clapped in the Tower, although if stupidity were a crime, you would be charged," the earl said irritably.

"I only meant to help you," Luca muttered sullenly, but he turned away from his brother-in-law, for the look Robert Minton gave him sent a chill through him. He suspected if his sister were not this man's wife, there would be no mercy shown him by the Earl of Lisle.

Upon reaching the home of the king's mother, they were greeted cordially by the lady's majordomo, who always traveled with his mistress and saw to her comforts. "My lord, sir, please come in. You were not expected."

"Is it possible that Lady Margaret can

make time for us?" the earl inquired politely, his tone implying that if she could not, they would gladly return when she could.

But the queen mother's trusted servant knew two things: Robert Minton was a great favorite of his lady, and the earl would not be here unannounced without good cause. He bowed to her guests. "I will tell her you are here, my lord," he said, and turning, hurried off.

They waited, Luca growing more nervous by the moment. He dreaded the king's mother learning of his foolishness. It was no secret that she was very protective of her son and had played an important part in seeing him made king. What would she think of what Luca had done, even if his intentions had been good?

The majordomo returned. "Her ladyship will see you, my lord," he said, directing his words to the earl.

"Come!" Robert Minton ordered his brother-in-law.

Lady Margaret was awaiting him in her privy chamber, surrounded by her ladies. "Robert!" she said, her usually stern face lighting with a smile. "What are you doing in London? And Master Pietro d'Angelo, it is good to see you again."

Both men bowed politely to the king's mother.

Bending to kiss her cheek, the earl whispered in the lady's ear, "If you would, dear madame, send your ladies away, for what we have come to say must not become open knowledge."

Luca stood quietly. Several of the queen mother's ladies were young and pretty. Normally he would have flirted with them. Today he did not dare to do so.

"Ladies," the king's mother said, "I would be alone with my guests. The day is fair. I would suggest a walk in my gardens. When I wish your presence, I will call you back."

The women and girls all rose from their places, curtsied to their mistress, and left the privy chamber. One directed a smile at the earl as they went. He nodded politely, although not with great interest.

"That is Catherine Talcott," Lady Margaret said, "the girl I considered for you before you met your Lucianna. Now, my lord, what is it you wish to tell me that requires such privacy?"

"My brother-in-law has, without meaning to, involved himself in a plot, madame."

"A plot?" Instantly, Lady Margaret was fully alert.

"He was approached by several men at a

local inn he frequents," the earl began. "They claim they seek to gain the release of Clarence's son from the Tower."

Lady Margaret's face darkened. "Will these people never cease in their attempts to destabilize the country?" she asked of no one in particular. Then she looked at Luca. "They sought your aid? Why?"

"They knew I had been a soldier, my lady," Luca said. Then he rushed on to say, "I meant no treason! I only sought to learn the identity of those behind such a nefarious scheme."

"And have you?" Lady Margaret queried him sharply.

"Alas, no, madame, I have not, but it is not for lack of trying," Luca told her. "When the earl learned of my involvement, he hurried to London with my sister to insist I go to the king and warn him." Luca realized that for the first time since he was a boy, he was truly frightened. The king's mother was a powerful woman, and this was her son of whom they spoke. He knew how his mother would react should anyone dare to threaten one of her children with bodily harm.

"I thought it best to come to you first, madame," the earl broke in, "and solicit your advice in this matter. I will see that

Luca is sent home to Florence immediately if the king will forgive him his stupidity."

"Nay," Lady Margaret said, surprising them both. "He must continue to involve himself with this plot, but you will keep me informed at all times of what these traitors are doing," she said, piercing the young man with a hard look. "I will, with your help, Luca Pietro d'Angelo, put an end to this sort of treason once and for all. Henry cannot be constantly besieged within his own realm. The Earl of Kildare in Ireland has welcomed a pretender to England's throne who cries to all who will listen that he is Clarence's son." She sniffed derisively. "And it is said there are no snakes in Ireland."

"But Clarence's son, the Earl of Warwick, is in the Tower," Robert Minton said incredulously. "I thought all knew that."

"Well," Lady Margaret said dryly, "whether the Irish do or not, they will be crowning this fellow in Dublin, we have been informed. Sooner or later this summer, there will be an invasion. We do not need the true Edward, Earl of Warwick, escaping the Tower and racing about the countryside, causing havoc at the same time as well." She turned and looked at the earl. "I think it best we keep this from my son for now, Robert. I see no need for him to worry further. Master Pietro d'Angelo will continue to attempt to learn the perpetrator of this latest plot so we may end it before it gets out of control."

"Is this wise, madame?" He had never questioned a decision of hers before.

"Probably not, Rob, but if Luca simply disappears, his fellow conspirators will grow nervous, and heaven knows what they will do.

"We need to know where this comes from. At least with this pretender in Ireland, we know who he really is, and who is behind him. He will prove troublesome, it is true, but we will prevail."

"Who is he?" the earl asked, curious. Until she had spoken of it, he hadn't heard of a pretender, but then he had been in the country on his estates, trying to enjoy his new wife's company.

"His name is Lambert Simnel. He was born in Oxford. His sire is a shoemaker or a baker or some such. You know Oxford is the home of lost causes, and a traitorous priest named Symonds conceived this particular plot. The boy, Simnel, is well favored, and even has the look of York about him. He was sent to Ireland shortly before we arrested the priest, but of course Margaret, Dowager Duchess of Burgundy, and sister of the late kings Edward and Richard, as well as to Duke Clarence, supports this pretension. She is such a bitter woman. She will send troops to help this pretender, for she hates my son for defeating her brother," the king's mother explained. "Still, that must not concern you. I am interested in learning who is behind this plot that your brother-in-law is involved in, Rob."

"Madame," Luca said, "I swear on the blessed Mother, on Santa Anna, my family's patron, that I meant no harm. I did not solicit these men. I thought only to help the king by exposing their plot."

"You should have exposed it immediately," the earl snapped.

"Nay, he was clever to realize that those coming to him were not capable of crafting such a plot, and to attempt to learn who was behind them," Lady Margaret said, half excusing the young man. "Press them for a name, Luca, and continue on so I may root out the chief traitor. You will then go home a hero, and I will commend your bravery and your cleverness to the Medici." She now favored him with a small, wintery smile.

"Lucianna believes that someone was attempting to forge a breach between myself and the king in order to gain favor for themselves," Robert Minton said.

"That too is possible," Lady Margaret agreed. "Using your foreign wife's family to discredit you would be of benefit to an ambitious man. It would also keep the king from forging trading ties with Florence, as he has been hoping to do. But we can only speculate until we find the perpetrators of this nefarious plot."

The earl nodded in agreement. "Shall Lucianna and I return to Wye Court?" he asked Lady Margaret.

"Remain for the interim. Your fields are planted and will not be harvested for some weeks. I understand your longing for home, Rob, but stay until this matter is settled," Lady Margaret said.

He bowed. "As you wish, madame. Shall I recall your ladies now?" the earl inquired of her.

"Yes," she answered him, and he did so.

The queen mother's women streamed back into her privy chamber, chattering, the older women curious at their mistress's need for privacy, the younger ones more interested in flirting with Luca who, now relieved of his burden, was more than happy to oblige them. After a few moments, the earl said they would take their leave. When they had departed, one of the older women asked Lady Margaret what her favorite earl and the young silk merchant had wanted.

Lady Margaret shrugged. "The young Florentine will soon be required to return home by his father. He came to tell me himself, and thank us for our custom. I thought that exceedingly polite, but then these Florentines do have exquisite manners."

"Surely the earl's wife will not again step into the shop?" Cat Talcott said. "It would be unthinkable."

Lady Margaret's ladies all nodded in agreement, some frowning with disapproval.

"Nay, of course, Lady Minton will not become a shopkeeper once again," Lady Margaret said. "They have trained an assistant who will carry on for the Florentine silk merchants. I am right glad of it, for the Milanese have given up and prepared to leave London."

"Their silks were not as fine, I am told," one lady said. "How clever of the Florentine woman to train an Englishman to the task."

"Yes," Lady Margaret agreed. "Robert gained a most clever wife when he wed Lucianna Pietro d'Angelo."

Cat Talcott turned away.

"Do not look so sour, Cat," one of her friends remarked. "You will get wrinkles before your time," and the other girls giggled.

"He should have been mine," Cat Talcott said softly.

"Our lady will find you another husband, Cat," her friend reassured her.

"I don't want another!" the girl said.

"We cannot always have what we want," her friend replied.

Chapter 14

Lucianna was waiting anxiously for her husband and brother to return from their visit to the king. Luca, however, went to the shop while the earl returned to his wife's London house. Dunn and Gerd had hurried out to take the two horses into the stables. The earl found his wife waiting in the little hall of the house.

"What happened? Where is my brother? Oh God! He's been arrested!" she half sobbed.

"Nay, nay," he quickly reassured her, going to the sideboard to pour himself a goblet of wine. "We did not go to the king. We went to Lady Margaret first," he told Lucianna. Then he quietly explained what had happened, concluding, "As it is believed he is not quite ready to go, I thought it better he return to the shop. We wish it to appear as just another day as far as Luca is concerned."

Lucianna nodded as she processed everything he had just told her. "Is Luca in any danger?" she asked him finally.

"He could be if they realize what he is about, but as that is quite unlikely, I would say probably not. I do not believe anyone important would have involved a foreigner in their treasonous enterprise. I do not believe he is being watched, but a bit of caution does not go awry."

"I cannot leave London until I am certain my brother is free to return home. While my first loyalty is now to you, to your king, I still have a loyalty to the family of my birth," she told him seriously. "I need to know with certainty that this is over and done with, that my brother is safely on his way home without any stain of disloyalty tarnishing him, my lord. His actions were foolish, but Luca is a man of honor."

"I would not disagree with you," he said, then told her, "Lady Margaret has requested we remain until this matter is concluded."

"The king's mother well understands family alligiance," Lucianna said, "and who she may and may not trust."

"She pointed out the lady she had in mind to wed me to," the earl told her, taking her mind from her brother immediately.

"Is she pretty?" Lucianna asked. She felt a

jealous spark ignite.

"I didn't really notice," he foolishly replied.

"Liar!" she accused. "No man is told that he might have wed this maid and does not look at her. She was pretty then. How pretty?" What was the matter with her that she was suddenly so possessive?

"In the usual way," he admitted. "Hair the color of a chestnut. A bit of a turned-up nose, and a too-thin mouth. Not like my wife's lush lips," he said, reaching for her.

Lucianna evaded his grasp. "Her eyes?" she demanded. "What color were her *usual* eyes, my lord?"

"I actually did not get close enough to see their color," he told her truthfully. "Fair-skinned, so I would imagine she is light-eyed." He kept his expression serious, but he was frankly enjoying her jealousy. So far his wife's passion was confined to the physical. She did not use words to express her emotions as a rule. Her open jealousy conveyed a great deal more to him than she had ever before revealed.

"If you set us side by side," Lucianna continued to press him, "would you still choose me?"

"God, yes!" he exclaimed without hesitation. "I far prefer the wife I have with her golden red hair and blue-green eyes."

"You are a wise man," Lucianna murmured, smiling, well pleased. Moving closer to him, she slipped her arms about his neck. "You may kiss me now," she told him, grandly pursing her lips at him.

Robert Minton resisted the urge to laugh, or to tease her. He instead accepted her invitation, wrapping his arms about her, giving her a long, deep kiss. Then he chuckled, saying, "I am pleased to see you are capable of jealousy, *amore mia.*"

"Of course I can be jealous," she told him. "Florentine women with Venetian mothers can be very jealous in the right circumstances. However, my lord, I was merely curious this time."

He took her hand in his. "I have loved you almost from the first moment I saw you, Lucianna," he told her. "I shall never stop loving you, my beautiful wife." He now raised the small hand in his hand to his lips and, turning it over, kissed the delicate skin of her sensitive wrist.

His loving words, the touch of his warm lips, both sent a thrill racing through her. "I am so fortunate in your love," she admitted candidly, realizing how much she was coming to love this strong man. Yet she could not bring herself to say the words she knew would fill him with happiness. She was not quite ready yet to give him all of herself. Their marriage was new. It had been quick. Should she have waited?

Waited for what? she asked herself. For Lady Margaret to give him an English wife? To lose him forever, or finally relegate herself to being his mistress? She was Lucianna Pietro d'Angelo, daughter of a Venetian princess. She could not have yielded herself to him had he been wed to another. She might not have been born noble, but Lucianna knew that her manners and her morals were far superior to many who had nothing else to recommend them but their noble blood.

Suddenly she realized he was leading her from the hall. "Where . . ." she began, and then she smiled at him, nodding. They were going upstairs to their bedchamber, where they would continue this discussion of love and marriage.

"I thought we needed more privacy if I am to continue kissing you," he said, "and kissing seems to lead to . . ."

"I know where kissing leads to," she told him. "It is fortunate that we left Balia behind at Wye Court. Now our trysts are private."

"Servants know everything," the earl said

as they entered their bedchamber. He turned to close the door and lock it so no one would come in upon them unintentionally.

"It is true," she agreed, slipping into his arms again. Reaching up, she stroked his handsome face. It was rough with the new beard that had been growing for the last several days. "I do not know if I like you bearded or smooth-shaven," she said. "Your beard scratches me."

"Scraping my face smooth while we were traveling would have proven time-consuming," he replied. "And at this moment I have no plans to defer my wicked intentions towards you for any purpose, madame."

"I have not asked it of you, my lord," Lucianna murmured.

He had been slowly pushing her across the bedchamber towards their bed as they spoke.

She felt the edge of the bed against the back of her legs, and she let him shove her gently backwards. Looking up at her husband, she held out her arms to him, smiling. Briefly he laid himself atop her and they kissed again. As they did, he rolled them onto their sides. Lucianna's tongue entwined naughtily with his tongue, and she felt his need for her increasing with each heated, playful stroke.

They spoke not a word. His hands moved to push her skirts up. Her hands began to unfasten his shirt laces. He stroked the inside of her thigh, and she almost purred. She loved his touch. He cupped her mound and gently squeezed it. The heat and dampness from it excited his senses. So did that facile little tongue of hers, now teasing his ear.

"Volpe femina!" he growled against her lips.

"Tormentore!" she hissed back, pressing herself against him.

He loosened his breeches with a hand, releasing his hungry, swollen member. Passion had been denied as they traveled, as there had been no time to enjoy it with his bride. But now she lay eager beneath him, and they both understood there was no more time for niceties. He drove himself into her wet heat, his groan of pleasure mingling with hers. "*Jesú,* you feel good!" he told her.

Beneath him Lucianna laughed softly. "May I return the compliment, Husband?" she asked softly.

He began to move on her. Very slowly at first, for he did not wish to conclude this delicious interlude too quickly. But their combined lust was just too great for both of them. Wordlessly, she encouraged him to increase his thrusts. Her breath began to come in short pants. Her legs wrapped themselves about his torso, allowing him deeper access. With the strength that could only be exhibited by a man of experience, the earl was able to hold off his own pleasure until he saw his wife gaining it. With a groan he exploded, his boiling juices filling her eager and welcoming womb.

"I love you!" he told her as his heart began to slow itself back to a normal rhythm, and he kissed her gently.

"I love you too!" Lucianna heard herself admit aloud as she curled into the curve of his arm. "I should have said it before, but I could not quite voice it."

He did not inquire as to why she struggled to speak her love of him to him, for he had always known she felt it. Lucianna was a proud woman. Better he not question her. "I am glad you love me," was his simple response, and his arm tightened about her.

After some minutes had passed, Lucianna said, "We cannot remain here all day, my lord, and do not ask why not. You know the answer to that. Do you think Lady Margaret will tell the king you are in London?" she wondered aloud.

"I think tomorrow we must present our-selves to him. He will learn we are here sooner than later, and he will wonder why we have not come to pay our respects. I will say nothing of this plot we have discovered. I am certain his mother will speak to him of it, and if he wishes, he will question me further. I would learn more of this pre-tender, for if he invades the realm, then King Henry must drive him from it. I will have to join him, Lucianna."

"Is this the English way, then?" she asked him. "My father supports the Medici fam-ily, but if they went to war, he would not join them. But then, the Medici are not the rulers of Florence. They are an important family, it is true, but we are a republic. Even when the pope threatened to excommuni-cate everyone in Florence, we made our decision to ignore him as a city," she told him.

"King Henry's marriage to the heiress Princess Elizabeth of York, and the subse-quent birth of their son, Arthur, has settled a quarrel between the Lancaster and York families that had raged for years," the earl explained to his wife. "The country is finally settling down and cannot be roused by tricksters. This Lambert Simnel claims to be the son of the Duke of Clarence, but that lad is in the Tower. He has been ever since King Henry overcame King Richard. The Irish either will not accept that or are simply enjoying making trouble, and deluding the ignorant. I suspect the latter."

"I have never met any Irish," Lucianna said. "If they came to Florence, they had no need of silk."

"Nay." He smiled. "The Irish have no need of silks. They are great fighters, however, and enjoy nothing better than causing difficulties for England."

"Perhaps if your kings would cease their interference in Ireland, the Irish would not be so eager to make trouble for England," Lucianna said, and then she smiled at his surprise.

"I thought you had never met any Irish," he said.

"I haven't but for one. For two years we had a tutor who came from that place. He told us stories of the last king of all of Ireland, a man named Brian Boru. And there was a princess called Red Ava who wed an English lord. Our tutor's name was Master Cormac. He went to Rome with Giorgio, our brother. He was very devout, and my parents liked him greatly. Is it not true that the English interfere in Ireland, my lord?" she asked him innocently.

He did not give her an answer, saying instead, "It would be unwise to voice such sentiments before Lady Margaret or the king."

Lucianna smiled. "You have without saying given me an answer, my lord," she told him.

Robert Minton chuckled. "What a vixen, *volpe femina,* you are, my Lucianna."

Luca returned home in midafternoon.

"Why have you departed the shop so early?" she demanded of him. "When you return home, our father will not allow such a thing."

"Baram is there to close up, and there is little business on a sunny summer's day," he said. "I will take my meal, and then go to the tavern to see if I can conclude this business so I am free to return to Florence. I am not of a mind to endure another English winter."

Lucianna shook her head. Well, he would shortly be her father's problem. Giovanni Pietro d'Angelo would not tolerate a second son ignoring his business. He would take Luca in hand, and Lucianna almost laughed. Their seemingly gentle father could be very hard when he wanted something, and he wanted his world to run smoothly.

Why were her siblings so troublesome?

Marco, with more interest in his mistresses than his trade. Bianca, running off with an infidel. Francesca, widowed and refusing to marry again. Her youngest sister, Giulia, insisting that everyone now call her by her second Christian name, Serena, and refusing to answer to any other. Only Giorgio and she could be called respectful children. Then she reconsidered. Well, perhaps only Giorgio. She had, after all, wed without gaining their blessing first, although she knew that her father would be pleased, for he had really sent her to England for the purpose of seeing if the Earl of Lisle truly loved her. Though her mother would fuss, she would be content to have her third daughter wed into the nobility, even if it was English nobility. And to a close personal friend of its king, moreover. Oh yes, Orianna would give them her blessing as well.

Luca took his meal with them, and then arose to go.

"Be careful," Lucianna cautioned him, but said nothing more.

He bent by her chair, kissing her cheek. "You worry too much, Sister mine," he teased gently. Then with a nod to his brother-in-law, Luca left them.

"I wish we could go home," Lucianna said. "I feel safer at Wye Court than I do in

London now."

He nodded. "I am not much for the city either," he agreed, "but Lady Margaret has asked us to remain, and so we must. Tomorrow we shall go to court to be seen. It would seem odd if we did not."

"And if Lady Margaret and her ladies are there, you will point out this wench she thought to wed you to, my lord?"

"If you promise me you will not scratch her eyes out," he said with a wicked grin.

"I merely wish to see this creature the king's mother thought would make an acceptable wife for you," Lucianna told him. "You cannot deny me my curiosity, Roberto. I am a woman, after all."

The earl chuckled. She was indeed a woman — his woman, and he could imagine being wed to no other.

Lucianna could not sleep that night until she heard her brother's footfall upon the stairs and knew he was safely home. This business in which he had found himself frightened her. How could anyone seriously considering overthrowing Henry Tudor think such a mindless plan as freeing the young Earl of Warwick from the Tower would be successful? The boy was very well guarded, since he could indeed prove a threat to the king's tenure as England's king.

And why would anyone want to involve a foreigner in such a plot? The only reason she could think of was to place blame elsewhere, but why Luca? Had it been a simple coincidence? Or did someone, as she had previously considered, seek to tarnish the Earl of Lisle's good name and friendship with the king? Lucianna sighed, and resigned herself to the fact she might never have the answer to her questions.

Fortunately, much of Lucianna's wardrobe had remained in London, and so she had the proper garments to wear to court. It would hardly do to present herself looking like a country woman. For her first appearance at court, she decided to be elegant rather than subdued. The women would gossip more about her clothing than they would of her. Flawless manners would be appreciated, but for women it was her gown that would count.

With this in mind, Lucianna chose one of deep green silk. Its square neckline with a panel that ran the gown's length to its hem, the hem itself, and the cuffs on the gown's wide sleeves were embroidered in a green-and-gold braid. As this shade of green and gold were the favored colors of the Tudor family, Lucianna's choice subtly declared her loyalties to the ruler. The low-cut hip belt was of the embroidered material. She wore a single gold chain, at the end of which dangled a gold-and-ruby crucifix.

Cleva had helped her to dress and was enthusiastic about her mistress's choice as she slipped the round-toed shoes on Lucianna's feet.

"Will you come to London often, my lady?" she asked her.

"Now and again," Lucianna answered her, not wanting to disappoint and tell her housekeeper that she would never come if such a thing were possible. "I like Wye Court and the country. Yet I grew up in a city. Is that not odd? But you and the others will continue to keep the house for me. My family may wish to visit London now that I am to make my life in England."

Cleva was pleased to learn they should not all be put out on the street. "We shall endeavor to serve you in any way we can, my lady," she answered, the relief in her voice evident.

The earl approved his wife's gown with a smile. "My clever Florentine wife," was his pronouncement upon seeing her. He was dressed simply in silk hose, an embroidered doublet, a fine cotton shirt, and an ankle-length coat with wide, flared sleeves. His shoes were the finest leather, and from the gold chain he wore hung a pendant with his family's insignia: a stallion with head and front leg bent as if bowing, and above it a small crown and the words *Ever Faithful* edging it. It wisely espoused no faction — just loyalty to the ruler.

Lucianna curtsied, acknowledging his compliment. "I do not know if I like your looking so particularly handsome, my lord. Hearts have already been broken, if I am to believe your boasts," she teased.

"I could look no less elegant than my wife," he countered, and they both laughed.

Outside the house, the earl's horse was waiting for him, as well as Flynt and Ford, Lucianna's two litter bearers, smiling as they prepared to convey her. It seemed odd being carried through the streets again after riding from Wye Court, but it was a better mode of transportation, considering her gown.

When she reached the palace, her husband was there to hand her out, having already dismounted so his animal might be brought to the stables. The litter bearers would join others of their ilk awaiting their masters and mistresses.

"Your hand is like ice," the earl noted.

"I am perhaps a bit nervous," Lucianna admitted. "Coming into a royal presence is new for me."

"I know you have met the Medici," he answered, surprised.

"That is different. Lorenzo is no king," Lucianna replied, "and I have known him my whole life."

"I have known Henry Tudor most of my life," he replied. "I will not deny he is majestic, but you need not fear him, and the queen is a very sweet young woman." He rubbed the icy fingers between his two hands, and then he led her into the palace.

Lucianna hardly noticed where they were going until she found herself in a hall filled with people. Her husband was greeted, and she was inspected by curious eyes as he led her to where the king sat, a pretty young woman on one side of him, his mother on the other. Robert bowed as Lucianna curtsied to the monarchs.

"I did not expect to see you back in London so soon, Robert," the king said to the earl.

"There are matters we need to settle before we may retire to Wye Court, my liege," the earl said. "May I present my bride to you?"

Lucianna curtsied again as the king inclined his head towards her. "You are exceedingly pretty, madame," he said. "My mother speaks highly of you. Her praise is not lightly given."

"The Lady Margaret's favor honors me, Your Majesty," Lucianna replied, with a small smile.

Her response pleased the king, who sent a fond look towards his parent. "You are most welcome at my court, Countess."

They had been recognized and approved. They moved away from the seated king.

"Well done," Robert murmured to her.

"He is very serious," Lucianna said. "Is he always so grave?"

The earl nodded. "Even as a boy. He understood his situation far better than those about him did. He laughs now and again, but not often. His concern is for England, and for his family. He would not have any take him for less than he is," Robert explained.

"He said I was pretty. You say I am beautiful," Lucianna said.

"You are beautiful," her husband replied. "The king is not given to hyperbole. That he said anything at all is an indication of his regard. He does not often offer compliments to any, let alone a woman."

"Do you see this wench of Lady Margaret's here?" Lucianna asked him, pleased by his words.

He chuckled, and then cast about to see if he might spy Cat Talcott. "Let me see," he said, and was surprised to find her quickly. What was more, she was staring directly at him and Lucianna. "Do not make a show of looking, but she is there, just below the dais to the left," he said softly. He found her gaze a bit unnerving.

"The bold baggage in the lavender gown?" Lucianna asked him.

He chuckled. So she had noticed the stare. "Yes, the maid in the lavender gown."

"I think her hair more the dun-color of a plow horse, not chestnut," Lucianna said. "I am surprised Lady Margaret would have considered someone quite so ordinary for you."

"Her family connections are impressive," he told her, struggling not to laugh. Lucianna's jealousy had exhibited itself once again, and he was both flattered and amused by it.

"They would have to be," his wife responded dryly.

Now he did laugh. "You are jealous," he teased her.

"I am." She did not deny it. "I should be jealous of any woman who thought to have you for herself. You are mine, Roberto! *Mine!*"

"It is fortunate then that you are the only woman for me," the earl told her. "You are mine, *amore mia.* And only mine."

Now that they had paid their respects to the king, men who had known Robert Minton began coming up to him to be introduced to his beautiful new wife. She was paid extravagant compliments, and she found herself relaxing, laughing, and being admired for her charm and her wit. By the time the earl decided it was time to return home, Lucianna found herself less intimidated. She did notice, however, that there were very few women at this court, and afterwards she asked her husband why.

"The reign is new," he explained, "and it is still not secure. While their lords have been fighting all these years, the women have remained at home holding their estates, guarding their children. Many have never even been to court. The adherents of the Lancasters did not, as a rule, populate the court of York. In time that will change, when it becomes apparent that King Henry will not be overcome by any, but for now, most of the ladies you will see belong to either Lady Margaret's or the queen's households."

Lucianna could see the sense in that and nodded her understanding. "If everyone's estates are as beautiful as Wye Court, I should not want to come to court," she told him.

"It pleases me to hear you say it," Robert Minton admitted. "It has concerned me that, having been raised in a bustling city, you would miss London. I am glad you do not. Do you miss Florence, Lucianna?"

She shook her head in the negative. "Not so much that you should change your plan to steal me away," Lucianna teased him, but then seeing distress upon his handsome face, she added reassuringly, "My home is where you are, Roberto *mio*. I will always be content to be by your side, wherever that may be."

"No man should have a weakness," he told her, "but you seem to be mine, *amore mia.*"

Neither of them noticed Lady Margaret's maid-in-waiting, Cat Talcott, watching them enviously.

"He makes much of her," a girl standing next to her said. Like all of Lady Margaret's maids, she knew their mistress had once considered the Earl of Lisle as a possible husband for Cat. Cat had been furious when she learned the earl had married. Then, upon learning who it was he had wed, she had been even angrier.

"You imagine it," Cat replied tersely.

"Give over, Cat," her companion said. "Any fool can see they are in love with each other. I think it is very romantic."

"Love? Why would such a nebulous emotion brought about by the eagerness of cock and cunt to join have anything to do with a marriage? Marriage is about status, land, gold, and gaining new allies from other important families for your own."

"If all he wanted to do was couple with her," the other girl said, "he would not have wed her, would he? And if she were as low as you persist in believing she is, she would have been honored and content to be just his mistress. Our good lady will find another for you, Cat. Or you will wed your father's choice when you return home. Respectable women must be married, and you are already seventeen, the oldest of us all now. I expect you will go home before the winter."

"You know nothing," Cat Talcott snapped at the girl. "I will have Lisle sooner than later, you may be certain. I do not mean to permit that foreign shopkeeper to have the earl I was promised."

"Lady Margaret never promised him to you," her fellow maid-in-waiting said. "She said he might be an eligible choice since his lands are near your family's, but she never promised he would be your husband. It was you who decided that, Cat Talcott, and frankly I am glad the earl married his true love. She is probably already with child. We are all right sick of hearing you brag how you would have the finest husband of us all." Then the speaker left Cat Talcott staring at the departing figures of the Earl of Lisle and his bride.

"Will you never learn to conceal your emotions?"

She looked up to see her cousin, Sir Ralph Sand.

"Do you still moon after your earl who isn't your earl?" he taunted her wickedly. "His countess is quite a beauty. Even the king noticed and remarked upon it."

"You find her attractive? I think her features common," Cat said.

He laughed aloud. "Oh my, we are piqued, aren't we?"

"The king was being courteous," Cat replied.

"Courtesy is to greet a favored friend's bride pleasantly, not remark to all listening on her beauty," Cat's cousin answered. "I doubt he would have had you anyway, and that should have proven far more embarrassing, my pet."

"I will have him in the end," Cat told him. "No one takes what I have marked as mine."

"Indeed, Cousin? I should like to see just how you will accomplish your impossible goal," and he laughed again.

CHAPTER 15

The plot in which Luca Pietro d'Angelo found himself involved seemed to drag on, reaching no conclusion. He was wary of questioning the conspirators too closely, lest they become suspicious of him. Luca attempted to withdraw his company from them.

"I have studied your map of the Tower," he said to them. "I have shown you the best way to enter unseen. You no longer need me."

"Nay," the man who usually did the talking said, "we need you to come with us on the chance we lose our way."

"I know the way no better than you," Luca said. "If your map is correct, then the way I have indicated to you is the best way. I can be involved no further, as I have no interest in who your king is. I will shortly return to my own city."

"But you are cleverer than we are, and

341

you can speak with any we might meet without rousing suspicion," the man protested.

"If you are wise, you should avoid meeting anyone in that place, lest they know you are about some mischief," Luca responded. "You asked me to find you an obscure way into this Tower of London. I have studied the plans you gave me, and indicated how you may go. I will do nothing more." Then he pretended to grow suspicious of them. "Are you in the pay of that scurvy merchant from Milan? Do you seek to involve me further in your plot that I might bring dishonor on my guild?" he demanded to know, glaring at them.

"No, no, good master!" the conspirator protested. "We know naught of whom you speak."

"Then who has put you up to this?" Luca insisted. "Neither of you, it would seem to me, should have a quarrel with your king, or any reason to commit treason, for this is treason of which you have been speaking. You do understand that, don't you?"

His two companions shrugged. "We mean no treason. We were approached by another who told us to ask for your aid," the one who always spoke said finally.

"What did he look like?" Luca asked.

" 'Twas not a man, good master. It was a serving woman," came the answer that caught Luca by surprise. "We met her but once. She instructed us but once, and we saw her no more."

"Did not such an occurrence seem odd to you?" Luca queried.

"She paid us each a gold piece," the man explained. "I would do anything for that kind of coin, even if I cannot spend it. If others knew we had such wealth, they would think we had obtained it illegally, or seek to steal it from us."

Luca wanted to laugh, but he did not. What a pair of dolts that they would agree to attempt treason by helping to free the young Earl of Warwick, and not even realize what it was they were being asked to do. "Did this serving woman tell you what to do if you could obtain my help?" he asked them.

"Oh yes, master. We were to breach the Tower with you and free the prisoner. The old woman said you must be with us, for you would know best," the hapless conspirator said.

Luca shook his head. "We will not meet again," he said, getting up to leave them.

"But we cannot do this without you!" the man protested.

"You cannot do this at all," Luca replied dryly.

"What if the woman seeks the return of her coin?"

"Threaten to expose her as a treasonous bitch," Luca told the pair, and then he departed the tavern to go home. He had no intention of returning. Once his brother-in-law knew there was no danger of any treason, the earl would inform Lady Margaret. Then Luca might return to Florence while travel was still a pleasant prospect.

It was still reasonably early when he arrived at his sister's house. He found Luci-anna and Roberto in the hall, discussing their day. "I bring good tidings," Luca announced, joining them. He took the goblet of wine his sister offered him. "This plot is nothing, my lord," he told his brother-in-law. Then he explained his words.

"*Jesú!* Mary!" the Earl of Lisle swore when he had heard the tale that Luca related to him of his early-evening meeting. "A bigger pair of fools I have yet to hear of, Luca."

"I would send to arrest the pair and clap them in the king's prison for a brief sojourn just to bring home the foolishness of what they involved themselves in," Luca said.

"They were driven by greed," the earl

responded. "To make this public in any way would do no more to cause the king worry. I am curious as to who put them up to it, however."

"I believe they really do not know," Luca said.

"It was a woman," Lucianna said, and the two men looked at her, surprised. "It was a woman," she repeated.

"Why do you say that?" the earl asked his wife.

"Would a man send his serving woman to recruit two such villains?" Lucianna asked. "I think not."

"Have you offended any lady during your time here?" the earl inquired of Luca.

"Nay, my lord. I have confined my amours to serving women, and have had no opportunity to meet ladies of quality. I am always busy with the shop, or riding for exercise outside the city," Luca said.

"I surely have not offended any husband, brother, or father."

"Nor would such a person have gold with which to tempt others," Lucianna observed wisely, "or have concocted such a silly scheme, or one that, if they were caught, would attract the authority of the king. I still would consider if you have any enemies, my lord."

"We all have enemies," her husband said, "but there should be none who would seek to harm me. I am no threat to any, nor have I threatened others."

"Then unless we unravel the mystery of who would seek to harm any of us individually, or as a family, we cannot know," Lucianna said.

"I will inform Lady Margaret of this turn of events tomorrow," the earl said. "Then perhaps we may arrange for Luca's return to Florence. Your father is certain to need him back, and by the time we hear from him, the weather may not be as salubrious for travel."

The following morning, both Lucianna and her husband visited Lady Margaret. She dismissed her ladies, telling them to walk in her garden. Cat Talcott lingered behind, making certain she was the last to leave the king's mother. The other women and girls were ahead of her, and she waited until they had gone into the gardens before returning to listen outside the door of Lady Margaret's privy chamber.

"This plot was no more than a fraud," she heard the earl say. "Whoever thought to engineer it meant no harm towards the king. Whether they sought to damage my reputation, or my wife's, or her brother's by association, I cannot tell you, madame. I should like to be able to, but alas, the two conspirators who approached Luca knew no more than that a serving woman had given them each a gold piece to involve Luca in a plan to enter the Tower illegally and remove Warwick. They had never seen the woman before, nor have they since."

"A woman's ploy," Lady Margaret said slowly. "Who have you or your brother-in-law offended?"

"Luca swears no one, as do I. I have been much too busy since Lucianna came to England with courting her. It is curious that you would believe a woman is involved, for my wife said the same thing."

"Did you indeed, madame?" Lady Margaret said, with a small and wintery smile. "Does your brother speak true, or does he attempt to hide his pecadillos from you?"

"Luca speaks the truth, madame," Lucianna said. "Remember that we are twins, and I always have known what he is thinking. He has always confided in me alone."

The king's mother nodded. "Have you made an enemy, madame?"

"Not to my knowledge, madame. The only females with whom I have any congress are servants. There has been no opportunity for me to make friends with any. My closest companion is my serving woman, Balia, who has been with me several years."

Lady Margaret understood. She was a woman whose time had been taken up guarding and guiding her only child's safety and future. She had no brothers or sisters, and if truth be known, she trusted no one but herself and her son. Trust was something that could be betrayed. She had learned that at an early age when the first marriage contract arranged for her had been dissolved. A great heiress, daughter of John Beaufort, the Duke of Somerset, she had been married at twelve to Edmund Tudor, and found herself a widow at the age of fourteen, several months before her son was born. She had never feared for herself, only for her child. She had done everything for him. In the end, she had seen him obtain the crown of England.

"I am relieved, then, to learn this is just some foolish mischief, and not a serious threat to the king," she told her two guests. "I think that Luca Pietro d'Angelo may return home safely now, but first he must identify the two miscreants for me. Perhaps a little torture will loosen their tongues further. Foolish or not, I would know the architect of this plot that was no plot."

Listening, Cat Talcott was horrified by her

mistress's words. Then she realized that the two bumbling fools her serving woman had recruited did not know the woman, nor from where she had come. She hoped, nonetheless, that they had already fled when the silk merchant refused to attempt to go with them to the Tower. Perhaps she would do well to send the wench packing, but no. She needed her servant.

Moving away from the door to Lady Margaret's privy chamber, Cat Talcott went to discreetly join the other ladies. Hopefully they would not have missed her. If only she had been able to implicate the silk merchant in a plot against the king. It would have for certain tarnished the reputation of his sister, and the earl would realize his error. Lady Margaret would see that the marriage was annulled. The foreign woman would be sent packing.

And when that happened, she, Lady Catherine Talcott, daughter of the Earl of Southwold, would become the wife of Robert Minton, the Earl of Lisle. Ever since she had overheard Lady Margaret discussing such a possibility with an older lady in her household, Cat Talcott had dreamed of such a marriage. They were well matched as far as bloodlines went, and her dower portion was respectable. She was perfect for him.

Certainly the foreign bitch could not be, but she had obviously bewitched Robert Minton. Now Cat would have to think of another plan to rid herself of her rival. And she would.

Lady Margaret called her page to her from the garden, where he had been amusing her ladies with a song. "Thomas, fetch me the captain of the guard," she told the boy. They waited, and when the soldier appeared, Lady Margaret told him, "Send a small troop of men-at-arms with Master Pietro d'Angelo. He will take you to an inn to point out two traitors to His Majesty. Arrest them, and put them in the Tower for questioning."

"What if my refusal to aid them has caused them to flee?" Luca wondered aloud.

"More than likely they have not," Lady Margaret told him. "They are greedy fools who, I suspect, agreed to aid in this plot only for the coin put in their hand. Still, I must make certain of that myself. However, I cannot help but wonder why someone would conspire in such a foolish intrigue."

"I doubt our two miscreants will know, madame," the earl said. "As I said, my wife says this is a woman's doing."

"Interesting," Lady Margaret replied thoughtfully. Then she dismissed her two visitors, who joined the men-at-arms, leading them to the tavern Luca visited each evening.

As the king's mother had predicted, the two were already drinking their coin away. Luca quietly pointed them out and departed before they might see him. He did not bother to watch, concealed, as the two were dragged protesting from the tavern. That evening, he returned to have the tavern keeper tell him that "his two friends" had been arrested that same afternoon.

"They were no friends of mine," Luca said. "They thought because I was a foreigner they might get me to buy them drinks. I am a respectable silk merchant and do not consort with men like that. Do you know why they were arrested?"

The tavern keeper shrugged. "Who knows, with men like that?" he said. "More than likely they offended someone. I asked one of the soldiers where they were being taken, and he said the Tower."

"This Tower," Luca responded, pretending ignorance, "it is a prison for scum?"

"It is a prison for all manner of men, and sometimes women," the tavern keeper said dryly. "Best you never see the inside of it."

"I'll be returning to Florence shortly," Luca told him. Then he took his mug of ale and found a seat in a corner.

Lady Margaret sent the next day to tell the Earl of Lisle that torture had gained no answers. The two bungling conspirators could not tell the king's mother who had required their services. There was no real treason involved at all, as Lucianna had suspected.

"Now can we go home?" the Countess of Lisle asked her husband.

"We will go home," he told her.

Luca's passage was arranged. Her brother would depart London in a week for Florence. The earl and his wife would go home on the morrow.

"It is unlikely we will see each other again," Lucianna told her twin brother. "It is important that I give Roberto an heir, and I will not leave my child to travel." They sat together in the hall of her London dwelling the evening before his departure.

He nodded, understanding completely. The safe and loving childhood that they had shared with each other and their siblings had come to an end for them. Only their youngest sister, Serena, remained at home. Luca knew he would marry sooner than later and have his own family. It was the way of the world. Still, he had always hoped that Lucianna would remain near him. Having shared their mother's womb, and much of their lives together, he was saddened to realize it was very unlikely they would see each other again. "You will write?" he asked, knowing she would but wanting to be certain.

"I will," she replied. Then she smiled, teasingly. "Will you?"

Luca laughed. "Now and again," he promised. "You know I am not much of a correspondent, Sister."

"Now and again will do, Luca," Lucianna said. Then she said, "There may come a time when our mother can no longer write to me, and I should not like to be entirely cut off from the family of my childhood."

"Does Francesca write?" he asked her.

"Francesca?" Lucianna sniffed. "She is too busy ruling her son's duchy to bother with a younger sister. And Giorgio's ambitions are entirely focused on gaining the red hat of a cardinal. Having been in Rome all these years, he considers little else. Or so our mother writes."

Luca chuckled. "However, if he gained a cardinal's biretta, our mother would consider it every bit as prestigious as a good marriage for one of her daughters. She would shout it to any and all who would listen to her. It is not likely, though. Our sister Bianca's scandalous behavior has touched us all."

Lucianna said nothing. Her brother did not understand the situation the way she did. Her elder sister's second union was for love. Love was important, as Lucianna had discovered. While her own first marriage had not been the horror that poor Bianca's had been, both of them had chosen their own second husbands. It was Bianca's choice of an Ottoman prince that had caused the scandal that would have harmed her sisters' chances at marriage, except for their determined mother. Yet her second daughter was a duchess, and now the third was a countess.

Lucianna's twin brother, however, had always been particularly close to their mother. She had doted upon him, especially after having birthed her last child, another daughter. Lucianna knew that Orianna would be very happy to see Luca come home. As for her twin brother, she knew he would be delighted to be back in Florence, even if he was no longer a military officer.

"I will miss you," she told him.

"And I, you," he responded.

"You will take care of our parents, Luca. Marco is more interested in his women, and our youngest sister will eventually be wed.

They will need you," Lucianna told him.

He nodded. "I will remain at home, even if I wed, to see they are cared for, but of course our mother will never admit to any need."

Lucianna laughed. "No, she will not, nor would I. Our mother is a proud lady, Brother, but you will see she never realizes that you are looking after her welfare when she needs such care." Lucianna rose to embrace her brother. "We go at first light, which comes early at this time of year. Be safe and be happy always, Luca, my brother." She kissed his cheek.

"And you be happy as well, sister mine," he said, returning the kiss. He dared say nothing else, for he realized that he was feeling an actual pain at the knowledge he was unlikely to ever see his twin sister again in his lifetime. He wondered if she felt the pang as well.

In the early light of the predawn, the Earl and Countess of Lisle departed London for their home at Wye Court. While there was less urgency for this trip than their previous one to London, they were both eager to resume their ordinary lives. Once home, they settled back into the pattern of their everyday life. The earl spent his day managing his estates while his countess spent her time overseeing her household and the village, which was her obligation as well.

Lucianna found that this new lifestyle, while vastly different from her previous responsibilities, seemed to suit her very well. If there was one thing missing, it was a child, but Balia assured her the child would come. Especially considering all the time Lucianna and her husband spent together in their bed. "You have been wed but a few weeks, my lady." Hearing this tart observation, young Mali giggled and then blushed when Balia shot her an outraged look.

The king sent to Robert Minton to tell him that the pretender had been crowned King Edward VI by the Irish in Dublin. There was bound to be war eventually, and it came quickly. The forces of the Yorkist rebels had landed in Lancaster, and they had already begun their march over the Pennines. The Earl of Lisle was summoned to join the king's forces.

"Why must you go?" Lucianna asked him. "Men of property do not go to war in Florence. That is why Lorenzo keeps an army."

"In England," he explained, "it is a man's duty, be he of high station or low, to support his king in battle. This will be over quickly, and these Yorkist pretensions must be put to rest once and for all. This should end it, although I would have thought the battle we fought at Bosworth several years ago ended it."

"Is it possible this boy is who he says he is?" Lucianna wondered aloud.

"Nay, he is not. King Edward's sons disappeared from the Tower and were never again seen."

"How long will you be gone from Wye?" Lucianna inquired.

"However long it takes to defeat these rebels, *amore mia.* I like it no better than you, but I cannot refuse to go. And I must take with me a small troop of men, most of whom are unlikely to return, for the fighting will be hard, Lucianna. This is a battle for a kingdom."

Her mother had never had to face her husband going off to a war, Lucianna thought, but then she was not her mother. And she was no longer living in Florence. She was English, and living in a northern land where loyal subjects joined their king in battle.

"You cannot know for how long you will be gone," she said. "Will Worrell be able to manage in your absence? What should I know that I do not, Roberto? What must I do to help and keep Wye Court safe?"

"Worrell will see to the land and the stock,

but you will have to oversee my records, which include the births of beasts. There are at least two more heifers almost ready to calve. Worrell will tell you if they are bull or female, and you must enter that in my books. We grow and make almost all of what we use and need. You will know what you need should a peddler come to the village. I offer hospitality to any who come peaceably, and so must you, even if I am not here," he explained.

"I understand," she said. "And hopefully you will not be gone long." Wars, she knew, could last for months. "But how am I to recognize friend from foe? I would not unknowingly give hospitality to a Yorkist rebel, my lord."

"The battle will be more north," he said. "It is unlikely any Yorkists will come this far south, for we are too close to Wales, the stronghold of the Tudor family."

"Who leads these rebels?" Lucianna asked, curious.

"The Earl of Lincoln, one of the last of the Plantagenets. King Richard made him his heir after his own son died. And I suspect Lord Lovell is involved too."

The names were familiar but actually meant little to her, as she had not become involved in the court. Lucianna nodded.

"Do you think they can win?" she queried her husband.

"In war, no one can be certain who will win," he replied. "The king has sufficient forces, but so, I suspect, do the rebels." What she was really asking him was whether she thought he could come home safely, but of course he could not answer her one way or another. He put his arms around her. "This is likely to be quick, *amore mia*. And hopefully it will be the last of it."

"I hope so," Lucianna said softly. She didn't want him to go, but then what woman sent her man off to war willingly? She could not make it more difficult for him by weeping. She wasn't the only woman in England now with a husband going off to war.

He left the next morning, taking twenty men with him. They were men-at-arms for the estate. He would not risk the lives of the untrained.

The earl noted as they rode that the countryside about them seemed unsettled with this new possibility of war. He reached the king's forces on the fourteenth of June, going at once to pay his respects to the monarch, noting those others about the king who were given to gossip.

Henry Tudor had been taught almost from the moment of his birth to be wary of others. He gave his trust to few, which, given the men who populated the court, seemed wise to Robert Minton. Everyone came to gain something for himself, for his family. It was the nature of man. Therefore, it was better to be cautious, the king had once told Robert Minton, and the earl agreed.

John de Vere, the Earl of Oxford, nodded to Robert Minton. "How many men did you bring?" he asked in practical tones.

"Twenty, all mounted," the Earl of Lisle replied. "I am a small estate, de Vere, as you surely know."

"You came," was the dry reply.

"I will always come when the king asks it of me," was the reply.

"Many profess loyalty, but . . ." the Earl of Oxford, replied with a shrug.

Robert Minton nodded, understanding. There had been so much war in England for years that, for some men, being asked to choose a side was difficult. But he knew a man could not always be right, which was why in many families one son would support one side and another son would champion the other side. "We will overcome Lincoln and his band of traitors, my lord," he said, knowing something positive was expected of him. That simple sentence would be enough.

They marched towards the enemy the following day without encountering them. On the morning of the sixteenth of June, outside of the village of Stoke, they finally came upon them. The rebels were lined up in a straight line upon the edge of a steep hill. They were surrounded on three sides by the river Trent.

Robert Minton swore softly under his breath. It was a virtually impregnable position. Having to fight their way uphill was going to be very difficult, and it was bound to result in a serious number of casualties. But then he heard Oxford exclaim, "*Jesú!* Is Lincoln mad?"

A gasp of shock arose from the men around them. The rebel forces were giving up their position of relative safety on the high ground and charging towards the king's forces. The battle was enjoined and raged on for the next several hours. The royalists were outnumbered by the rebels, but the royalist troops were better trained and better equipped. No quarter would be given by either side, and when the battle came to an end in the early afternoon, more than four thousand rebels were dead, but only one hundred of the king's men had perished.

The king did not wait to pass judgment

upon the survivors. The rebel leaders not killed in the fighting — and most had been, to their credit — were immediately executed. The Irish lords and their surviving men were pardoned and told to go home to Ireland. Henry Tudor was no fool. He would need these lordlings to keep the peace in the Ireland he ruled. As for the pretender, Lambert Simnel, the king spared him as well.

"He does indeed have the look of York about him," Henry Tudor said, "but he is innocent of deceit and has been used by ambitious men. God has seen to the right of it, so I will take him into my household as a servant. Give him to the cook as a turnspit."

The pretender fell to his knees and thanked the king for his clemency. Henry smiled, one of his rare and wintery smiles. He had shown his fairness by punishing only the truly guilty, and pardoning the less guilty. It was just the sort of behavior his clever mother would have exhibited. Some of the king's lords thought the surviving rebels had gotten off too easily, and murmured about it among themselves. The Earl of Lisle kept his own counsel.

"Will you not remain with me, Rob?" the king asked him later that evening when the others had gone to their own tents.

"You do not need me, Henry," the earl said, using the king's Christian name. Although he was permitted to do so, he rarely did. "But Wye Court needs me, and my wife needs me. You have chosen your counselors well. The queen you wed has given you a fine son in Prince Arthur. While I considered Bosworth the end of the conflict between Lancaster and York, this battle two years after will certainly end it for good now."

"There will always be those who yearn for Edward's sons. As long as no bodies are found, they will continue to hope," the king said.

"Can you be certain that they are dead?" the earl asked daringly, which he never had before.

Henry Tudor shrugged. "I honestly do not know, Rob. I did not order such murder, nor would my mother, and Richard loved those lads as much as his own boy. If Edward of York and his younger brother, Richard, are dead, it was not my doing, and certainly not my wish."

"It is to be hoped then that this pretender will be the last of your troubles," Robert Minton said. "Will Your Majesty give me permission to depart with my men tomorrow?"

The king sighed. "Is she as amenable as she is fair?" he asked his friend, curious.

"Yes," the earl told him. "But stubborn too. She wants a child now, and I need an heir. I will not get one remaining with you."

"Hah!" The king barked a short laugh. "Nay, you will not. Very well, Rob, you have my permission to leave on the morrow."

"I will always come when you call, my lord," the earl reassured the king quietly. "If you need me, I will be there." He arose and bowed.

"Go home, then, to your lovely wife and your Wye Court. Perhaps one day I will come and visit you there so I may understand why you love it so much." The king waved him off.

"You can see the hills of Wales from my lands, Henry, and you will be welcome should you ever come." But Robert Minton knew that Henry Tudor was quite unlikely to ever come to Wye Court. He bowed again, and then turning, departed the king's presence.

Joining his men, he told them, "We leave for home come the morning, lads. You have done well, and we have been fortunate to return with all of those we came with riding upright, not slung across a saddle." They cheered him, knowing how lucky they all had been. They were not fighting men by nature, and they would be glad to return to their peaceful homes.

CHAPTER 16

The Earl of Lisle had arrived home to discover that his wife had gone missing the day before. Balia was frantic with worry. Worrell, his bailiff, was racked by remorse for having allowed the lady to ride the estate without an escort.

"She was only going to the far cottages, my lord. She did not wish to trouble me, she said, when we were short in the fields because of the king's war. She should have been safe, my lord. She should have been safe. 'Twas just a short distance, and she was a-horse."

"Why was she going to the far cottages?" the earl asked. What mischief was this? Perhaps Lucianna had been correct when she said the plot to involve Luca was an attempt to strike out at Robert Minton.

"She said she was told that the two motherless children of a worker had the spotting sickness," the bailiff said.

"She wanted to confirm that," Balia put in, "lest it spread to others and we have so much sickness that the crops be neglected."

"Who brought your lady the information, Balia?" the earl asked.

Balia turned to Mali. "You were with her when she received it," she said. "Who was it?"

"Blacksmith's lass," Mali said immediately without hesitation.

"Has anyone asked her from where she got her information?" the earl inquired patiently, and when heads shook in the negative, he said, "Fetch the blacksmith's lass to me, Worrell."

"Praise God you came home today, my lord," Balia said. Her eyes were red, and it was obvious she had been crying. "I have been so worried, but I knew not what to do."

"There is a reason for my lady's absence," he said, reassuringly, but he was feeling far from reassured. He could not imagine who would steal the wife of an unimportant nobleman. There had been no rumor of bandits in the region.

The blacksmith's lass was frightened. "I ain't done nothing wrong, my lord," she sobbed when brought before the earl.

"Cease your howling," Robert Minton

said sternly. "I simply wish to know who told you to tell my lady that there was sickness in the far cottages, girl."

"He give me a ha'penny, my lord, he did. I can buy ribbons when the summer peddler comes," she replied.

Jesú save me, Robert Minton thought. The wench was stupid beyond belief. His fists clenched by his sides.

Seeing it, Mali quickly said, "Who give you the ha'penny, lucky girl? Wish I had a ha'penny for ribbons." She grinned at the blacksmith's daughter.

"Never seen him before, Mali," the girl answered. "I was tending Ma's geese when he come upon me. Was riding a fine horse too he was. 'Wench,' says he, 'can you take a message to the countess? I'll give you a ha'penny if you do.' Well, of course I tell him I can. The lady is ever so kind, and when she rides out each day, she greets me by name. 'Good day, Nelwyna,' the lady says to me. Imagine! She knows me by my name."

"She's a good mistress," Mali said. "Tell me more."

"Well, he gives me the ha'penny and warns me if I don't tell the lady there is sickness among the children in the far cottages, he'll be back for his coin. Then he rides off.

Shortly afterwards the lady comes riding through the village. 'Good day, Nelwyna,' she says to me. 'Good day, my lady,' I reply. 'I have been told there is sickness among the children in the far cottages and thought you should know.' She thanks me and rides off in that direction. That's all I know, Mali."

"Did she reach the far cottages?" the earl asked his bailiff.

"She did not, my lord. When Balia notified me that the lady had not returned home, I went myself to seek her."

"No children are sick there, are they?" the earl asked, knowing the answer even before he spoke.

Worrell shook his head in the negative. "Nay, my lord, there are no ill children in the far cottages."

"And you saw no sign of the countess or her horse?"

"No, my lord," Worrell said uncomfortably.

Balia's face began to crumble. She began to pray in her native tongue, and he heard pleas to Santa Anna, the Pietro d'Angelo family's own patron saint.

Taking the tiring woman's hand, he looked her directly in the eye and said, "I will find her, Balia. Whoever stole her must proceed with caution. They cannot go far."

"What if they kill her?" Balia half sobbed. She was attempting to keep calm, but she was not succeeding.

"There is no purpose in killing her. She has been taken for one of two purposes. Either for ransom, or because someone believes that I can influence the king. I can, but pray it is a ransom. I can pay a ransom, but no one, save his mother, can really influence the king."

He wasn't surprised to see that Balia didn't look particularly reassured. Now he would have to gather a party of men and seek out his wife. He considered where she might be taken and held, for all the lands about were his. Then he recalled an old stone tower in a wood.

It would be a perfect place to keep a captive.

"Gather a party of men," he told Worrell. "I think I know where my wife may be. And someone get me a fresh horse."

The earl rode out with a dozen men by his side. His destination was several miles distant. They were a short distance from the wood when a rider came into sight, and behind the rider's horse a man, hands bound, was being led. Robert Minton spurred forward, and then, upon seeing who the rider was, began to grin. It was his missing wife, and she had obviously taken prisoner the person who sought to kidnap her.

"Lucianna!" he called, and she waved, smiling. Their horses met.

"What happened?" he wanted to know. "Where have you been? Balia is near hysteria with worry and fear. And who is your prisoner?"

"I am tired and hungry," Lucianna said. "Can we go home first, and then I will explain everything that I can? I have no idea who this *idiota* is. It was not hard to gain his trust and free myself."

"Give his lead to Worrell," the earl said, and then spoke to his bailiff. "Bring him to the hall when you get there."

"Aye, my lord." And he took the rope his mistress held from her.

The earl and countess rode ahead of the others, reaching the hall first. Balia wept openly upon seeing her mistress. Lucianna soothed her and asked for something to eat, for she had not eaten, she told them, since the previous day before she went out on her ride. The tiring woman hurried to bring her wine, bread, and cheese as the younger woman sat comfortably near the fire. It might be summer, but the evenings were apt to be cool.

He let her eat, but it was obvious he was anxious to learn whatever she might know.

Finally, Lucianna swallowed a last bit of wine and began. "It seems that someone, though my captor would not say who, would like me dead. I am fortunate my enemy sent the fool because he decided he might attempt to enjoy my favors before he strangled me. He did not. It took several hours before his pains subsided, for I kicked him quite hard," she explained matter-of-factly.

"He did not bind you?" The earl was surprised. What kind of an assassin was this fellow that he did not immobilize his captive?

"Nay, he did not. After I wounded him, he drank quite a bit of wine from a flask he carried, and then the sot fell asleep. When I was certain he was slumbering deeply, I found the rope he should have used on me and bound him. He was so drunk with his wine and the pain, he never even awoke until the following morning.

"He was not pleased to discover his situation, I can tell you. I would have left him there the day before, but the night was upon us by the time I was able to free myself. I thought it better to bring the villain along with me. I'm sure you'll be able to learn more than I certainly could. Thank you for coming to find me, Roberto."

"You are mine, *amore mia,*" he told her.
"No one takes what is mine, Lucianna. I
shall indeed find out from your prisoner
who wants you dead, and more importantly,
why."

They were both curious to learn the
answers they sought when Worrell came into
the hall with the man. "Kneel before the
earl, scum!" Worrell commanded in a hard
voice, and pushed the fellow to his knees
before he might protest.

"Your name?" the earl asked sternly.

The prisoner shrugged. "It matters not
now," he said. "I am Sir Ralph Sand."

"Why do you want my wife dead?" Robert Minton inquired.

"I don't. Damned waste of a beautiful
woman, if you ask me," Sir Ralph Sand said.
"I don't suppose you'd be willing to offer a
man a bit of wine, would you? It was a dusty
trek across your lands."

"After you answer my questions, you may
have wine," the earl told him. "If you don't
want to harm my wife, then who does?"

"Ah," Sir Ralph answered, "now here is
where answers become difficult, my lord.
Do I speak truth, or do I maintain family
loyalty? Would it satisfy you if I said it is a
lady who was disappointed that you wed

elsewhere, and thinks by ridding you of this inconvenient wife she may take her place? Or will you insist on having a name of me?"

"A name, sirrah!" the earl told him. "I was not pledged to any other when I chose to wed my wife. I courted no other. Who is this vile female who would resort to murdering an innocent woman?"

Sir Ralph was silent as he debated how far the earl would go to gain an answer.

Lucianna leaned over and murmured something in her husband's ear. Then she looked at Sir Ralph Sand and said, "It is Catherine Talcott, isn't it, sir?"

"I will neither confirm nor deny it," was the answer she received.

"It is easily proven, and especially if you are her kinsman," the earl told Sir Ralph. He shook his head. "Lady Margaret never even spoke to me about such a match. Why would the wench think otherwise?"

"She overheard the king's mother speaking with one of her women about such a possibility. From that moment on, the lady made up her mind to have you," Sir Ralph Sand said, his words actually acknowledging the relationship with Catherine Talcott.

"Why on earth would she ask you to do such a deed?" the earl said to his prisoner. "Since you linger about the court yet were not with the king, I can only assume you are no soldier."

"The act of kidnapping the lady and strangling her seemed a simple task. As everyone who is acquainted with me knows, I am only fit for simple tasks," Sir Ralph explained.

"Give him some wine," the earl said. He had learned all he needed to know from this man. "Then lock him up. In a few days I shall take him to London and present him to Lady Margaret for her judgment," Robert Minton said.

"*We* will take him to Lady Margaret," Lucianna told her husband. "If you think I shall miss the opportunity to punish this wench myself by making a small spectacle of my rank as your wife, you are sadly mistaken, Roberto."

Sir Ralph burst out laughing. "Lady," he told Lucianna, "nothing could be a greater punishment than to see another with something that this lady desires for herself."

"Take him away," the earl said impatiently, and Lucianna smiled archly as she stood by her husband's side. When they were alone again he said to her, "You are amazing, *amore mia*. Were you not afraid?"

"I was at first," Lucianna admitted. "He came upon me masked, and would have tied my hands had I not cried I would fall off my horse if he did. So he tied me to the horse instead, which is why I could not flee him. He brought me to a rather crumbling-down tower in a wood, and releasing me from the horse, he forced me inside, but he was so intent upon having me he forgot to tie my hands. He kept staring at my breasts," she explained.

"An error he undoubtedly came to regret," the earl noted dryly.

"Once he was incapacitated, I realized how easy it would be for me to escape. The rest you know."

"We are fortunate that stupid chit did not send a skilled killer," Robert Minton said. "I am angry the wench would be so presumptuous as to believe I would have her."

"I am certain she convinced herself that I stole you away in some wicked and unfair manner," Lucianna said. "While it allowed her to justify her own actions, she will now learn otherwise." She shivered. "I am still chilled. Though it be June, England has not the warmth of Florence." Then she paused, realizing he was actually home, and he had been gone but a few days. "Is the battle over, my lord?" she asked her husband. She hoped so.

"Over, and won," he assured her, smiling.

"Henry Tudor's throne is safe. The remaining Yorkists are routed, pardoned, or fled. We are invited to court when we would come," he told her, wondering what she would answer.

"First we must have a son or two," Lucianna responded. "Then I will consider visiting the court. Your friendship with the king should be maintained. Who knows how it might benefit our children one day."

"Ah," he said with a smile, "now you are beginning to think like a wife and a mother."

"I hope I will not turn into my own mother," she fretted.

He laughed aloud. "Orianna simply wants what she perceives as best for her children. All women do, *amore mia.* It is a wise woman's way to want success for her sons, and advantageous marriages for her daughters," he said, excusing his meddling mother-in-law.

"You are able to be so generous of her nature since she is not here," Lucianna reminded him. "Your heart would not be so generous if you had to deal with her every day, as my sisters and I did. Now she has only Serena left to match. I do not know what she will do when she has her youngest safely settled. Mayhap she will come to England."

"She will be most welcome," Robert Minton said.

"Hah! You say it because you think it an impossibility, my lord."

He laughed. "You are coming to know me too well, *amore mia*. And you are correct. I doubt your formidable mother will ever come to England. Travel would discommode Orianna too greatly. We are safe, and you are mine alone." He drew her into his arms and began to give her slow, deep kisses. *"Mine!"*

After a minute or two of such enjoyment, Lucianna said softly, "I think, my lord, that this conversation is better continued upstairs in our bedchamber, don't you?"

With a small smile he nodded in agreement, and hand in hand they ascended upstairs. Strangely, their body servants had conveniently disappeared. He bolted the door behind them, and by the time he had turned about, she was pulling off her garments. He joined her, drawing his own off quickly.

"We both stink of sweat and horses," Lucianna remarked, wrinkling her nose, "yet I have no desire to bathe now."

"Nor do I," he agreed as together they reached the bed.

"Mali can refresh the sheets on the morrow," she said.

"Enough housewifery, madame," he teasingly scolded her. "This is not the time for it." Then drawing her back into his arms, he began to kiss her once again with great passion. "What if I had lost you, *amore mia*? What if that stupid little bitch had sent someone more competent to do her wicked bidding? *I could have lost you!*"

"But she did not, and you did not, my own Roberto!" Lucianna reassured him. "I am here, and in your arms where I belong. I will never leave you willingly. *Never!*"

Oh yes! She was in his arms, and her naked body pressed tightly against his naked body. Was there a better feeling in all of the world than two lovers wrapped in each other's arms? Lucianna reveled in both the hard and soft sensation of it while his kisses wreaked havoc with her senses. Passion between two lovers had so much to offer.

When he finally released her lips, they were bruised with the sweetness. His hands began to explore her lush body, slowly slipping over the tempting curves of hip and breast. Unable to resist, even in his eagerness to join with her, he kissed, licked, and then suckled upon her nipples. The shiver that rocked her when he did always set his senses even more afire.

Until they had made love, Lucianna had never imagined a man's mouth upon her breasts. She had always believed them for nursing her children only. But when his mouth drew upon her, it but increased her desire for him even more, and she discovered herself eager for it. Her hands caressed the nape of his neck. Her fingers wound their way through his dark hair, and her lower body always responded with deep need for more than his lips on her sensitive flesh.

Lucianna sighed as he entered her, wrapping her legs about his torso as she eagerly awaited the final rhythm of their shared need. He did not disappoint, and she was soon dizzy with indescribable passion that filled her. She soared with delight, and she heard herself begging him not to cease. He obliged her until finally, with a gasp, the satisfied need burst for them both, his strong cock releasing its tribute.

It was at that very moment Lucianna knew in her heart that they had created a child. She cried out happily, but it was knowledge she would keep to herself for now. It was always possible she could be wrong, but her woman's intuition told her otherwise.

"Jesú, I love you!" he groaned as he rolled

off her, drawing her into the shelter of his arms.

"I love you more," she teased, gently content and happy in her secret. It would be a son.

The next morning, the earl sent a man to learn where the king's mother was residing now that it was summer. He knew she would not be in London. His man returned after ten days to say the Lady Margaret was residing near Cambridge. Her interest in the university was great, and the earl knew she planned to found and endow a new college there. Now that her son was safely enthroned, her interests had turned to learning, for she was a most scholarly woman and a supporter of the arts.

"It will be a long ride of several days," the earl told his wife. "We must travel cross-country. Are you certain that you would come?"

"I should come if I had to crawl all the way myself," Lucianna said. "I want to see the look on that little bitch's face when she realizes I am still quite alive. How dare she attempt to assassinate me!"

He grinned at her outburst. In her heart, Lucianna would always be a Florentine, and her mother's daughter. Her need for revenge must be met, or she would know no peace.

"We leave on the morrow," he told her. "No Balia. No Mali. Just you, me, and our men-at-arms."

She did not protest. "I will be ready at first light," she agreed.

The journey was long, but at least the summer weather made it easier than if this had been winter. Lucianna, however, would have gone no matter the time of year. The more she considered it, the angrier she became, realizing that this silly girl had tried to murder her and had no real assurance of ever gaining Robert Minton as her husband. She considered what Lorenzo di Medici would have done, had done, to such an assassin, and wished she possessed such power.

They managed their arrival in Cambridge in midmorning on a mid-July day. The earl sent to request an urgent audience with Lady Margaret, and was granted one that same day. There had been time to exchange their riding clothing for more suitable garments with which to meet the king's mother.

Ushered into her presence, Robert Minton bowed while his wife curtsied. He waited for her to speak, first noting that not all of her ladies were with her at this moment, and among the missing was Cat Talcott.

"It must be something very important, Rob, that you and your wife would travel to see me so urgently," Lady Margaret said. "I am told you were at Stoke with my son. I thank you for your continued loyalty to the king."

"I am grateful for the king's friendship, madame, as I am for yours," the earl began. "Therefore, it saddens me to tell you that one of your ladies has behaved in a most inappropriate and dangerous manner towards my family, towards my wife."

Lady Margaret's face became grave. "Say on, my lord."

"I have learned that the plot involving my brother-in-law was devised by a lady who believed that if she could discredit the Pietro d'Angelo family, I would repudiate my wife and be free to marry another, for this lady had hopes of being my countess, although I knew it not. When this misadventure failed, she sent her cousin to murder my wife, madame, and only his incompetence saved Lucianna."

Now Lady Margaret's usually calm demeanor showed anger. "Who is this woman, Rob? Who among my ladies would dare such a dreadful thing?"

"It is Catherine Talcott, madame," he answered.

When Lady Margaret saw two of her women nod at each other, she snapped at them, "What do you know of this?"

"My lady, we did not know the extent to which Cat would go to achieve her ends," one said, speaking for them all. "Had we been privy to such perfidy, we would have told you."

"What on earth ever made that wench believe she might be your wife?" Lady Margaret wondered aloud.

"You considered it once, I am told," the earl answered her, and the lady who was closest to the dowager queen nodded.

"You did, my lady," she said, "and from that moment on, all the wench could talk about was how she would be your countess one day. The other girls mocked her when it was learned you had wed your wife, and she was furious. I certainly never believed she would attempt to rid you of your wife, my lord. Never have I known such boldness."

Lady Margaret shook her head. "She had to have been listening at doors to have heard such a conversation," she said. "I know the maids will in order to learn secrets, yet as I never mentioned it to her, she was foolish to assume my consideration meant it would be done." She shook her head again, then said, "Someone fetch the wench to me. She is in the garden with the others. I will send her home, of course, with instructions to her father to see her married off as quickly as possible. You wish to confront her with the knowledge of her actions, my lord?"

"I do," the earl replied.

Lady Margaret looked at Lucianna, who had been silent all this time. "And you, madame? I suspect you know your presence will frighten the girl?"

A small arch smile touched Lucianna's lips. "I do, madame," she responded. "It is my nature to seek revenge of some sort."

"Of course," Lady Margaret answered, and they waited now in silence for the several minutes it took for Catherine Talcott to be fetched from the house's gardens.

She came, smiling to be called alone into her mistress's presence, for she believed it meant her importance was greater than that of the others. But seeing the Earl and the Countess of Lisle, she grew pale, forgetting even to curtsy to the king's mother as she looked to her.

Lady Margaret did not mince words. "How dare you!" she said to the girl. "How dare you execute plots and attempt the murder of an innocent woman? Do not bother to protest, for your cousin was caught, and he told all to the earl."

And it was then Lucianna, unable to contain herself any longer, said, "*Cagna! Volpe femina!* You dared? If this were Florence, I should rip your deceitful heart from your chest myself! I would scratch your eyes out so you would never cast them upon another woman's man! Thank the blessed Mother this is England, for it is your mistress who will pronounce your judgment." Then she slapped Catherine Talcott across her face as hard as she could before stepping back next to her husband.

"Your father will be told of this, mistress," the king's mother said. "You will depart my household today. I am advising him to marry you off as quickly as possible. You will never be welcomed at court again. You have disgraced yourself, but worse, you have brought shame upon my household. I will not forgive you." Lady Margaret turned to one of the older women. "Take her from my sight, and see it is done."

"Yes, madame."

Catherine Talcott was weeping now. "I only sought to be your wife," she said to Robert Minton.

"I have a wife," he told her coldly, and turned to take Lucianna's hand up in his to kiss.

With a sob, the girl fled the chamber.

"You will stay and have dinner," Lady Margaret said. It was not an invitation.

"We are honored, madame," the earl replied.

While Lucianna would have preferred the girl be punished more severely, she knew the matter was concluded to Lady Margaret's satisfaction, and she must be content with it.

They did not linger in Cambridge, beginning their return journey the following day. Much of the spring and the summer had already been wasted in service to others. Now home at Wye Court, they gratefully settled into their country life. Within the month, Lucianna was certain, as was Balia, that she was with child. The earl was delighted. The babe would come in the spring.

The harvest would be enough to sustain them through the winter. From London, Baram Kira reported that the shop of the Florentine silk merchants was thriving. England seemed to have settled into peace at last. Luca had reached Florence, her mother wrote. They were seeking a suitable wife for him. Serena, her youngest sister, was suddenly behaving in a less than cooperative fashion.

Lucianna laughed, and when her husband asked why, she showed him her mother's remark about her youngest sister. "I don't know why she thought Serena would be any easier than the others were."

"You married Alfredo Allibatore without question," he noted.

"There was no other choice for me," Lucianna replied. "With business being good again, Serena has an excellent dower to tempt an excellent suitor. Now that he has learned from the rest of us, I do not believe our father would let her be forced into a union she didn't want. We will not know until the deed is done." Lucianna rubbed her belly, which seemed to swell more each day. The autumn deepened, and then one day in early December an unfamiliar cart rumbled up to Wye Court.

Fflam, now the house's majordomo, stepped out to inquire of the driver, "What business have you here at Wye Court?"

"This the home of the Earl of Lisle?" the man asked.

"It is," Fflam answered.

"This wench says she has family here," the driver replied, indicating a girl by his side. "Well, get out, lass. You're here."

The girl struggled down from the cart.

"She promised me coin, for I have brought her all the way from Hereford," the driver told Fflam.

Fflam looked dubious. "Who are you?" he demanded of the girl. "Why should I pay this man for your transport?"

She told him, and, looking closely at her, he did not argue, but drew some silver from his purse and gave the pieces to the driver. "Come along then, lady," he said, leading her into the house. "Balia!" he shouted. "Balia!"

Lucianna's tiring woman hurried down the stairs and, seeing Fflam's companion, gasped with shock. "Mistress Serena!" she cried.

"Take me to my sister," Serena Pietro d'Angelo said. "And a bath, Balia. I have been traveling for days."

Balia did not argue, but hurried the girl to Lucianna's apartments, where she knew her mistress was sitting with Mali, sewing for her expected child. "My lady! My lady!" she managed to say before Serena pushed past her and flung herself at her sister's feet.

"I ran away!" Serena Pietro d'Angelo said. "I will not be married to some French count who wants nothing more than my dower and to save his vile reputation," she declared dramatically.

Lucianna burst out laughing. She could but imagine her mother's chagrin. Poor Orianna. This last of her daughters was obviously proving more difficult than all the other three had. Well, they had decided their own futures in the end. Why shouldn't Serena? "Welcome to Wye Court, Sister," she said, with a smile.

EPILOGUE

The Countess of Lisle gave her husband his first son in April, with her husband and youngest sister by her side. There were several other children — three sons and two daughters — who followed over the years. Together, they lived a long and happy life.

Henry Tudor, known as King Henry VII, ruled in peace until his death in 1509. Lady Margaret died in the same year. The king was succeeded not by his firstborn son, Arthur, who died at sixteen, but by his second son, Henry VIII. The Tudor dynasty ended in 1603 with the death of Henry VII's granddaughter, Elizabeth I. It had lasted but one hundred and eighteen years.

ABOUT THE AUTHOR

Bertrice Small is the *New York Times* bestselling author of fifty-five novels and four novellas, as well as the recipient of numerous awards, including a Lifetime Achievement Award from *Romantic Times.* She lives on the North Fork of eastern Long Island in Southold, which was founded in 1640 and is the oldest English-speaking town in the state of New York. Now widowed, she is the mother of a son, Thomas, and grandmother to a tribe of wonderful grandchildren. Longtime readers will be saddened to learn of the passing of Finnegan, her long-haired black kitty. Sylvester, her eight-year-old black-and-white bed cat, has been joined by a white kitten with black markings who lives up to her name, Delilah. Readers can contact the author at www.bertricesmall.com, bertricesmall@hotmail.com, or P.O. Box 765, Southold, NY 11971.